Atlantis Quest

ENTANGLED PUBLISHING, LLC

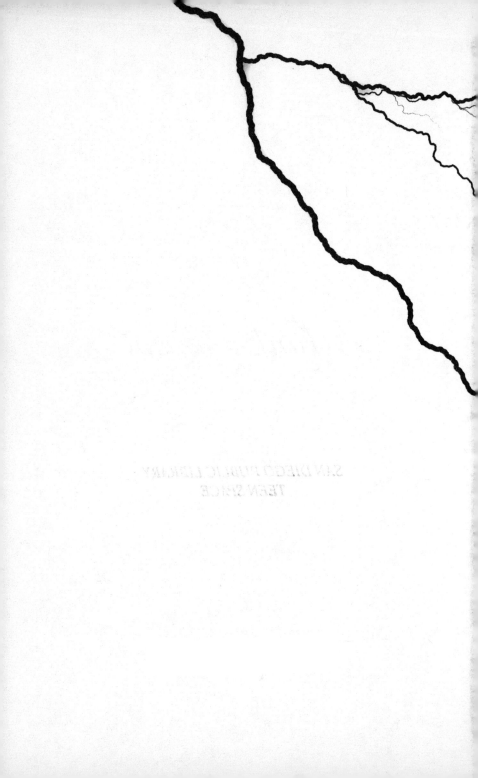

Atlantis Quest

Gloria Craw

Entangled Publishing, LLC
2614 South Timberline Road
Suite 109
Fort Collins, CO 80525

Entangled Teen is an imprint of Entangled Publishing, LLC.

Visit our website at www.entangledpublishing.com.

Edited by Liz Pelletier
Cover by Kelley York
Interior design by Jeremy Howland

Print ISBN 978-1-63375-283-2
Ebook ISBN 978-1-63375-284-9

Manufactured in the United States of America

First Edition March 2016

10 9 8 7 6 5 4 3 2 1

To my mom, Susan, and my dad, John.

Chapter One

Ian's words played through my mind... *It's okay to fight dirty,* he'd said. *Aim for the joints, the bridge of the nose, just above the kidneys. The goal is to inflict maximum pain while conserving as much of your own energy as possible.*

Parting my low ponytail down the middle, I pulled and tightened the elastic that held my hair away from my face.

"Maximum pain," I whispered, getting into fighting stance.

I punched with a right, followed with a left, and then kneed the heavy bag hanging in front of me as hard as I could. It swayed back and forth.

"How did that feel?" I asked.

Predictably, the bag said nothing, so I drove my elbow into it twice and then stepped back to get my water bottle. I gulped down about half the liquid and smoothed the front of my workout shirt. I didn't look the most ladylike, but sweat and ugly clothes were necessary.

Hitting a bag full of sawdust was good practice, but it felt different than hitting another person. Sadly, I had firsthand knowledge about burying my knuckles in someone's flesh.

Capping my water bottle, I put it back on the floor and took up position for another punching sequence. Hitting people seemed the least of what I'd done over the months since my senior year of high school started. At seventeen years old, I could say with complete honesty that I'd killed a man. Of course, I'd opened some kind of portal to death that allowed my dead mother to cross over from the other side and help me do it. But the fact remained, it was me who'd reached into his mind and crushed the life out of him. I'd done it for the greater good.

The descendants of Atlantis, or dewing as we called ourselves, were a species similar to humans, but according to genetic research and our advanced science, hybrid human-dewing combinations weren't possible. Sebastian's existence proved that to be wrong. He was a mixture of the worst aspects of human nature—selfish, greedy, cruel, and narcissistic—combined with dewing characteristics, like prolonged life, high intelligence, and mind control capabilities. A very dangerous mix.

Sebastian's hybrid nature introduced his negative characteristics into our dewing shared consciousness, and they spread like a virus. They turned a highly evolved people, who respected life and abhorred violence, into a power-hungry warlike threat to their own kind and humans.

Someone needed to stop the disease from taking over. Destiny, which I'd never consider my friend, determined that someone was me.

An unfortunate side effect was that I had a crystal-clear memory of what happened that night, and my subconscious kept using it as nightmare material. I'd probably wake up in a cold sweat as least twice a week for the rest of my three-hundred-year-long life.

Trying a new kick combination, I over-rotated my hip and lost balance. Knowing I was going to fall and not wanting to land flat on my back, I tucked my shoulder so it wouldn't hurt as badly. Just as I expected to make contact with the mat, someone caught me under the arm and pulled me up.

Surprised and still off-balance, I took a sharp breath and stepped on his foot.

"Crap, Alison," Ian hissed. "That hurt."

"Sorry." I panted, moving off his gray Converse. "Are you okay?"

He bent down to check the damage, and a lock of his light gold hair fell forward. Genetics hadn't been fooling around when they put him together. He was dewing like me and one of the most beautiful people of any species I'd ever seen. His features were perfect—deep-set eyes, high defined cheekbones, and a strong, straight nose. The color of his eyes was a striking turquoise and they were framed by thick golden lashes that would make most girls jealous. His best asset, though, was his teasing smile. It made my insides melt and drew me to him like a magnet.

"I might limp for the rest of my life," he said, testing his foot, "but I'll live. Remember to center yourself before the kick, then you won't get thrown backward. Try it again."

He was only an inch or so taller than my six feet, so his breath tickled my ear when he took up position behind me. He put his hand on my hip to angle me properly in front of the bag, and I dragged in a breath.

"You okay?" he asked me with wink.

He knew exactly how his touch affected me. I both hated and loved that he read me so clearly.

I pushed him back, centered my weight, and kicked the bag. It landed perfectly that time.

"Good," he said. "Try it again to make sure you're feeling it right."

I did and then asked, "What are you doing here? I thought I was meeting you at FatCats for pizza after work."

"This is work?" he asked, looking around the odd space we stood in. The back room of the Shadow Box bookstore had once been a graveyard for unsold books, ancient invoices, and electronic equipment no one knew how to use anymore. Lillian, my boss, had cleared it out, so I would have a space to train. It was just one of the many kindnesses she'd shown me since revealing she was also a descendant of Atlantis.

"I finished my shift half an hour ago," I said, "but this is work, too. Lillian said I can kick the crap out of this thing until six."

"When it's not kicking the crap out of you," he teased.

"You caught me at a bad moment. The only bad moment
I've had today, by the way."

He pulled a face. "Well, I just had a bad moment. Your
boss made me take the trash out. I think there was two-day-
old Chinese food in it. The smell was…I don't know how to
describe it, but it was not good."

"What doesn't kill you, makes you stronger." I grinned,
elbowing the bag. "You'll survive."

I caught a glimpse of an evil twinkle in his eye, and then
he said, "Think fast, McKye."

That was all the warning I got before his right fist came
flying toward my face. I blocked with my left arm and threw
my own punch. It didn't land.

At first glance, Ian looked a bit lanky. Appearances
were deceptive. He had more than his fair share of muscles,
strength, and speed. I'd seen him fight to kill, and it was
mind-blowing. His greatest asset was quickness. Most of the
time, his opponents couldn't see his fists coming in time to
avoid them. And when he landed something, it was with a
lot more force than his lean frame suggested was possible.

We'd sparred together a lot over the past few months,
so I wasn't surprised by the punch he threw. He always
went easy enough not to kill me, but he'd gotten over his
reluctance to hit a girl. I was glad about that. I didn't like
pain, but I wasn't afraid of it. Pain was a teacher that helped
me learn faster than anything else could.

Bouncing back, I prepared myself for a kick to his upper
thigh. He read the move and swept my leg out from under
me. I fell on my side and tucked to roll up. Before I could

make much progress, he jumped toward me with his arms and legs spread out like a flying squirrel. I turned my face, preparing for impact, but he caught his weight on his arms instead of body-slamming me into the mat.

Grabbing me just under my rib cage, he started to tickle. I squirmed and pushed at him, but he was too heavy to shift, and he knew my weak spots. The sound of my laughter echoed off the walls. "Get off," I wheezed. "Get off."

"Make me, tough girl."

I knew his weak spot, too. The backs of his knees. I stretched until I could reach them and then tickled until he was laughing as hard as me.

"Can't breathe, can't breathe," I managed through our mutual laughter.

Smiling, he rolled off me. "Next time, don't mess with the master."

"Who's the master?" I asked.

"Ridiculous question. Me."

That was one of the things that made Ian…Ian. He had confidence. He was only half kidding when he called himself the master. In his mind it wasn't boasting; it was a statement of fact.

He slid his hand over mine while our breathing slowed, and I laced my fingers through his. The two of us had been through a lot together. When I say a lot, I mean heavy-duty stuff…life-and-death stuff. It was our friendship that had kept me sane since the night I fought and killed Sebastian. He was special to me in a way no one else was.

Ian didn't shy away from telling me he wanted to be

more than friends, nor did he let it get awkward between us when I resisted.

That was another thing that made Ian…Ian. He didn't get embarrassed.

When it came to how he felt about me, I think he assumed I was in denial. With time, I'd admit he was awesome and fall properly in love with him. But I already knew he was awesome. I also knew that if I let myself, I *would* fall totally, deeply, and irreversibly in love with him.

The problem was it didn't matter how I felt about him, because I could never be with him…no matter how much I might want it. I'd seen things and felt things that left me knowing we weren't meant for each other. It had destroyed a piece of me when I figured it out, but it was a fact.

He squeezed my hand. "You're getting better," he said. "You're defending yourself on instinct instead of thinking about each move. That's an important step."

"It's starting to feel more natural," I admitted. "I suppose I should thank you for all the times you've tried to punch me."

"Are you kidding me?" he asked with shining eyes. "I've enjoyed every minute of it."

I let go of his hand to hit him in the stomach. He choked out a breath, though I hadn't hit him that hard.

"Why are you here?" I asked again.

"I'm supposed to invite you to dinner. My parents request the honor of your presence at our house this evening. Apparently, there are issues they need to discuss with you."

He made quotation marks with his fingers as he said

"discuss." Air quotations were never a good sign.

"Any idea what the issues are?" I asked.

"No, and they're being weird about it. I think it's more than how are you doing in school, Alison. Donavan will be coming by, too."

I groaned. I'd only known Donavan for a couple of weeks. He was a cousin of Spencer's and was going to take over supervising the security guys protecting my family. Which was wonderful, except when he was around it usually meant I was going to get my butt kicked in an entirely different way.

The light clips of Lillian's steps echoed into the room. She stopped to stare down at us with aged eyes, her short white hair glowing like a halo in the suspended light. She looked a little bit like an angel, but I knew better.

"I'm locking up in half an hour," she said in a voice without inflection.

Ian smiled up at her. "Ah, my favorite reader of human thoughts. You're always so warm and welcoming."

Her response was to blink once. It might have been her way of laughing or her way of flipping him off. It was difficult to interpret Lillian's reactions to things. Mostly because they were all the same. I loved her in spite of it.

There were reasons why she came off as cold and distant. I didn't know all the details, but she'd gone through something terrible in the past. Whatever it was had hurt her enough that she'd withdrawn from everyone she knew and loved. Now she kept her distance as a defense mechanism.

Though she'd never actually said it, I knew she cared a

lot about me.

Three years prior, she'd figured out I was dewing and quietly gone about helping me. She'd given me a job at the Shadow Box, allowed me the space I needed to deal with my situation, and generally made sure I kept my sanity.

On a few rare occasions, she'd opened up to me. Mostly to advise me not to follow the path she'd taken. She urged me to take chances, to trust people and to love them. She'd said there was no guarantee they'd stay, but if they left, I'd still have the memories.

I got to my feet and rotated my stiffening shoulders. "I'll practice for another five minutes and clean up," I said. "I'll be ready to leave in twenty."

Ian didn't move from the floor. "I'll wait here," he said, continuing to smile up at my boss.

She narrowed her eyes and pointed to the corner. "See those boxes? They need to be stacked."

"And you want me to do it," he said with a long-suffering sigh. "You should fire Alison and hire me instead."

Her hazel eyes had seen many, many years of life, and her unflinching stare could bore a hole into your soul. "You talk too much," she replied.

Ian got to his feet with the grace of a cat and put his arm over her bony shoulder. "You love me anyway," he whispered. "I know I'm your favorite."

She moved away from him and out of the room.

Ian rubbed his nose when she'd gone. "She's really warming up to me."

"What makes you think that?" I asked.

"I can tell these things. Maybe I can get her to say five sentences in a row tonight. The record is three, but I aim high," he said, then left to find her.

And that was the third thing that made Ian…Ian. He loved a challenge.

Rolling my weight to the balls of my feet, I kicked and then punched the bag again.

Meeting Ian and his cousin Brandy had changed me. I'd been hiding from Sebastian in plain sight for years, dressing in blah clothes, barely talking to anyone, and staying away from social situations at all costs. The McKyes, my adoptive human family, meant everything to me. I'd withdrawn from the world to protect them. Sebastian had hunted me down anyway and threatened to torture and kill them if I didn't help him in his delusional plan for world domination.

Then Ian and Brandy came along and offered to help me take Sebastian out. Not only that, but Brandy had helped me get my life back. I felt awkward and even a little afraid at first, but she introduced me to people and pushed me to get involved in things again. She stuck by me the entire time. Eventually, I'd gotten back a bit of the happy, social girl I'd once been, despite moments of sadness because my life would have to change soon.

Breathing hard I kicked, spun, and elbowed my lifeless opponent for the last time. Then I walked to the small bathroom at the back of the store to clean up and change back into the clothes I'd worn to school.

I saved the hardest part of getting ready for last. Grabbing the brush I kept in the medicine cabinet, I started to detangle my mass of dark brown hair. It was thick, heavy, and long. Straight as a pin, it hung to the middle of my back. Dealing with the last snarl, I put *get a haircut* on my mental list of things to do.

When I stepped out, Ian and Lillian were waiting at the back door.

Lillian had her jacket on and her purse over her arm. "You usually stay late on Fridays," I commented. "Is something wrong?"

"My car wouldn't start this morning," she replied. "I took the bus in. I asked Ian to take me home."

He opened the door, and I chuckled when he mouthed the words "help me" behind her back.

Chapter Two

While Ian drove out of the parking lot with Lillian in the passenger seat, I stayed behind to text my mom. I wanted to let her know there'd been a change of plans, and that I was going to have dinner at Ian's house. She proceeded to ask a million questions about my day at school and what I'd done at work.

Her constant concern and overprotectiveness used to bother me. It could still get annoying, but I appreciated it in a way I hadn't before. I wouldn't always have her around to nag me.

When I was finally ready, I took the drive to Ian's slowly.

Time was something I had more than enough of. The average dewing lived three hundred years. Plus at about twenty years old, we started aging at a snail's pace.

My special DNA gave me some pretty amazing recall. If you asked me what I'd been wearing three years ago on the same day, I could have told you. Not only that, but what I'd eaten for dinner and the time I'd gone to bed that night.

Another cool component was how quickly my body healed. I'd never been sick for more than twenty-four hours, and when I cracked a rib as a kid, it fused back together in a few days.

Then there was the mind control thing I could do. That was an entirely different level of freakish.

With few exceptions, the dewing could connect their mind to a human's and manipulate their thoughts. The term we used for it was "joining." I was a thoughtmaker and could join a mind to implant thoughts. Mine was the only kind of joining that worked on dewing minds as well as human minds.

Seeing Ian's place ahead, I pulled up to the gate and entered the code.

He called his house "the compound." His parents were the clan chiefs of the Thane clan and had more money than Midas. It was actually a contemporary-style mansion that fanned out in cube shapes, corners, and windows. It sat high on the east side and had an amazing view of the Las Vegas Strip.

I drove their long driveway and parked behind the house in the less formal lot there. After cutting my engine, I walked to the back door and let myself in. The others were in the big room that Ian called "disaster headquarters." If troubling news was going to be discussed, it generally happened there.

Spencer and Katherine were sitting at the glass table in the corner of the room.

Katherine gave me a welcoming smile that was a little too big. Spencer smiled, too, but instead of looking welcoming, he looked apologetic. I didn't like it. They were being weird. Something was up.

"I ordered Thai from Take Me Out," Katherine said. "The delivery man should be here soon."

"Okay," I replied, thinking it was kind of funny that even sophisticated Katherine ordered takeout from dodgy places sometimes.

Ian was across the room. Like always, he seemed mildly surprised to see me.

Dewing had a unique energy force that only we could sense. It felt like a vibration against your skin and served as a kind of beacon, letting other dewing know you were one of their kind. From the feel of it you could tell gender, approximate age, and which clan they were from.

I was an anomaly, because I didn't have a vibration. I could feel others, but they couldn't feel me. Ian thought it was probably because I'd been raised by humans and I was sort of behind the learning curve. He thought I'd catch up eventually and be like all the rest of them.

Whatever the reason, Ian hadn't fully adjusted to the abnormality and was usually taken a bit aback when I showed up.

A slow smile tipped up the corners of his mouth as I walked to him. My heart flip-flopped. In a white T-shirt that was a little tight across his shoulders and a pair of worn jeans, he was amazing to look at.

"Hey," I said.

"How's my favorite thoughtmaker?" he asked.

"If you mean your only thoughtmaker, I'm fine."

He leaned in, so close his breath brushed my cheek. "You're the only thoughtmaker I care about."

It was a corny line and might have been creepy coming from someone else. Because Ian said it, it was just cute and funny. I pushed him away.

"You were right," I said. "Your parents are acting strange."

He nodded. "They've been whispering to each other since I got back."

"Some kind of crap is about to hit the fan."

"Unfortunately, I agree."

We turned to look out the window. The lights on the Vegas Strip shone like colorful jewels sprinkled over black velvet.

"I'm getting tired of this view," Ian said with his Australian accent surfacing for the first time in a while.

"How can you get tired of something so ostentatious?" I asked.

"Because it's ostentatious. Give me the beach, some sunshine, and a surfboard. I'd be a lot happier."

Spencer and Katherine had houses in several cities around the world, but the one Ian had grown up in was in Sydney. He never complained, but I could tell he missed his friends and surfing. I got the impression his parents were antsy to move on, too.

Their tie to Vegas was me. Since I'd killed Sebastian and concurrently saved Ian's life, they'd stayed to look after my human family.

The intercom buzzed, making me jump. "It's just the food," Ian said, squeezing my shoulder. "You're sure jittery."

I was. The atmosphere was too strained for my liking.

When we sat down to eat, Katherine wouldn't look me in the eyes, and Spencer, who had a seemingly endless supply of energy, was uncharacteristically quiet.

I chewed and swallowed *pad thai* until I couldn't take the tension anymore.

"Let's just get the bad news out of the way," I said. "Tell me what's going on."

Chapter Three

I almost choked when they told me. "Am I hallucinating right now?" I asked.

Ian paused with his chopsticks to his mouth. "How much MSG is in this?" he asked. "Because I can't have heard that right."

Katherine squared her shoulders. "You heard correctly."

"Nikki Dawning almost got me killed," I said. "You can't seriously want me to go looking for her."

Ian shook his head and laughed. Not the amused kind of laugh…the *you've got to be kidding me* kind of laugh. "You'd have to look underground anyway," he said caustically. "Nikki is dead."

"She's not," Spencer replied while turning a glare on him.

"If she's not dead, she doesn't want to be found," I said

in a voice laced with dislike. "She disappeared the night we fought Sebastian and hasn't been heard from since. She's been missing for three months."

"Maybe she hasn't contacted anyone because she can't," Katherine suggested.

Ian took another bite of food. "Here's a thought," he said. "Maybe she can't contact anyone because she's dead."

Apparently, he'd tested Spencer's patience enough. "Stop it, Ian," he snapped. "We're being serious, and frankly, it has nothing to do with you. We're asking for Alison's help."

Ian's back went ramrod straight and his mouth tightened. The worry line just above his right eyebrow, the only imperfection on his face, deepened. "It has everything to do with me," he replied. "I found Alison. I brought her into this. She wouldn't be sitting here eating bad Thai food if it weren't for me. I owe her. We all do, and I'm not going to be silent while you ask her to do something this dangerous. Especially when it involves Nikki Dawning, who pretty much wrapped her up like a birthday present and turned her over to the master of evil."

Spencer leaned toward Ian in an intimidating sort of way. Ian leaned right back. From their turquoise-colored eyes to their blond hair, father and son were mirror images of each other. Spencer was a powerful man in a powerful position. He was used to getting his way. Ian, who would inherit the clan chief position after him, was just as stubborn and did not intimidate easily.

Katherine looked at them and breathed a long-suffering sigh. "Let's make a deal," she said. "Ian, you be quiet for two minutes. Then you can tell your father how you disagree with everything he said."

Ian shoved back in his chair and threw his hands up. "Fine," he replied. "Go ahead and talk. You were just saying something about Nikki being dead."

For a moment, I thought Katherine might reach over and slap him. Which was completely crazy because I'd never even heard her raise her voice to him. She was always collected, calm, and serene. Watching her expression change from empathetic to angry was impressive.

One look at his mom and Ian got the message. He might bait his father, but he wasn't going to tangle with her. My already-deep respect for Katherine rose another notch.

She turned her lovely amber eyes on me. "We believe Nikki has been kidnapped," she said.

I glanced at Ian and figured he was thinking the same thing…karma had come back around to kick her square in the butt. Jazz hands.

Kidnapping wasn't new to me. Sebastian had drugged and abducted me, too. And it was Nikki who'd told him where to find me. She'd been responsible for putting my family in the biggest danger.

"Perhaps what comes around goes around," I said.

"You may never forgive her for what she did," Katherine said. "I'm not suggesting you should, but you wouldn't want her to be hurt if you could stop it."

I kept chewing, thinking maybe Katherine didn't know me as well as she thought she did. Nikki had screwed me over, and I'd seen enough of her at school to know she wouldn't hesitate to throw even a *good* friend under a bus if it suited her. I wasn't the kind of person to throw another under a bus, but if Nikki landed there, I wasn't in a hurry to help her up.

Spencer and Katherine exchanged a look. I figured they hoped I'd show more sympathy. Instead, I kept eating. The kuay tieu was surprisingly good.

"You should know Nikki's parents got a package yesterday," Spencer continued. "It had pieces of her in it."

"What, like hair or something?" I asked, only mildly interested.

"Fingers," Katherine replied.

The food in my throat turned to acid and started crawling back up. "Gross," I muttered.

"The blood was relatively fresh," Spencer added. "It happened recently."

Ian shifted position. Undoubtedly, he wanted to ask questions, but his two minutes of silence weren't up.

I swallowed deeply. "How can you be sure they were… Nikki's?"

"Amelia confirmed it," Katherine replied. "And a mother would know."

"Someone from the Truss clan has her," Spencer said. "Katherine saw it."

Katherine was a futureseer. She joined a human mind and caught glimpses of what would happen to them. Most of the time that future involved a dewing as well. I'd been told she was never wrong. I had bet my life on one of her visions before. I trusted her, and that made it worse.

"Whoa," I said, putting my hands up. "Someone from the Truss clan has her?"

Katherine nodded. "I saw her in an airport," she said. "Someone was gripping her arm to prevent her from leaving. They were Truss. No doubt about that. I heard him say, 'When you're clan chief, you can do what you want with her.'"

"The Truss are a mess," Spencer added. "Sebastian had no children, so there's no clear heir to the chiefdom. Twenty of the oldest clan members called the Elders have been trying to hold things together, but it isn't working. Sebastian's pride, ambition, and greed have infected them. Many of the Truss have been fighting over land and assets. There have even been a few murders. If someone doesn't take leadership, reestablish order, and uphold our rules and traditions, we worry there will be more blood spilled."

Katherine held her hands together so tightly that her knuckles turned white. "Murder of any kind is beyond atrocious," she said. "Our population is too small to survive another rash of them. Not to mention the thousands of years we have respected human life and civilization. We will be at risk of exposure, too. Humankind is unlikely to hold our lives in such regard."

The dewing had evolved faster than humankind. Not only was our technology centuries ahead, we were socially and emotionally advanced. We hated bloodshed, both human and dewing. Our policy was to live and let live, one of many reasons Sebastian and his viruslike tendency to slaughter people was such a huge problem.

"The Truss Elders don't trust us," Spencer said. "Let's face it, some of them hate us. They have very little desire to come back to the clans. They see it as losing autonomy and freedom. But for the greater good of the dewing and humans, it's the right thing to do. Our survival depends on it."

I understood where he was coming from. It was possible we could become an extinct species. A pair of dewing could only have two children…one to take the place of each parent. If we didn't survive long enough to have kids, our population would decrease and never recover that number. Fewer Truss meant fewer pairs, which meant fewer children…which meant fewer of all of us.

"The Elders condescended enough to let us know they'll decide on a new clan chief before the end of spring," Katherine said.

"We know names of the candidates, but nothing about their personalities, political beliefs, and plans for the future," Spencer said. "We need personal observation to find out about those things, but of course, the Elders don't want our interference."

"In my vision, someone said 'when you're clan chief,'" Katherine added. "That leads us to believe whoever has Nikki is one of the candidates. That's part of the reason we want you to find her."

"What will you do if you don't like who the Elders appoint?" I asked.

"We have ideas," he replied.

"You'll kill them?" I surmised, my stomach churning

Thai food. "I thought we were done with that."

"If the Elders choose someone like Sebastian, a much greater number of lives may be lost. We have to do what's best for all the descendants of Atlantis."

Spencer's lips mashed into a thin line. "We'll do it quietly, and because the infrastructure and security Sebastian established has crumbled, we can do it in a way that won't be traced back to us."

I gulped. "When you say *we,* I hope you aren't including me. I don't regret that Sebastian is dead, but I do regret killing another living being. It haunts me. I'm afraid it always will."

"We'll keep you out of that part of it," Spencer said. "I promise."

I continued to feel unsettled and anxious, but I said, "So you want me to casually stand around the Truss candidates and listen for information about Nikki."

Ian pointed to his watch for permission to speak. He'd been quiet long enough, so Katherine gave him a nod.

"Why does it have to be her?" he said angrily. "You use humans as spies all the time."

Katherine shook her head. "Humans work well sometimes, but they report a myriad of things that we have to sort through to get relevant information. It would be a lot more difficult—and time-consuming—to get the right kind of information out of a human report. Alison knows what we're dealing with. She'll know what to listen for."

"As far as we're aware," Spencer added, "she's the only one of us who doesn't have a vibration. She feels completely human. She could be in the middle of a group of Truss, and they would never suspect she's dewing."

"Some people know about her," Ian protested.

"Only ten of us, and it's in their best interest to keep her identity a secret," Katherine said. "Most everyone else thinks the daughter of the White Laurel is just a myth."

"It's too dangerous." Ian clenched his hand into a fist.

"There are precautions in place," Spencer said. "We have made arrangements for her to stay with someone. His house is off location, so she won't be spending nights where the Truss are meeting. We don't expect problems, but he's agreed to protect her if it comes down to an essence fight."

"I'll protect her," Ian interjected, "because if she's going, I'm going."

"We expected you'd say something like that," Katherine replied. "But the place we've arranged for Alison to stay at, the only place within reasonable driving distance, is less than a mile from where the Truss will be."

Spencer gave him a stern look. "You can't get that close, Ian. There's a chance, slim as it may be, that one of the older Truss will feel and identify you. They distrust the Thane clan more than any of the others. It's possible they'll pack up and leave before we can get the information we need."

"Theron's vibration won't concern them," Spencer followed up. "His family has had a place up there for years."

"Theron," Ian said disbelievingly. "You asked *Theron* to look after her. He hates your guts."

Spencer shook his head. "Be that as it may, he agreed to help."

"Why don't you just napalm the Truss?" he asked with disgust. "They've been nothing but trouble for decades. They're weak now. Maybe it's time to finish them off."

"It's not like they had any problem murdering my clan," I added.

It was true. My clan, the Laurels, had been the most vocally opposed to Sebastian's plans. He'd ordered the Truss to kill them. Within just a few short weeks, every member of my clan had been murdered.

Katherine shot us both a cutting look. "Every life is precious," she said. "Shame on both of you for speaking so lightly of it. I sympathize with Alison, but vengeance won't bring her peace."

Spencer shook his head. "The clan chiefs explored a napalm type of option several years back. Aside from the fact that genocide is revolting, we can't kill them off. The survival of our species depends on keeping them around."

He ran a hand over his forehead and then pinched the bridge of his nose before continuing. "As far as we know, the Elders are considering three couples to lead them. The first is especially concerning to us. Not because of what we know about them, but because of what we don't know. Yvonne and Robert Truss are the youngest of the candidates, which might make them easier to work with, but for the last ten years, Sebastian employed them. I have to wonder how much of his ideology infected them."

Katherine focused on me. "He makes this sound as though it's all about politics. But Nikki's parents are our closest friends. They've been a mess not knowing what happened to her. Now they know she's alive, but someone is hurting her. Every day they can't help is more excruciating than the next. Imagine your parents in the same position."

She'd hit the right button. I hated Nikki Dawning, but I did feel for her parents. They'd been nice to me. And if they were my parents, I *would* want to help them.

"I'm not saying I'm in," I stated, "but what's your plan?"

Katherine looked at her hands. "We'd like to send you on a ski vacation. Yvonne, Robert, and a few of the others are staying at a luxury resort in Colorado called the Ledges. They have a seventeen-year-old daughter, Phoebe, who will be with them. The Ledges caters to a more mature demographic, and since you and Phoebe are the same age, we hope you can befriend her. If you spend time around her, you should be able to get close to Yvonne and Robert. Maybe they'll let something slip about Nikki, if they have her."

"So, to recap," I interjected, "if I agree to do this, I won't get to spend Thanksgiving break with my family. I'll be spending it with some guy I don't know, watching a bunch of Truss who may have helped murder my clan. All while looking for someone I hate."

"We know this will be difficult for you," Katherine said in a voice full of regret. "If we could do it another way, we would."

"We'll probably need you to do the same with the other candidates, too," Spencer added.

I laughed. "How am I supposed to do all that in one week?"

"You can't," he replied. "We'd like you to look at the others during Christmas and spring breaks. We can get your parents to agree to you vacationing with us during those times."

I could hardly believe what they were asking of me. I had limited time left with the McKyes. Every holiday and every break was precious time I could spend with them. Time I would never get back.

"There's a problem no one has addressed," Ian said. "She's been told more than once how much she looks like her mother. One of the Truss might recognize her."

"I really don't think you will be recognized," Katherine responded, looking at me. "The people who have commented on the resemblance knew who you were before they met you. They were expecting to see a resemblance."

"Whether they recognize her or not, they've killed human spies before," Ian said. "They'd probably kill her, too."

I saw real sorrow and regret in Spencer's eyes as he looked at me. "If I could do this myself, I would," he said. "You're smart; you learn fast. You've proved you're resourceful. You're also the most powerful thoughtmaker I've ever met. I believe you have more energy bottled up inside you than even your mother had. I don't like the position this puts you in, but you're more likely to be able to do this than anyone else. We need your help. And when I say we, I mean all the descendant of Atlantis."

In the silence that settled around us, I heard a voice say, *There is more to this than they think. What happens to your parents, your brother, and your brother's children depends on what happens to the descendants of Atlantis… The two worlds are connected and will be until—*

No one else heard it, but I recognized the voice. It was my dead mother speaking to me. Her warning that my brother was in danger felt like a knife cutting me deep.

I put my head in my hands. "Until what?" I murmured.

"Did you say something?" Ian asked.

I shook my head. Telling him that the dead spoke to me would take too much time to explain. Ultimately, it didn't matter what I said. If both humankind, including the McKyes, and the dewing, including Katherine, Spencer, and Ian, needed my help, I had do it.

"When do you want me to go?" I asked without enthusiasm.

"I've booked a flight for tomorrow," Katherine replied.

"There's no way my mom is going to let me leave for Colorado tomorrow. She'll need a few days to adjust to the idea."

"She's already agreed," Katherine said. "We had a nice conversation over lunch today. It came up."

"Of course it did." I sighed.

Chapter Four

$\mathcal{I}$ was finishing my food when I felt another dewing park in front of the Thanes' house.

"Donavan is here," Spencer said.

"Fabulous," I grumbled. "I'm a little stiff from training, and now he's going to beat me up some more."

Ian put his arm around my shoulders. "You can tell them you won't practice tonight," he said.

"I wish," I replied, shaking my head, "but I've got to learn to essence-fight. I need to train with someone who doesn't care about hurting me."

"Hey," Donavan said, swaggering in. "It smells like food poisoning in here. Processed food will kill you."

"Not really," Ian replied. "We can survive a lot worse."

Donavan had a military-type bearing. He shook

Spencer's hand, but it wouldn't have surprised me if he saluted him.

"How did it go today?" Spencer asked.

"Good. I think the guys you hired to watch the McKyes are going to work out great. They're all experienced, and you're paying them enough to make it more than worth their while. They'll report to me if anything seems the slightest bit off."

"Good," Spencer said.

"I came by to give you my first report."

He pulled a carefully creased and folded paper from his pocket and handed it to Spencer.

"Thanks, I'll check it over tonight."

Donavan looked at me. "Are we going a round tonight, Alison?"

"Sure," I replied, trying to sound excited about it.

It was a familiar drill. Ian and Spencer moved the sofas off the Persian rug, so I could fall without hitting my head. I took up my position in the middle, and Donavan stood across from me.

"Put your fists up," Ian suggested.

"Why?" I asked. "We aren't going to hit each other."

"Maybe it will make you feel strong," he said, but he didn't look very hopeful.

"Fine," I said, taking up a fighting stance and preparing for the energy Donavan was going to pound me with.

My body began to warm as I pulled together all the energy I could access in my mind. When I felt it start to boil under my skin, I was ready.

Donavan threw his energy at my neck. The force of it made me suck in a breath, but I was decent at protecting myself. I pushed back with my own energy until it equalized between us. He aimed at my ribs next. I anticipated it and pushed back before his energy could connect.

It went back and forth like that until Donavan surprised me by sending his energy against my shins. I crumpled to my knees. Next, he hit me upside the head, and I rolled from my knees to the floor.

Ian who had been pacing the entire time, said, "That's enough."

I sat up and shook my head in an attempt to stop the ringing in my ears. Donavan extended a hand and helped me up. "Sorry, kid," he said.

"Don't be," I replied. "This is like eating eggplant. It's good for me and will make me stronger in the end. Even if I nearly choke to death swallowing it."

He gave me a tight smile and walked away.

Ian guided me with his hand on the small of my back. "You have no idea how much I want to beat him to death right now," he whispered as I sat on the sofa.

Katherine brought me a glass of water, which I gulped down. The room was warmer than normal from the heat Donavan and I put out during our sparring.

"You're improving," Spencer said. "You lasted for five minutes that time."

Five minutes sounded pretty pathetic. The problem was I couldn't throw my energy out at an opponent like the others could. I was constantly in defense mode, and with no rest between punches, I tired quickly.

"Well, I gotta git," Donavan said on his way out the door. "It's going to be a busy day tomorrow. Good to see you, Alison. I look forward to next time."

Spencer sat next to me. "Do you want me to work some of the kinks out?" he asked.

I nodded. He was a healer and could join my mind to trigger a release in my muscles and soothe my nerve endings.

I felt a small jolt as his mind joined mine, and then it was like he set butterflies loose. Their wings touched the places I hurt and gently eased the pain.

I closed my eyes and breathed deeply, letting the magic work.

When I was relaxed and pain-free, he asked, "Better?"

"Yes, thanks."

"What do you need?" Katherine asked. "I'll get it for you."

"I just want to lie down," I replied. "On the floor."

Ian snorted. "Why on the floor?"

"The tile is cold. It will help me cool off."

He smiled at me and helped me down. Getting a pillow off the sofa for my head, he said, "You're so weird."

I wasn't offended. Ian called me weird a lot. It had sort of become a term of endearment.

"Will you be okay down there while I go over a few things with my parents?"

"I'll be fine," I replied.

It had been a long and exhausting day. As my body cooled, I fell asleep.

I awoke to find Ian's face inches from mine. "Are you still alive?" he asked, smiling at me.

I yawned. "I am. I think."

"We're going to make a late visit to Bruce and Amelia," Katherine said from across the room. "We'll be home in an hour or so."

Ian helped me to my feet while she pulled her jacket on. Coming to hug me, she said, "Have a good night."

She let me go, and Spencer thumped me across the back a few times. "You're doing great, Alison. Your mother would be proud."

When they'd gone, Ian pulled me close. I rested my head on his shoulder and breathed in the clean minty scent that was unique to him. "Bad Thai food, agreeing to look for your mortal enemy, and a fight that didn't end well," he said. "Thanks for coming to dinner."

I smiled, thinking it would have been a lot worse if he hadn't been there.

"Speaking of my mortal enemy," I said still hugging him in a *friendly* sort of way. "She'll grow her fingers back, right?"

"Yeah. It'll take some time. Maybe a year to restore them perfectly. But at the moment, I don't really care about Nikki's fingers. I care about you. Are you going to be okay after your day full of sparring?"

"It depends on what you mean by okay. Physically, I'm recovering fine. What I'm not okay about is the Truss. I just can't get away from them, and thinking about it makes me want to hit something."

I felt his breath on my cheek as he chuckled. "I think there's a big wrench in the garage. Do you want me to get it for you?"

"There's nothing in this house I wouldn't feel terrible about breaking. Do you have anything else to distract me?"

He hugged me tighter. "We could make out," he said, teasingly. "That would be distracting."

I pulled back enough so I could see his eyes. He smiled down at me expecting my reluctance. We'd kissed before and it was…amazing. I saw fireworks and the whole bit. Not exaggerating. But we'd talked about it afterward, and I told him it wasn't going to happen again.

Like always, Ian was up for a challenge and kept nudging me toward another kiss, or two, but I knew we'd never likeness, and I didn't want to make things more difficult for either of us in the long run.

"What would your parents say?" I asked.

"At this point they'd probably cheer."

Likeness was a pairing between a male and female dewing. It wasn't a phenomenon based on love. It couldn't be controlled or stopped. It was permanent and connected the two so strongly that if one died the other would, too, usually within the year.

You could be in love with someone one moment and then *bam*…attach to someone else the next. Almost as strangely, you could be platonic friends with someone, have zero attraction to them, and then in a second be locked to that person for the rest of your life. You could even be walking down the street minding your own business, randomly come across another dewing, and likeness to them without even knowing their name.

Laughing, I pushed him away and went to get a soda from the fridge.

"I think I have something else to distract you," he said, leaving the room.

I took my drink back to the sofa and stretched out my legs.

Ian came back carrying an old book. It was leather bound, and the edges of the pages shone with gilding. I'd seen another book like it—the Laurel book that recorded my genealogy. Lillian kept it in a vault at the Shadow Box.

He sat next to me and opened it on his lap. "This was written in 1040 AD," he said. "It's pretty amazing."

I moved his hand away from the delicate paper and handwritten words. "You shouldn't touch it without gloves. Lillian would smack you down if she saw."

"Settle down, nerd. The pages have been sprayed with a special preservative. Lillian knows all about it."

"Oh."

"How well do you read Old English?"

I looked at the written words in front of me. The ink had bled and blended some of the letters together. "I understand Chaucer, but this is almost unrecognizable as writing."

"It takes some time to adjust to the calligraphy," he agreed. "This is sort of like a history book about our origins. My mom wants you to have it for a while. It might answer some of your questions."

His parents were concerned because I hadn't asked a lot

about our kind and our history. I had a reason for putting it off. In the time I had left with the McKyes, I wanted to concentrate on them and my human life. When that time was over, I'd have centuries to learn about the dewing.

Obviously sensing my hesitation, he said, "You can't hide from this part of yourself forever."

"I know. I am curious, but please let me decide when the time is right."

He nodded slowly.

"I'd probably better get home," I said. "It will take a while to convince my mom to let me go skiing."

"My mom told you she took care of it."

"We're talking about Deborah McKye here. The woman who looked into getting a tracking chip put on my brother's molar."

"Right. I forgot about that." He pushed a strand of my hair behind my ear, and continued, "You can change your mind about doing this thing."

The worry line above his eyebrow was back again. I reached up to smooth it out with my thumb. He caught my hand. "Why do you always do that?"

"You have that mark because of me. You got it when you saved my life."

His eyes softened, and he kissed the palm of my hand. I tensed up on the outside, but on the inside I was melting. "Well, I like the mark, so you can stop trying to make it go away."

I had to sternly remind myself that my sanity depended on staying in the friend zone with him.

He leaned toward me and rested his forehead on mine. "Just so you know, Theron is great, but he doesn't fight as well as me. I want to be the one there for you."

I let my eyes close. "You'll only be ten miles away."

"Yes," he replied without enthusiasm. "Staying with his human friend whom I've never met."

"Maybe she's really nice," I suggested.

"What if she's not?"

"You're nice. She'll like you."

"I suppose you're right," he replied, with a joking twinkle in his eyes. "I am pretty irresistible."

I smiled at him because he was only telling the truth. Getting up, I checked my pockets. "Where did I put my keys?"

"You dropped them when you were practicing with Donavan. I put them on the table next to the door."

"Thanks," I said.

"Wait. I'll get my shoes and walk you to your car."

When he'd left the room I thought again about my mother's words.

There is more to this than they think. What happens to your parents, your brother, and your brother's children is dependent on what happens to the descendants of Atlantis... The two worlds are connected and will be until...

"Until what?" I asked again.

As I expected, there was no answer.

Chapter Five

On the drive home, I prepared myself for what awaited—my mom was no one's fool. Especially when it came to her children. She was controlling in an annoying but loving way, which was nearly bulletproof. It was going to take some effort to convince her I wouldn't break a leg or fall into a mountain crevasse while skiing in a place as "dangerous" as Colorado.

It wasn't only my safety that concerned her; she was also worried about my mood swings. Most of the time I was pretty happy, but then something would remind me why I had to leave Vegas soon, and I'd fall back into my old withdrawn self.

My dad was a physician, a really good one. Over the years, he may have been curious about why I never caught colds and how quickly I healed, but he'd gotten particularly interested when I'd come home with a head injury three months ago. A cut that should have scarred instead healed without leaving a mark. Several times, I'd caught him looking at the spot with a confused expression.

Whether it was my ability to heal quickly or something else, he had questions. And if he asked them, I wouldn't be able to give the answers. Not honest ones.

I could thoughtmake him into ignoring my ability to heal, but not forever. Other people would start noticing and might say something about it. Not to mention that I'd stop aging in a pretty noticeable way when I hit twenty.

The best thing for everyone was for me to get some distance from the McKyes. That meant going out of state for college and then disappearing from their lives for good. Knowing that broke my heart.

I hobbled a bit when I walked into my house because I was still a little stiff.

The aroma of falafel hung in the air when I went inside. It was my mom's new favorite dish…it was not one of mine. She'd gone from vegetarian to vegan a few weeks before and was determined to drag the rest of us along with her.

Super glad I'd eaten lots of MSG-infused Thai food with the Thanes, I went to join my family in the kitchen.

My dad was standing by the fridge with a bag of carrots in his hand. He noted the slight hitch in my step, and his brows drew together. "Are you okay?" he asked. "You look a little sore."

"I went to the gym with Ian," I lied. "I think I pulled

a muscle in my calf or something. Don't worry, I'll be fine tomorrow."

I sent the same thought into his mind. His expression cleared, and he crunched another carrot.

Mom was sitting cross-legged on the floor by our table. It was a surprise to see a bunch of my clothes spread out in front of her. My skis and snowboard were leaning against the wall.

"You're back earlier than I expected," she said, glancing up at me. "I thought I'd have you all packed up before you got home. Alex is only just getting the travel suitcase out of the garage now."

I think my mouth might have dropped open. "You're letting me go? I thought I'd have to beg."

She folded one of my shirts and said, "Katherine and I had a nice lunch today at the new vegan place near my gym. She mentioned what a responsible girl you are. And I had to agree. Not many girls your age save up to buy their own car, let alone pay their own insurance."

"Very responsible," my dad said around a mouthful of carrots.

"She also reminded me that you'll be eighteen in three months. I think I have to let you experience some of the world on your own. Small steps like vacationing with them will be perfect."

Dad winked at me. "Wonders never cease," he muttered just loud enough for me hear.

I hid a chuckle. Though he'd never say so, he thought she was a bit overprotective, too. I appreciated that he empathized with me.

Alex came in from the garage lugging our biggest, ugliest travel suitcase. "This thing is an embarrassment," he said, laying it down next to my mom. "It doesn't even close right."

Mom patted it and eased it onto its side. "We've had this longer than we've had you kids," she said with fondness. "It's been all over the world. There's still a lot of use in it. No sense cluttering a landfill with perfectly good luggage."

Alex pushed his red hair out of his eyes and gave me a long-suffering look. Mom had also gone ultra-green. She recycled everything she could, including things she shouldn't.

"Don't worry," my dad said. "I have a roll of duct tape in the garage. You can strap it together with that."

Alex shook his head. "Pray the power goes out at the airport. If it's dark, no one will think you're homeless and looking for a place to sleep."

Dad watched Alex push his too-long hair away from his eyes. "Either you get a haircut this weekend, or I'll take a pair of clippers to it while you're asleep," he said.

My brother gave him the kind of look that implied *good luck with that, Dad.* Then he turned his glare on me. "This totally sucks," he said. "You get a ski trip, and I get stuck at home eating tofu turkey."

"You can hardly tell the difference," my mom muttered.

Alex made a face.

"You get to come golfing with me and the boys," my dad said in an attempt to lift his spirits.

Alex sat down and put his head in his hands. "Tofu

turkey and golfing with senior citizens… I hate my life."

I reached over to pat his leg. "I'll bring you back a snow globe."

He peeked out from under his hair. "I hate you, too," he muttered.

He didn't, though. Alex and I were close. We'd spent a lot of time together during my years of social withdrawal.

Our old dog, Tsar, came wandering in and lay on the floor next to me. I scratched behind his ears while his brown eyes looked lovingly at me.

The light caught some glitter on a sweatshirt my mom was folding. I'd never worn the awful bubble-gum-pink thing, and I didn't intend to start. In a panic, I reached for it, but Mom evaded me. "I can pack my stuff," I said, trying to stop her from putting it in the case.

Like she hadn't heard me, she tucked it in. "Remember to layer before you go outside," she said. "You'll be more insulated that way."

Alex gave me an evil smile, knowing I hated to be lectured.

"I thing you've outgrown your parka and ski pants," she continued, "but Katherine said the resort has a clothing boutique. I'll send some money with you. You can buy new things when you get there. I just hope you'll be able to find ski pants that fit."

"Thanks for reminding me that I'm enormous, Mom."

"There's no shame in being tall, sweetheart. Especially when you're mostly legs. The girls at my gym would kill for your figure."

"Until they figured out how hard it is to find pants long enough and sweaters with sleeves that go all the way to their wrists," I mumbled.

Dad breathed a loud sigh from across the kitchen. "Why can't I have an Oreo now and then, Deborah?" he grumbled. "A little flavor never killed anyone."

"No, but high fructose corn syrup is as addictive as some drugs."

"According to who?" my dad asked.

"According to an article in *Go Holistic,*" she replied. "By the way, I know about your stash of Ding Dongs in the garage. Go get one of those. Enjoy it, because I'm throwing the box away tomorrow."

My dad's shoulders slumped. "You found my hiding place?"

My mom kept packing. "You're too predictable."

"Come on, Alex," Dad said, "I'll share the last of my addictive Ding Dongs with you."

I smiled as they trailed out of the kitchen and then scooted up next to my mom. I would miss her while I was gone.

Putting my arm around her shoulder, I wondered for the hundredth time what I would have done if she hadn't come into my life. She'd taken me into her home and into her heart when I was eight. By that time, I'd been in and out of so many foster homes I almost couldn't connect with people anymore. It must have seemed a daunting task to bring me back from that, but she hadn't given up. She showered me with affection until I'd come to life again. I really couldn't have loved her more.

She checked her work. The shirts and pants were folded and tucked in tight. "Well, that's the last of it," she said.

There were so many clothes in the case I could have gone two weeks without washing. "I'll be super cozy," I assured her.

She tried to smile, but it didn't reach her eyes. For all her bravado, she was still worried for me. She would always be the same overprotective mother.

I formed the thoughts, *Relax. Alison will be fine,* and slipped them between the worries already in her mind. The uneasiness in her eyes cleared.

"I promise I'll text or call every day," I said.

She patted my cheek. "If you don't, I will."

Her phone rang. Pulling it from her pocket, she looked at the screen. "It's work," she said. "I have to take it."

"No problem," I replied. "I'll finish up."

I closed the lid on the suitcase and tried to latch it, but it wouldn't hold. So I went to the garage in search of duct tape. Dad and Alex were leaning against my car eating Ding Dongs and Twinkies.

I laughed at how dejected they looked. "If you want, you can hide your snacks under my bed while I'm gone," I offered.

Alex spit crumbs as he said, "That's a good idea. Maybe I don't hate you after all."

Dad perked up and opened his tool chest to get a roll of silver duct tape out. He handed it to me and kissed me on the forehead. "If I don't see you before you leave tomorrow, have a good time and don't worry about your mom worrying about you. Alex and I will keep her busy."

"Thanks, Dad," I said, turning to go back inside.

"Don't forget my snow globe," Alex added, spitting more crumbs.

"I won't," I assured him. "I'll get the ugliest one I can find."

I stayed up for a long time, thinking about how lucky I'd been to get adopted by the McKyes. Ian would have called it destiny.

The concept of destiny was important to the dewing. Sometimes, the way Spencer, Katherine, and Ian spoke about it made me think it was their version of God. Some omnipotent force who'd mapped out the course of our lives eons ago. I'd been raised to believe in choices. Choices were what made life interesting. Destiny and choices didn't seem to go together, but the dewing believed in making choices, too. They just thought destiny knew what their decisions would be far in advance.

If destiny did determine things, then being abandoned by my parents, getting passed from home to home, and finally having to leave the only family that had loved me was just the map my life followed. If I accepted that, I had to accept that whatever destiny was; it didn't care about my pain, loneliness, and fear.

If I believed in destiny, I would hate it.

Chapter Six

The ring of my phone woke me up the next morning. Rolling over, I picked it up and checked the time. It was seven o'clock, and Lillian's name showed on the screen. I answered with one word, "Why?"

"When are you coming by the Shadow Box?" she asked.

I sat up and pushed the hair out of my face. "It's Saturday, my day off."

"Katherine left a bag here for you. I think it's full of things that will change how you look."

Still in a sleepy fog, I asked, "Like a disguise?"

"Come find out," she replied.

"I'll be by in about an hour."

"No later than that. I'm closing up at ten."

Lillian never closed the store early. "Okay," I said,

confused.

She hung up before I could ask more.

I took a shower and got dressed in the warmest clothes I had left. There wasn't a lot to choose from since my mom had packed so much. I had to settle for a pair of jeans that were worn at the knees, a faded hoodie, and a pair of old Vans.

I didn't want to wake anyone up, so I tiptoed down the stairs to the kitchen. It turned out no one was home. Mom had left a note on the table.

> Dad and Alex went to the clubhouse for breakfast. I'm filling in at the gym this morning. Have a good time. Be sure to check in.

I scribbled "I love you guys" at the bottom, grabbed a handful of granola, and headed for the garage and my car.

Technically, the Shadow Box didn't open until nine, but Lillian had left the door unlocked for me. When I went in, she was sitting at her messy desk with her eyes glued to her laptop. From the look of concentration on her face, she was on the trail of a rare book. Chasing down old and valuable volumes was the real source of her income. Running the Shadow Box was more like a hobby for her.

Hoping to get her attention, I let my backpack drop to the floor.

"I'm finishing this deal," she said.

"Okay," I replied, strolling over to a grouping of corduroy club chairs at the front of the store. When I sat down, a spring poked me in the hip. I adjusted my position and noticed Lillian must have hired a window painter to create a holiday scene on the glass. There was a snowman in one corner and a Santa Claus in the other. Blue and white snowflakes bordered the top.

"Festive" wasn't a word I'd use to describe the Shadow Box. Having the window painted was likely a first time ever event.

Across the street, the owner of the Tiny Cup Teashop had put a Closing our Doors for good, Liquidation Sale sign up. The teashop was on a long list of stores in the neighborhood to call it quits. What small businesses that remained were struggling to hold on. Lillian hadn't said so, but if I were a betting girl, I would have put money down that the Shadow Box was running in the red. Business had been even slower than normal over the past few weeks.

"Got it," Lillian said.

"Is it something great?" I asked.

"A sixteenth-century Italian tribute. I'm going to make an excellent profit. The seller went lower than I hoped he would. I just have to put in the payment information and the transaction is done."

She finished at her computer, went into the back room, and came back carrying two cups of tea. I thanked her when she handed one of them to me. When she wasn't looking, I put it on the table next to me. After almost two years, she still didn't remember I hated tea.

Motioning toward the street outside, she said, "It looks like a ghost town, doesn't it?"

"It's still early, and normal people sleep in on Saturdays. Business will pick up in a few hours."

Her hazel eyes met mine. "You don't believe that any more than I do."

She was right, but I wasn't going to admit it.

She blew on her tea, took a delicate sip, and then reached for a bag near her feet. "These are the things from Katherine. You should probably look through them."

I took the bag, hoping whatever Katherine had put in it would make me appear a whole lot different than my biological mother. Ironically, I didn't know what she looked like. The dewing tried not to get caught in pictures, because it would be hard to explain to an old acquaintance why you looked the same at sixty as you did at thirty.

Opening the bag, I found a manila envelope. I pulled airline tickets and new ID out of it.

"According to this driver's license, my name is Ali McCain," I said. "Apparently, I'm from Arizona."

Ali McCain had dark hair like mine, but her eyes were black-brown. She also had a rocking good tan. The kind my naturally pale skin could never achieve.

I pulled a contact lens case out of the bag and opened it up. Two very brown lenses floated in a watery solution.

"You should have a bottle of pills in there, too," Lillian said. "They'll change your skin color…make it a couple of shades darker."

I found the bottle. The pills inside were enormous. "Is it possible to swallow these without choking to death?" I asked.

"Those things have been around for a long time. No one has died yet. At least not that I know of."

"That's comforting," I muttered, putting the ID in my pocket. "Even with dark eyes and a new complexion, a Truss might recognize me," I commented.

"I doubt it. I knew you for more than a year and didn't make the connection between you and your mother until Ian told me who you were. The resemblance is all in the eyes. That pale blue-gray color is unusual. Besides, she was petite with white-blond hair. You're the opposite."

I was taken aback. "You knew her?"

"I didn't *know* her. I met her once."

"You never felt like you should mention that to me?"

"Why…is it important?"

"Well, yeah," I replied. "What did you think of her?"

Lillian shrugged. "I thought she talked too fast."

"That's all?'

She nodded and pointed at the pill bottle in my hand. "You should swallow one now. It takes a while for the full effect to set in. There's should be a blue pill among the others. It's the reverse dose. When you swallow that one, drink lots of water. You'll basically pee the color out."

"That's disgusting," I replied.

In the bottom of the bag was the book Ian tried to give to me the night before. I wasn't happy to see it. I felt like I was being pushed again.

Leaning forward, Lillian caught a glimpse of it and she drew a sharp breath. "Can I look?" she asked with something close to reverence.

Turning pages, she stopped at one with a beautiful illustration on it. Thanks to an art history class, I had a soft spot for art. Lillian rotated the book so I could see. The inked and colored drawing showed a map of the island of Atlantis. It was southwest of the very bottom of England.

The picture piqued my interest.

"I expected the island to be in the Mediterranean," I said. "Not out in the middle of nowhere."

"The island was isolated but our people weren't," she replied. "Our maritime technology was centuries ahead of humankind's. We sailed and had settlements in many different places. Several of them were on the coast of the Mediterranean Sea."

She pointed to a dot marked with the word "Laurel." "Do you recognize this?"

"Of course, it's my clan name."

"The fifteen original cities were each named after one of the clans."

I looked at the arrangement of dots. The Dawning, Vasitass, Stentorian, and Ormolu lived in the northern hilly region. The Illuminant, Bethex, Calyx, and Klamant lived on the eastern coast and in the plains. The Thane, Elysis, and Truss lived in the middle. The Laurel, Falco, Gallem, and Hezida lived on the west side of the island.

I let my finger rest lightly over the city marked Laurel. There weren't any of them left for me to know, but they were still a part of me.

"It's a beautiful book," I said. "And probably valuable."

"It's priceless," she replied.

The muscles in my shoulders tightened. "Why did she send it in the bag? About the last thing I want to do is fly to Colorado with a priceless book in my backpack. Can you keep it in the vault until I get back?"

Lillian thought about it. "No. If Katherine wants you to take it with you, that's what you should do."

She reached for her teacup, and I saw the corded scar that formed a V in her palm. We all had the mark, but it was uglier in Lillian's palm. It got that way with age. The V in my palm was a faint blue color, sort of like it had been drawn lightly with a blue pen. I'd learned early on to curl my fingers in a bit to hide it. All the other dewing I knew had variations of the same habit.

The mark had bothered me before I learned its significance. Now I associated it with Atlantis and a connection to my ancestors.

"There should be one other thing inside," Lillian said, pointing to the bag. "It will look like a tan tissue square."

I checked and found what she was talking about. "What is it?"

She took the paper from me, pulled a backing off, and laid it over my palm. I watched the V fade away and the edges of the tissue disappear into my skin.

"How…is that possible?" I asked, turning my hand back and forth.

"Our technology. You can only wear it for a few days because the material restricts oxygen flow to your skin. It will peel off on its own."

I nodded my understanding. A spring in the chair was

poking me again, so I shifted uncomfortably. "I think you need new furniture in here," I commented.

"I'll be two hundred eighty-three in March."

Rapid subject changes weren't unusual for Lillian. I'd learned to adjust. "I'll throw you a party," I replied.

"Who would come? And anyway, I won't be here in March."

"Are you going on a trip to celebrate?"

"I'm moving...to Ystad."

I blinked. She'd never mentioned moving before.

"You're moving?" I asked to clarify.

"To Ystad," she repeated. "It's in Sweden. I'm closing the store before I go."

I took a deep steadying breath. I'd never thought about Lillian leaving. She was probably the closest thing I had to dewing family. I hated the idea that she might move.

"Did you just pick that place off a map?" I asked, keeping my voice as even as I could.

"I was born in Ystad. It's where I spent some of my happiest days. I want to feel the wind coming off the sea and listen to the sound of the gulls in the air. I want to go back to where I started...in the time I have left."

I gulped as I considered what she was really saying. "In the time you have left?" I asked.

"I could die any time now."

I shook my head and huffed. "You don't look sick."

"I'm old," she replied. "Aging for us isn't what it is for humans. Our hair goes gray, and we get wrinkled, but the rest of us doesn't gradually slow to a stop. It's a sudden thing. One day we're here, the next we're not. Maybe it's a blessing…maybe it a curse. I'm not sure. All I know is that I want to go home before it happens."

My mind was whirling. "When are you leaving?"

"In February. I'll start an inventory clearance sale after the first of the year. I should have all the loose ends tied up quickly."

"I don't know what I'll do without you and the Shadow Box," I said.

"You won't be around much longer, either. You'll graduate from high school in the spring. Then I assume you'll go to college and from there, someplace the McKyes can't find you. At that point, I think you should go to the Thanes."

Spencer and Katherine hadn't said so officially, but I figured if I asked, they'd take me in after college. The problem was, I didn't know if I wanted to live with them.

Lillian watched me for a moment. "You're not sure about a future with them in it, are you?" she asked.

"I'm not."

"I may be able to help clarify a few things for you," she said.

I knew what she was offering. As a reader she could join a human mind to see emotions. I was dewing, but having been raised human, my mind was susceptible to her joining, too.

"I suppose it wouldn't hurt," I replied.

There was a slight jolt of energy when her mind joined mine. The feeling as she worked, I equated with putting

Legos together. She found thoughts and feelings that matched and clicked them together.

"You're uneasy, and it's not just about the trip to Colorado," she said. "You're conflicted. Probably over Ian." When I didn't deny it, she continued. "You're happy when you think about him, but you feel grief, too. You know he's in love with you, but you're scared of loving him back. You think…no, you're *sure* loving him back will cause you pain. You believe he'll likeness with someone else and you don't want to see it when it happens."

The pressure of our mental connection eased as she let me go. "Does that help?"

"Yes," I replied softly.

"When you've lived as long as I have, you learn some things," she said. "One is that you can be sure of only one thing: death. The situation between you and Ian may work out different than you believe."

I knew it wouldn't, but I appreciated that she cared enough to say so.

"If you want, you can come stay with me in Ystad," she continued. "As long as I'm still breathing, you will have a place to stay."

It was an enormous show of trust and affection for Lillian to open her home to me. Tears stung my eyes, but I didn't let them fall. Lillian wouldn't like that show of emotion. "Thank you," I said. "You don't know how much that means to me."

She sipped her tea. "I think I do. I also think you'd be better off with the Thanes."

Chapter Seven

There was a surprise waiting for me at my car. He was dressed in a gray Henley, dark jeans, and his usual Converse.

"Hey, what are you doing here?" I asked.

"You've been spending too much time with Lillian," Ian replied. "'Good morning, Ian. How are you? You look like a god.' That's how polite people greet each other."

I laughed. "Okay, good morning, Ian. You look like a god."

"Better," he replied.

I leaned against the side of my car. "So, why are you here?"

"To say good-bye and tell you good luck. We may not see much of each other much for the next few days."

I felt a twinge of separation anxiety, which came as a

surprise. We'd been together almost every day since school started. I hadn't realized how important his presence was to me.

"You okay?" he asked. "You've gone a little pale."

"I'm just not looking forward to sleeping on some stranger's couch for a week."

"Theron is a good guy…well, in most ways."

"Uh…I don't like how that sounds."

"He's been going through kind of a rough time," Ian replied, shuffling his feet.

"What type of rough time?"

"He…broke some important rules. He's serving a year's isolation and suspension because of it. Isolation means he can't travel more than a hundred miles from his primary residence. Suspension means he has limited access to technology."

"So, it's punishment. It's like getting sent to dewing jail."

Ian nodded. "He's our age but incredible with computers. He graduated from MIT when he was fifteen. A couple months ago, he hacked into some federal databases and got caught by one of our own. If he'd been found out by humans, it would have put a lot of attention on him, and consequently on us. That's a big no-no."

Exasperated, I sucked in a breath. "I can't believe it. Your parents are sending me to stay with a criminal."

"Theron didn't hurt anyone. I think he only hacked the Feds because it was a challenge, and it kept him busy. My mom calls him a restless soul. Trust me. He's harmless."

"For his sake, I hope you're right. Because if not, I'm

going to punch him in the throat and then go after your dad and do the same thing."

Ian's eyes twinkled. "You're cute when you're trying to be scary."

"I am scary. I put an end to the biggest evil we've—"

I stopped talking because Ian had stepped in front of me and slid his hand behind my neck. I knew what he was going to do. I also knew I should turn away, but I didn't. I let him move closer, I didn't look away when his eyes lingered on my lips, and I didn't tell him to stop when his lips touched mine. Instead, I moved even nearer until there was no space between us. I reached up and ran my fingers through the golden-blond hair that curled up at his shirt collar.

Part of me was disappointed in myself. I'd given in. The other part of me didn't give a crap and wanted the kiss to last forever.

He moved his hand from behind my neck and held mine. When the V marks in our palms touched, a jolt of energy shot through me. I jumped back like I'd been scalded. "What happened?" I asked, looking at my hand.

"I kissed you. I thought you knew what that was, but I can define the word for you if want."

"I don't want you to define it, because that was more than a kiss and you know it." I touched my lips, which were still tingling.

He wrapped his fingers around mine and moved them. "Don't wipe our kiss away," he said.

"We shouldn't have done that."

"I disagree. I think it's exactly what we should have

done."

I dropped my gaze so he wouldn't see the sadness in my eyes. "It makes things confusing and complicated."

I left out the part about being heartbreaking, too.

He let out a long breath. "There's more to it than that, Alison. There's something you're not telling me. Why don't you just spill it, so we can talk things through?"

The answer was that if I told him, it would hurt and could destroy our friendship.

I moved around and opened my car door.

"Okay," he said, his shoulders slumping a bit. "I suppose it's time for you to run away like you usually do. Have a safe trip. Tell Theron I said hi. I'll call you tomorrow morning."

I closed the door and started my engine. I couldn't leave him like that, though. After rolling down my window, I said, "I'm sorry, Ian."

He smiled a little. "You'll tell me eventually. Like everything else with you, it's just a matter of time.

Chapter Eight

It was six o'clock when my plane touched down at the airport, and I was exhausted. The flight that should have taken me a few hours took six instead. Halfway through, we had to land because of mechanical trouble. My fellow passengers and I sat around a dirty airport while it got worked on.

After breathing recirculated air and sitting on seats with who-knows-what spilled on them, I wanted to shower, change my clothes, and go sleep somewhere. Walking through the poorly lit jet way, I rubbed my dry eyes and hoped I'd find Theron quickly.

The moment I stepped off the escalator on the first floor, I felt a weak dewing vibration. It was so slow that I had to pay close attention to narrow down who it was coming from.

The lucky guy was leaning against a wall by the luggage

carousel. He was making a fist and letting it go over and over again. When he turned slightly, I got a good look at his face. A passing impression that I'd seen him before ghosted through my mind.

I started walking his way, and he made a fist again. He was good-looking, tall with broad shoulders that practically screamed muscles. His hair was brown and cut short. Darkish eyes framed by thick lashes and a brooding, impatient expression added to the appeal. To sum it up, he was the tall, dark, and dangerous type.

Stopping at his side, I asked, "Are you expecting someone?"

His eyes traveled from my face to my feet and back up again. Then he stepped away from the wall. "Hello, coz," he drawled.

I didn't have cousins. Feeling a little sick at the idea that I'd approached a Truss, I backed away.

"Sorry," I said. "I thought you were someone else."

He grabbed my elbow before I got too far. Then he turned his hand over so I could see the faint V mark on his palm. "You got the right guy. I'm Theron Falco, your babysitter for the week."

I narrowed my eyes to look as menacing as possible. "I don't need a baby—"

"Yeah, yeah. You're going to tell me you don't need a babysitter and that you're capable of taking care of yourself, but it's not true. If things take a turn and you get yourself in trouble, I've been ordered to put my neck on the line for you."

"Consider yourself unordered," I growled before heading toward the luggage carousel to find my suitcase.

"So, you're Grace Laurel's kid?" he asked, following me.

"That's what I've been told."

"Isn't it interesting that everyone knows your mother's name, but they don't know a thing about your father? It's like he never existed."

I couldn't believe it. I'd know this guy for less than a minute and he was talking about my father in a way I found offensive.

"Do *you* know his name?" he taunted.

"Of course I do."

"What is it?"

When I didn't answer, he asked again. "What was his name?"

If I hadn't been so irritated I would have kept my mouth shut, but I wasn't in my right mind. "His name was Saul," I hissed. "And don't say another word about him."

I glared at him. He was angry, too, though I couldn't understand why. He was the one who'd been rude to me.

Gradually, he relaxed. "I didn't think the Thanes would tell you. To dewing like them he was insignificant."

I stood stock-still, unsure if I should hit him for his second rude remark.

"Do you want me to get your bag?" he asked.

What I wanted was to knee him between the legs, plant my elbow in his spine, and watch him writhe on the floor in pain, but I started going through luggage looking for my suitcase instead.

"What does it look like?"

"It's ugly. The ugliest one you've ever seen."

I spotted it and waded through a sea of suitcases to get it. It didn't have wheels, so I had to lug it over the larger items like car seats, golf bags, and skis.

"You look different than I expected," he commented.

"What did you expect? A three-headed serpent?"

"I thought you'd look more like your dad. He was in and out of my life when I was a kid."

I turned to him. "What?"

He flicked his fingers. "I knew him. I used to call him Uncle Saul. But now isn't the time to discuss it."

"Why not?"

"For one, we're standing in a public airport. For another I just decided I don't *want* to discuss it."

So that's how things were going to work between us. If Theron was going to be a plain-speaking jerk, I was going to unleash the demons of mockery and scorn on him.

Squaring my jaw and lifting one eyebrow, I said, "You're ninety percent asshole, aren't you?"

He put a hand to his heart. "That hurts. I'm ninety-eight percent asshole."

I found my snowboard and then settled a glare of hate on him.

He was unfazed. "Listen, I want to get out of here," he said. "We can do that faster if I carry something. Do you want to let me help or not?"

"What I would like is someplace else to stay for the week," I muttered. Then in a louder voice, I said, "I got it."

"Suit yourself," he replied, walking ahead, "But I only ask once. Don't expect me to slow down while you schlep your stuff. You can find the car by yourself."

I would have flipped him off if my hands hadn't been full with my things.

Chapter Nine

The lights of the city faded in the rearview mirror as we drove away from the airport. Leaning my head against the cool glass of the car window, I looked at the sky. Bright moonlight lit the snowflakes that floated like pieces of cotton through the air.

"I forgot how beautiful falling snow is," I said quietly.

He drummed his fingers on the steering wheel. "Until it turns to slush, and all the cars driving the interstate end up in a ditch."

Twenty minutes together and I already knew I was going to loath every moment I had to spend with this guy. "It's still pretty," I muttered.

"What exactly about snow makes it pretty?"

"It's white, it floats through the air, and every piece is

different."

"You just described a fly ball and bird poop," he replied.

Great. I'd be living with a jerk who thought snow was like bird poop. *Charming.* "Do you think puppies are ugly, too?" I asked.

"It depends on the breed."

I stared at his profile. His features were nice, but his skin looked green from the console lights. He reminded me of an ogre. I didn't want to share a roof with a ninety-eight percent asshole ogre.

"Is there anywhere else I can stay?" I asked.

"Nope."

I let my head flop back against the headrest and sighed. "I don't know what you have against me. You obviously don't want to 'babysit' me. That should probably hurt my feelings, but it doesn't because I don't like you. I don't like anything about this situation. I'd rather be at home with my friends, watching ridiculous horror movies and eating my mother's vegan pizza with fake cheese. Unfortunately, that's not an option."

He was quiet for a moment, and then I thought I heard him chuckle. "Fake cheese?" he asked.

"It's made with coconut oil instead of milk. It doesn't taste bad, but it feels like wax in your mouth. It's terrible. You should try some."

"Maybe I will," he replied as if he liked the idea.

I folded my arms across my chest and concentrated on the falling snow.

"Okay," he said. "I admit we got off on the wrong foot."

"It wasn't me that got off on the wrong foot. It was you. Aside from the fact that you insulted me and then my father ten seconds after I met you, you know my entire clan was murdered. Calling me coz was just…cruel."

His brow furrowed, and he shook his head. "That's Spencer for you. Never tell the whole truth when half will do."

"What are you talking about?"

"He didn't tell you your father was Falco."

"That's because he was a Laurel. His name and dates are in the genealogy volume."

"Right, but your father was adopted into the Laurel clan after he likenessed with your mother. That's how it works with us. When a pair are from different clans, they choose one and swear loyalty to it. Your parents chose the Laurels, but he was originally a Falco like me."

I looked at him in disbelief. Not disbelief of what he'd said. He had no reason to lie about it. It was incredulity that I might really have living relatives.

"I did exaggerate a little," he admitted. "I'm not your cousin. Not your first cousin, anyway. Your dad's sister was my uncle's aunt or something like that."

I felt a wary sense of hope. "I have an aunt?"

"Uh…not anymore. She and your grandparents… passed away."

"Of course they did," I huffed as my rising hopes collapsed. I hadn't known about my father's family for more than two seconds, and they'd been taken from me, too. "Destiny wouldn't have it any other way," I whispered softly.

Theron glanced at me and then started to drum the steering wheel. He seemed a little ashamed. Maybe he'd figured out how awful some of the things he'd said to me were.

"That's Greenvale," he said, nodding toward some lights in the distance. "It's the nearest town to my place and the Ledges. That's where Ian is staying. There's no hotel, but my friend Stacy agreed to put him up. I suppose she'd put you up, too. But her place is small, and you'd have an hour commute up the hill each day. There's also a chance you'd fall into a ravine trying to negotiate the road during a snowstorm."

There was an exit ahead. He turned his blinker on. "Speak now or forever hold your peace," he said.

I'd been honest when I told him I didn't like him, but I really didn't want an hour commute in bad weather to get to the Truss. Maybe if I stayed away from him as much as possible it would be okay.

"Well, Spencer wouldn't like it if I change plans," I said.

"There is that. He'd probably come for my head, but I'd take his off first."

He was joking…probably. "I don't want to be the reason for that," I said. "We'll try it. If I can't stand you, I reevaluate."

"Sounds good."

He took the exit, turned right, and gunned the gas.

My hands tightened into fists. "You're going too fast," I said in a squeaky voice. "You told me the roads get slick with slush."

"They do, backseat driver, but I have to get a running start or we won't make it up the first incline."

The engine roared and my stomach churned. I had to swallow hard to keep my airplane peanuts from coming up. When the road narrowed and started to get curvy, I got light-headed.

Trying to divert my attention, I watched the tall evergreens get increasingly thick as we climbed. But then they disappeared on the left side of the road and there was nothing to stop us from driving off and rolling down the steep hillside.

In my mind, I watched a cartoon version of Theron's Land Rover, with me in it, flipping end over end down the mountainside.

When the back wheels slipped, Theron made a growling noise and shifted something.

"We're going to die, aren't we?" I asked.

"Relax," he replied. "I drive this road all the time. I know what I'm doing. Besides, if we drive off the hill we won't stay dead. We might break every bone in our bodies and be in a coma for a few months, but we'd heal."

"That doesn't make me feel much better," I replied through my teeth.

When the road straightened out a bit, he said, "Spencer told me to give you the layout of the Ledges. So here goes. The lodge is a five-level building just off the main road. The bottom level is mainly shops. There are two restaurants and a spa there, too. Six big conference rooms take up the second floor. Above that are the guest rooms. Additionally, twenty private cabins are spread around the property. It's a members-only resort with security staff on site. They're all plainclothes, but don't be fooled. Half of them are former military."

"Why so much security?"

"Because the people who stay there are either famous or very wealthy. Usually both. Those things breed curiosity, stalkers, and sometimes violence. The guests are willing to pay a high price for privacy and safety. "

"How did my alter ego, Ali McCain from Arizona, score a ski pass to a private resort overnight?" I asked.

"Spencer and Katherine have friends in high places."

"It's hard to believe the rich and famous travel this terrifying road, risking their lives just for time away from the public."

"They don't. They helicopter in. You'll drive, but you have to go through a search at the security gate. You might get lucky. They do pat-downs sometimes."

I rolled my eyes. Unfortunately, it was too dark for him to see. "What will they be looking for?"

"Cameras mostly. They want to keep the paparazzi out. They'll try to take your phone but Spencer said your joining will get you around that."

"Thoughtmaking my way through the gate will be easy."

Theron negotiated a sharp curve in the road, and I squeezed my eyes closed. "I've always wondered how that works," he said.

"Don't worry, I'll show you before I go."

"Why does that sound so unpleasant?"

"Because it will be."

By the time he slowed and turned into an opening

between the trees, my fingernails had dug indentations in the skin of my palms.

He stopped the Land Rover in front of a rustic-looking cabin. It appeared surprisingly cozy. Smoke came from the chimney, and a lamp was shining in the window.

"Welcome to Hotel Falco," he said. "Continental breakfast included, as long as you consider cold cereal continental."

I opened my door, stepped down, slid on the packed snow, and landed on my butt.

"Ooh, that hurt," Theron said, glancing my way.

"Thanks for the compassion," I replied, pulling myself up by the door handle.

He looked at my shoes. "Vans? You might as well be barefoot. I hope you packed some boots."

I brushed snow off my backside and gingerly made my way to the back of the car to get my stuff.

For the first time, I saw a hint of sympathy in Theron's expression. "Go inside," he said. "You'll freeze solid before you can haul your things up the stairs. I'll get it all."

My toes were numb and my tailbone hurt, so I didn't argue.

Letting myself in the door, I checked out the space.

My first impression was that it was really small. My second impression was that it was cute. Little old lady cute. There were homespun rugs on the floor, checkered curtains at the windows, and two wooden rocking chairs flanking a fireplace.

The charm of the place was marred by the piles of things stacked in each of the four corners. There were tools and electronic odds and ends in one corner. Snowshoes, cross-country skis, canteens, and backpacks in the second. The TV and about a million books took up the third. And an art easel on top of a canvas drop cloth was set up in the fourth.

The most impressive part of the room was a huge fireplace with happy little flames dancing inside.

After taking my shoes off, I hung my coat on a hook behind the door and went to sit near the warmth.

I was nearly thawed out by the time Theron came in carrying my suitcase. He shook snow from his spiky hair, stamped his feet, and hung his coat. "I put your board on the porch," he said. "The overhang will keep it dry until tomorrow."

"I'd say thanks, but you're shaking snow all over my Louis Vuitton luggage."

He looked down at the disaster that held my clothes. "Louis Vuitton doesn't do duct tape. Come on, I'll show you your room."

I followed him down a dark hallway. He stopped halfway to the end and pushed a door open. "This is it," he said. "Make yourself at home."

It was a tiny room with a twin bed against one wall and a dresser against the other. There were shelves with knickknacks on them all over the room, and the bed had been made up with a beautiful red-and-white quilt. It was the kind that had been patched and stitched by hand and would cost hundreds of dollars to buy. There wasn't a lot of walking space, but it was super cute.

"This place is adorable," I said. "I mean you could do

an episode of *Hoarders* with all that stuff in the living room, but the bare bones are really great."

His gaze softened. "My grandparents built it. It was one of their vacation spots. My grandma called it her Snow White cottage."

"I can see why," I replied, smiling.

I'd been right about a little old lady decorating the place.

"What's in those?" I asked, pointing to two boxes next to the bed.

"I'm not sure. Katherine had them expressed into town today."

I stepped in and laid my backpack on the dresser.

"The bathroom is across from you," he said. "The towels are under the sink. There's food in the refrigerator if you're hungry."

"Thanks," I replied, like a good guest should.

"Okay then. It was sort of nice meeting you, Jillian Laurel."

He'd called me by my dewing name. "Jillian Laurel doesn't exist," I said sharply. "I'm still Alison McKye."

He looked thoughtful. "Are you telling that to me or to yourself?"

I honestly didn't know how to respond.

He turned his back to me and walked out. The impression that I'd seen him before came back, only stronger. I quickly ran through my memories but still couldn't find a match to anyone that looked like him.

I closed the door, thinking I was just overly tired and imagining things.

Chapter Ten

*T*en hours later, I was ripped from a nice dream by Theron knocking on the door. When I didn't answer immediately, he knocked louder.

"Go away," I said. "The sun isn't even up."

"What?" he asked. "I can't hear you."

Realizing my voice was muffled by blankets, I pushed them off my face. All I could see was my own mess of hair.

"I said go away," I repeated.

"No. I'm going to give you ten seconds. Then I'm going to throw your phone into a snowbank. You left it in the bathroom and it keeps ringing. The train whistle's driving me crazy."

He was probably kidding about the snowbank, but after some of our less-than-friendly interactions, I couldn't be sure.

Bracing myself for the cold, I threw the covers off and ran to the door. I opened it to see Theron wearing an exasperated expression on his face and a flannel shirt. It was red-and-black checked.

"Where's your beard?" I asked.

"What are you talking about?"

"You look like a mountain man. Except they have beards. Tangled ones, with food in them."

His lips tipped up in a predatory smile. "You like insults first thing in the morning?" he asked. "That's my favorite game." He pointed to my hair. "What kind of animal is living on your head, because it looks like it's trying to eat your face."

"I'm hurt," I replied, pretending to pout.

I reached for the phone in his hand, but he evaded me and held it high. "Ask nicely, Amazon."

I started jumping for it, but Theron was tall enough to keep it away. Not many were. "You woke me up to give it to me," I replied. "Hand it over so I can hate you from under the covers where it's warm."

He raised an eyebrow. "My mountain man flannel is warm. What you're wearing is not. I can stand here for hours."

I stopped jumping and put my hands on my hips. I was freezing. "Please," I said with false sweetness.

He dropped the phone into my hand. "That's better."

"Just so you know"—I growled—"I'm not some animal you can train to do tricks."

He chuckled all the way down the hall.

I ran for the bed, crawled in, and checked my messages. Mom had called three times. Figuring she'd worked herself into a frenzy of worry, I called her back. I expected her to be waiting anxiously with her phone nearby. Surprisingly, she didn't answer at all. I left a message telling her I was fine and that I'd call later that night.

After a good yawn and stretch, I sent a request to FaceTime Ian. I'd promised to contact him, but I almost hoped he was still asleep. The kiss, electric shock when our palms touched, and my reaction afterward left me feeling awkward.

He was up. His image flashed onto my screen. "Good morning, Ian. You look like a god."

He laughed and ran a hand through his hair. I could see he'd just had a shower. The light gold color of his hair was a shade darker and wet around his ears. I had a serious weakness for that look.

"You remember the proper way to greet people," he replied. "I'll have you cured of all Lillian's ways in no time."

"It helps that I'm a quick learner," I replied. "I thought you might be sleeping."

His image bounced around while he pulled a T-shirt over his head.

"I'm going out to breakfast with Theron's friend in a few minutes. Since I'm staying in her house, she wants to get to know me better."

"I'm surprised Theron has any friends," I grumbled.

"Why do you say that?"

"Because he's rude, insensitive, sarcastic, a morning person, and he dresses like a lumberjack."

Ian chuckled. "The isolation and suspension must be getting to him. I'll come punch him for you if you want."

"Thanks for the offer, but I can punch him myself."

"Just be patient. You'll charm him with your weirdness like you did me."

I smiled at the backhanded compliment. "What's Stacy like?" I asked.

"She's…hard to explain. She definitely likes cats, though."

He turned his phone in a slow three-sixty. Everything from the walls to the bedding had some kind of cat print on it.

When Ian reappeared, I said, "That's horrible."

"I'm sort of afraid to sleep in here. They might come to life and eat me piece by piece or something. How are you doing? Are you feeling better about your secret mission?"

"Not really. When I have the time, I'm going to be pissed at you and your parents. None of you said anything about my father being from the Falco clan. Imagine the shock when Theron told me we're related."

Ian was quiet for a moment. "We wanted to give you some time to deal with everything else that's happened," he said. "Telling you Sebastian killed your Falco grandparents seemed like a little too much for you to process."

Suddenly, I couldn't swallow. Learning that Sebastian had spilled more of my family's blood stole my breath. This time he'd taken lives from another clan.

I made myself drag some oxygen in and said, "Theron

told me they were dead, not that they'd been murdered."

His eyes softened as he looked at me. I could see a pang of guilt in them and how much he hadn't wanted to cause me pain. "I'm sorry I didn't tell you before," he said.

"Well, tell me everything now."

"Sebastian thought your father's family might be hiding you. He made sure they weren't."

All I could think was that he'd killed them because of me. Then I imagined something even worse. "He tortured them first, didn't he?" I asked.

Ian wouldn't answer that question, which was answer enough.

"Ah…I feel sick," I said.

"Crap. Stacy is knocking at the door. I have to go, but I want you to find Theron. Ask him what happened. He can give you details I can't."

"I changed my mind," I replied. "I don't want to know anything more, and I definitely don't want to be around Theron."

"Do it for me, Alison," he pleaded. "You shouldn't be alone right now. If you don't want to ask him about your grandparents, ask him to repeat the conversation we had earlier. I updated him on a few things."

I could see some wisdom in what he was saying. At least if I fell into a catatonic state from an overload of grief, which wasn't completely out of the question, Theron would be able to monitor my vital signs.

"Okay," I said. "I'll find him."

"Promise me."

"I promise."

Numb to the cold this time, I went looking for Theron. He was sorting through the hiking stuff in one of the corners. He glanced up at me and then scowled. "A T-shirt and shorts in Vegas may be fine, but they won't work here. Go put some warmer clothes on. I don't want to look at your goose bumps anyway."

I ignored him and sat down at the table. Folding my arms on top of it, I hid my face. "Don't look at me then," I said.

"I'm serious. The heat in this place barely works well enough to keep the pipes from freezing. You'll catch pneumonia."

"I don't care. I'm going to sit here and you're supposed to be in the general area while I do it. I promised Ian."

There was a moment of hesitation, then I heard his footsteps cross the floor. A heavy blanket fell over my shoulders. "At least wrap up in this."

Because I'd started to feel the cold again, I pulled it tight around myself and rested my head in my arms.

"What's wrong?" he asked.

I tipped my head so I could stare at him with one eye. "I'm going to be perfectly honest, so prepare yourself."

"Okay," he replied.

"I *hate* destiny."

If previous experience was anything to go by, speaking ill of destiny was blasphemous. I expected Theron to look shocked or angry…especially because we weren't friends, but he didn't react at all.

"We have that in common," he replied.

I watched him sit down, trying to determine if he was being serious or mocking me.

"So tell me," he said. "Why do you hate destiny?"

"For a lot of reasons. The biggest one right now is that Sebastian Truss killed every Laurel but me and then turned to the Falco clan and killed some of them, too. And he did it because he wanted to find me. It's my fault people from your clan are dead. I suppose that explains why you hate me."

He looked shocked that I'd suggested it. "I don't blame you for what happened to your grandparents," he said.

I sniffed. "Really?"

"Really. And look on the bright side, you still have me, your amazing cousin."

"You're like my third cousin five times removed or something."

"It still counts."

I smiled a little. "I don't like destiny for a lot of other reasons, too."

"Do you want to tell Uncle Theron about it?" he teased.

"I thought you were my cousin."

"I'm offering to listen, take it or leave it."

"Okay, here's another one," I said. "Three years ago, I was a pretty normal kid, living a pretty normal life. Then I meet some guy who tells me I'm a different species and some other guy is hunting for me. He says I better hide so my family doesn't end up dead. Then I meet these people who explain what I am and what I can do. Great, right? No, because I'm not really dewing, my mind doesn't work like theirs. But I'm not human either. It's like I'm hanging in space swinging from two worlds. Destiny turned me into a freak."

"If it makes you feel better, you're not the only freak I know," he said.

"Can I meet the other guy? Because I'd like to form a support group."

He chuckled. "I'll introduce you sometime."

I drew a deep breath and sat up straight. "Sorry. I just unloaded my trash on you."

"I'm carrying my own trash. A bit more doesn't make a difference."

"Wow. Are you actually being nice?"

"Don't worry, it'll pass. In fact, I feel my old self coming back. Tell me how you got that frightening bedhead?"

I patted my hair. It had to be standing three inches high. "It's simple. Sleep with the covers over your face to keep your nose from freezing off. It would look good on you."

"Noooo thanks," he replied.

"I'm supposed to get an update on the situation at the resort," I said.

"I'll tell you, but not until you're dressed and your hair is tamed. I think I'm going to have nightmares about it."

"I hope so," I replied, getting out of the chair to go clean up. "Because I'm going to have nightmares about the shirt you're wearing."

The warm shower felt wonderful. I stayed under until the hot water ran out. Drying my hair, I thought about Theron. I couldn't figure him out. He'd been cruel the night before, sarcastic that morning, and then almost sympathetic at the table. The keyword was *almost*. I didn't like him, but I didn't hate him anymore, either.

I'd opened the boxes by the bed the night before. They were full of new clothes. Going through them had been like opening presents on Christmas morning. Along with snow boots and thick socks, there were new sweaters, jeans, and snow gear. Katherine had sent a parka, an insulated jacket, and pants as well.

I laid the ski clothes on the bed and noticed the tag under the arm of the parka. I had to sit down after reading it. The parka alone cost almost as much as my car.

When I was dressed, I went to find Theron. He was sitting at the table, weaving a spoon back and forth between his fingers. "Wow, you look spoiled," he said. "You'll blend right in."

"Guess how much this cost?" I said, holding the parka out.

He shrugged. "I have no idea."

"Two thousand five hundred dollars." I pointed to the ski pants I was wearing. "These cost one thousand five hundred. Together, that's as much as I spent on my car."

"You must drive a real junker," he replied.

"That's not the point."

"Look, you're going to be mixing with lots of people in expensive parkas. Your job is to blend in. Katherine sent appropriate things for that. You should trust her."

I thought about it. "Maybe you're right."

He pointed to a box of sugary cereal. "Continental

breakfast like I promised."

I think I squealed. "I haven't had Frosted Flakes in years," I said, pouring a bowl. "My mom refuses to have it in the house. She says it's addictive like drugs."

I ate one bowl and poured a second.

When I was full enough to care, I noticed Theron staring at me.

"What?" I asked.

"Aside from the fact that you're inhaling that cereal, you look like a different person today."

"Should I take that as a compliment? You didn't like the old me."

"It's just an observation."

I pulled a face at him. "What information do I need to know about the resort?"

"Word for word as they came from Ian's mouth, or summary version?"

"Summary, please."

He nodded. "Originally Yvonne had booked five rooms at the Ledges. Last night she booked ten more and two of the cabins. What Katherine and Spencer thought was going to be a small gathering is turning into something a lot bigger. They aren't sure what that means, but they hope you'll be able to shed some light on it. Your target is still the same. Get in good with Phoebe and hope she'll get you close to her parents."

"Any idea what she looks like?"

Theron reached in the pocket of his shirt and produced a flip phone.

"That's tragic," I said, nodding to it. "I didn't think they made those anymore."

"This is as much technology as I'm allowed. It's a piece of junk, but I can get pictures on it. One of Spencer's people took this. It's the latest Truss family photo."

He held the phone out for me to see. "Wow" was all I could say.

It showed a family of four entering a building. The father's and son's profiles looked normal. The mother's and daughter's did not. They had large noses that hooked down at the end. It was the kind of unfortunate facial feature that would always stand out in a crowd.

Theron flipped the phone closed. "You think you'll recognize her?"

"Yep. I guess we can go now."

He hesitated. "There's been a change of plans. I'm not going with you. Not today, anyway. So many Truss in one area is a big deal. Plus it makes the odds of them noticing me greater. Spencer thinks it's best for you to observe them in their natural state, not when they're worried about a dewing from another clan…even if that dewing is someone like me."

"I'm going in alone." I sighed. "Why did I not see that coming?"

He tossed me some keys. "Spencer had me get a rental car when I agreed to let you stay here. You can choose to think of it as a coincidence, if you want. I put your snowboard on the rack."

"Thanks, but if I'm on my own, I'll hang out at the lodge

all day. I've got a better chance of finding her that way."

"It's your ballgame now."

He pulled something out of his pocket and tossed it to me as well. It was another cellphone, a good one, not another flip phone.

"When you're at the resort, that's the phone you should use," he said. "My number is the only one programmed in it."

I nodded and put it in my pocket.

"You can't always rely on the signal up here," he warned. "You'll get a strong one at the cabin because I jacked up the satellite wifi before this place became my prison. The Ledges has a good one, too, but the trees and mountains on the road block it a lot of the time."

I nodded.

"It starts getting dark at four thirty," he continued. "Don't stay past five unless you let me know first. If you're not back by six, I'll come after you. Even if the roads look clear, go slow. Black ice is normal this high up."

My stomach tightened as I remembered our hair-raising drive the night before. "How will I find the resort if I can't get a GPS signal?"

He smiled at me like I was imbecilic. "There's only one road. When you get through the clearing, go left. The resort is a mile up the hill. You can't miss it."

Chapter Eleven

The drive from Theron's place to the Ledges was slow going. The snow had been cleared, but the road twisted and turned so much that I averaged about eight miles an hour. It was an enormous relief when I saw the lodge rising through the trees.

It looked like a giant log cabin, but the logs had to have been manufactured because I was pretty sure no trees grew long enough or wide enough to have built all five stories of the hotel.

The rustic ambiance was thrown off by a chain-link fence that ran around it. There wasn't barbed wire on the top, but the message was clear. If you're not invited, stay out.

I pulled my rented all-wheel-drive Subaru to a stop at the gatehouse, and a muscular-looking man stepped out.

"May I see your driver's license?" he asked.

I handed him my false ID, and he disappeared inside, presumably to check that the paperwork was in order. I used the time to scan the area. There were security cameras on the roof of the gatehouse and probably more along the fence. I figured they would be everywhere inside the lodge, too, which could complicate things if I had to do a lot of thoughtmaking. Whoever was monitoring the feed, especially if it included audio, might see fellow employees breaking the rules. I didn't really want to get anyone fired.

A woman came through the gate. She was dressed in normal-looking ski clothes, but when she unzipped her parka, I saw a baton hanging from her belt. It was sturdy enough to do real damage if she hit someone with it. Theron hadn't been lying about trained security staff.

The muscled guard came back out and handed me my license. Then he extended a finger scanner my way. "Not many visitors drive in," he said. "We keep prints on file just in case."

I almost asked *in case of what*, but it didn't matter. I didn't want my prints on file. The guard noticed me pause. "You can't get in without a scan," he said.

I could, but I was worried about the camera feed. Deciding to risk it, I joined his mind and put *the finger scan is complete* into it. He nodded like he'd done the job and returned the scanner to its place.

"Am I done now?" I asked.

"Not yet. I'll need to keep your phone and any other electronic devices you may have. You can pick them up on your way out."

I put my phone out like I was going to hand it to him, but implanted the thought *I have it. I'll put it away for her*, instead.

"Belinda will check your person now," he said.

Belinda was the woman with the baton. She wasn't going to touch me. I'd faked handing over my phone, so it was a little late to worry about cameras. I put *pat-down complete* into both of their minds, and that took care of it.

He opened the gate to the parking lot, and said, "Enjoy your time at the Ledges."

When I cut my engine and got out, I breathed in the cleanest air my lungs had processed in more than three years.

It had stormed the night before, so the snow would be fresh and fast. I told Theron I'd be staying in the lodge, but the conditions were just too perfect. If Phoebe liked to ski even a little, she'd probably be out. I decided I'd try looking for her on one of the runs first and then stake out the lodge for an hour or so.

After unloading my gear, I followed signs to one of the chairlifts.

Taking my place at the end of the line, I did some people watching. Aside from the fact that everyone had top-notch gear, most of the skiers were ordinary-looking. I'd almost lost interest when someone well known got in line behind me. My dad was big on news channels, so I was familiar with the man's face and voice. He was an anchor from CNN. I surmised from the resemblance between him and the young girl he was with that they were family. He saw me watching and sort of scowled, so I turned the other way.

A few yards ahead, I spotted an information board with a map on it that showed the layout of the ski runs. There were fewer of them than I'd expected, and they were all pretty short. I was going to get a taste but not the full experience of snowboarding, which was a disappointment.

At least the lift was good. It was state-of-the-art, took me up smoothly and at the perfect pace to enjoy the scenery below. Snow weighed on the branches of tall evergreens and sparkled in the sun. There was something wrong with Theron if he couldn't appreciate that kind of beauty.

When I slid off the lift at the top of the hill, I did a quick check of my gear and then pushed off. Momentum built as the forces of gravity took hold. Though I hadn't done it in a while, snowboarding was like riding a bike. You never forget how. Within minutes, most of my technique had come back.

Easing into a comfortable back-and-forth rhythm, I let my muscles warm. Then I picked up some speed. Noticing a high spot downslope, I cut toward it. I pulled my legs up to catch as much air as possible and landed smoothly.

That's when I felt two dewing ahead of me and identified them as Truss.

They were both women and not moving fast. I got a bit closer and then, trying not to make it obvious, looked them over. They were both wearing goggles, which obscured their faces a little, but neither of them had the nose I was looking for.

I cut to go around them, but the energy under my skin

started to heat in preparation for an essence fight. Without realizing what was happening, I'd become furious. It wasn't like I wanted to hurt them, but anger had turned my fight impulse into something I couldn't control.

Freaking out, I plowed off the run and into the deeper untouched snow. I stepped out of my bindings and sat down so my body would cool.

Bowing my head, I pinched the bridge of my nose and practiced some of my mom's yoga breathing exercises. I hadn't processed the thought at the time, but I'd wondered if either of the Truss had participated in the massacre of my clan. Their proximity, and the possibility they killed my family, made me burn with anger. Which meant there was a problem.

If I reacted to every Truss in that way, I wouldn't be able to get within yards of one, making hanging out with Phoebe impossible. Going back to the lodge didn't seem like a good idea after all, so I got back on my board and started down again.

I was pretty discouraged until I decided that regardless of my mission as a spy, I was going to take advantage of the snow and do one more run.

The next time down, a male Truss on skis passed me. Like before, the anger and heat came on, but not as strong as before. Still, it panicked me enough that I moved to the trees and sat. My energy returned to normal much faster, which was good.

I was curious if exposure to Truss was like building immunity. The more I was around them, the more my reaction would decrease.

I did a third run, hoping to test the theory.

There was another vibration ahead of me, and whoever it belonged to wasn't moving. They were sprawled out spread-eagle on the snow. I wanted to help but feared what my reaction might be if I got too close. Then I noticed her large nose, and it was bleeding. I'd found Phoebe.

Destiny had done me a huge favor.

I'd been told she was my age, which meant she wouldn't have been older than three when my clan was systematically murdered. She couldn't have been a part of it. I decided to take a chance, hoping with that knowledge my body wouldn't react. After getting off my board, I took slow steps toward her. My heat held steady, so I went all the way to her side.

"Are you okay?" I asked.

She sat up and rubbed under her hooked nose. Her glove came away streaked with red. Taking it off, she hunted in her pockets.

I pulled my scarf off and handed it to her to stem the bleeding.

"Use this," I suggested.

"No, I couldn't," she said in a voice loud enough to be heard in Canada.

Although surprised by the decibel, I continued to urge her. "I've got another. Just use it before your parka gets ruined."

I waved the scarf in her face until she took it. "Okay," she agreed.

"What happened?" I asked after a moment.

"Jacob freaking cut me off."

Her voice was still too loud, but not bone-rattling this time.

"Jacob?" I asked like I didn't know who he was.

"My brother. He likes to…joke around."

"It's tight on this corner. He probably didn't see you."

"Trust me. He saw." Moving her hand away from her face, she asked, "Has the bleeding stopped?"

I scrunched my nose and bent to look. "I think so. Let me help you up."

I reached out to her, but the moment our hands touched, I had to pull away. The heat and anger came back. I bent at the waist and counted my breaths.

"What's wrong?" she asked, sounding alarmed.

"Just light-headed," I lied. "All I've had to eat today is a couple bowls of sugary cereal."

She managed to get her feet under her and was almost standing when she winced and put a hand to her side.

"You're hurt," I said. "Maybe you should stay here. I can go for ski patrol."

She laughed. "You're breathing weird. Maybe *I* should go for ski patrol."

"We're both messed up," I replied, thinking it was funny, too.

"Anyway, I can't wait on the hill," she said. "I have to get back for dinner or my mom will kill me."

My temperature had returned to near normal, but I'd truly become light-headed.

"Maybe we should go down together," I suggested.

We made our careful way to the bottom and I asked, "How's your side?"

"I'll be okay by morning," she replied.

I smiled, knowing it was true. "I hope so. It would be a sucky vacation if you had to stay in your room with your ribs taped."

She kind of cringed. "This isn't a vacation. It's a week of meetings, followed by a ritualistic sacrifice."

I froze as I envisioned Nikki lying on a burning altar surrounded by Truss with pitchforks and stakes.

"Sorry," she said. "That didn't sound as creepy in my head as it did when I said it out loud. I'm actually here for a family reunion thing."

"Oh," I replied coolly.

"Thanks for the help," she said. "I'll have your scarf cleaned and then get it back to you. What room are you in?"

My quickly formulated plan had worked. She'd have to see me again when she returned it.

"I'm staying with…my grandmother," I improvised. "She lives down the hill. I've got a ski pass for the week, though. I could meet you somewhere."

"How about the lift tomorrow?"

"Okay. I'll be there around one o'clock."

"I'll find you," she said. "I'm Phoebe, by the way."

Things were getting off to a great start. "I'm Ali. See you tomorrow."

Chapter Twelve

I wasn't able to enjoy my success for long. I had a scary drive ahead of me. Not to mention an evening with Theron, whom I couldn't decide if I liked or not.

By the time I drove out the security gate, clouds had moved in and a fierce wind was gusting. I held the steering wheel in a death grip and negotiated the turns in the road at a crawl. Even so, I hit a patch of black ice and heard my own squeal of terror when the front wheels slipped. I got the car under control but might have suffered a heart attack in the process.

When I got back and opened the cabin door, a gush of warm air hit me in the face. It was wonderful.

Theron was watching something on television, while flipping a quarter into the air and then catching it. He glanced at me and said, "You're shaking from head to toe."

"That's because my life just flashed before my eyes at least a dozen times while driving back."

"City drivers. No sense of adventure."

"Well, this city driver deserves a pat on the back," I said, hanging my jacket. "I found Phoebe and talked to her. We're meeting at the chairlift tomorrow so she can return my scarf."

He flipped the quarter again. "Why does she have your scarf?"

"She wiped away a bunch of blood with it."

"Yuck. Are you sure you want it back?"

I shrugged as I sat in the empty chair next to him. "She's having it cleaned, and it's a good excuse to talk again."

"What's she like?" he asked.

"Loud and sort of bossy," I surmised.

"Did everything else go okay?"

"Ah…not really. When I'm around a Truss, I have some kind of allergic reaction."

He looked at me like I was speaking a foreign language. "Like hives or something?"

"No. I get angry and my essence starts to heat up."

"That will complicate things."

"I'll think of some way to control it. Or I'll just run away."

"It's your funeral." He shrugged.

"Have a little faith, Debbie Downer."

He pulled a face.

"I'm worried about all the security cameras up there,

though. I did some thoughtmaking before I went through the gate. I'm afraid if I keep doing it someone is going to get suspicious or fired."

Theron's quarter flew into the air again. He caught it easily. "I've got a solution for that problem, but I won't have everything set up until tomorrow afternoon."

Skeptical, I asked, "What are you going to do? Order a continuous supply of takeout for the security team, so they'll be stuffing their faces instead of checking their monitors?"

"Where did you come up with that idea?"

"I watch a lot of television," I said, motioning toward his screen. "The History Channel?"

He pulled the quilt off the back of his chair and threw it at me. It was warm from the heat of the fire and his body. It felt wonderful as I pulled it over my shoulders.

"You should watch, too," he said. "It's like school."

I snuggled into an armchair and watched for a minute. It was a documentary on Ben Franklin. I'd seen it before and was bored. There weren't a lot of exciting options in a cabin in the middle of the woods. The best I could manage was bugging grumpy Theron some more.

"Speaking of school," I said. "Are you in it?"

"After I finished at MIT, I studied art at Columbia for a year."

"Hence the easel," I said, pointing toward it. "I thought everything was ugly to you."

"I never said that. I asked you to explain *why* something was beautiful. Understanding beauty is an important skill for an artist."

He seemed to know his stuff. Impressed, I asked, "Did you do those canvases against the wall? Can I look?"

"Yes, and no. In that order."

"You're such a jerk."

"Yep."

My stomach growled loudly. "Dinner will be ready in half an hour," he said. "Can you wait that long?"

"Can I just have more cereal?"

"Nope. You only get cold cereal once a day at Hotel Falco. Besides, you'd probably finish the rest of the box, and I like cereal, too. I'm planning to give you a can of chili for dinner. If you're nice, I might even give you a spoon."

"Thanks for your generosity," I replied.

He nodded and got up and walked toward the kitchen. "You can change clothes or whatever. I'll hold the food for you."

"Is that your way of saying you don't like my current outfit?" I teased.

"It's my way of saying I don't like you getting the furniture wet."

I wanted to get out of my ski clothes anyway, so I went to my room, took off my insanely expensive snow gear, and pulled on one of the soft sweaters Katherine sent. It was a little tight, but I didn't care. It was marvelously warm. A pair of jeans and two pairs of socks later, I was pretty comfortable. Theron had said half an hour. I still had time, so I lay on the bed to stretch out.

Seeing that my phone was flashing with a message, I grabbed it to check. My mom had called and was anxious to talk to me. I dialed her cell phone, but yet again, she didn't answer. So, I dialed home and got Alex.

"Hi," he said with false enthusiasm. "Did you get my snow globe?"

"I've only been here since last night. I haven't had time. What's going on at home?"

"All the usual embarrassing stuff. I went golfing with Dad and had to fake laugh at all his friends' jokes. Then Mom made me go to one of her classes. I had to sit with my legs crossed like a pretzel while all her granola friends told me how much I look like her."

I laughed. "That's interesting since you're not genetically related."

"Exactly. I'm super mad that you left me alone with them. One of me and two of them doubles the crazy."

"Hang in there," I said. "Is Mom around? She left me a message to call back."

"She's on a run. Whatever she wants can't be that serious. She's been humming Christmas songs all day and cooking things. Whatever she's making smells good, but will probably give me diarrhea."

I choked out a laugh.

"I wish I was joking. I gotta go. Dad's asleep and I want to snag the remote before he wakes up."

"Okay. Tell Mom everything is fine here, and…"

"Gotta go," he repeated before hanging up.

I smiled. It wouldn't be the first time Alex sneaked the remote off my sleeping father's stomach so he could change the channel to anything that wasn't golf.

When I went back out, Theron was stirring something on the stove.

"Why don't you have a bathtub?" I asked, trying to look over his shoulder into the pot. "A hot bath would be heaven here."

With his free hand, he pushed me back a step. "I live in a cabin. Bathtubs aren't a necessity."

I leaned against the countertop. "Still, it would be nice, don't you think?"

"I'll put it in my expansion plans," he remarked drily. Nodding toward a loaf of bread on the countertop, he asked, "Will you put that bread on the table?"

I did, and the smell made my mouth water. He followed me and set bowls at our places.

"Sit. Eat," he ordered.

He didn't have to tell me twice. It was sort of like chili, but it was sweet as much as it was hot. And there were lots of vegetables, beans, and meat to make it filling.

"Like it?" Theron asked as I had another spoonful.

"Love it."

"Try the bread," he suggested. "Don't forget the butter."

I did and fell in love with that, too. "Did you make this from scratch?"

"Yep."

"Let me guess. This is your secret weapon. The one thing you cook really well. When you have a girl over, you make it for her, and she melts into your arms like this butter. I'm flattered you tried it on me."

He gave me his wicked smile. "If this was a secret

weapon designed for you, I would have poisoned it. And just so you know, I have lots of secret weapons. Until now this hasn't been one of them. Thanks for the idea."

I chewed more bread, watching him. I still wasn't sure if I liked him, but I liked that he was quick with a comeback. After a long day at the Ledges, it felt good to release some tension going back and forth with him.

"Where did you learn to cook like this?" I asked.

He pointed to a stack of books by the recliner. "I've read about a million cookbooks since getting stuck up here. Anything to keep my mind off the claustrophobia of this place. I have to eat anyway, so I figured I'd give it a try."

"Computers, painting, and cooking. Those are pretty different interests."

"Not really. There are creative aspects to all three."

"You're a badass computer hacking genius. You cook like a pro. How well do you paint?"

He shrugged and avoided eye contact. "Good enough that I've sold a couple of pieces."

"Is there anything you don't do well?"

His jaw muscles clenched and he scowled at me. "There are some things I can't do at all."

There was a half a second opening to ask what some of those things were, but it was gone before I said anything. He gave a look that warned he was done talking about it.

"Well, I'm happy you were bored enough to learn to cook," I said. "Can I have seconds?"

He nodded and got up to take my bowl.

"I can do it," I said.

He waved me down. "I got it. Did you call home?"

"Yep, I talked to Alex. He's my younger brother…well, younger human who I think of as brother. I shouldn't miss him, but I do."

"I have a brother. I could go the rest of my life without seeing him and be just fine."

That was odd. I'd learned enough about the dewing to know their family bonds were usually quite strong.

He brought more soup, sat down, picked up his butter knife, and started twirling it between his fingers like a baton.

"Are you considering stabbing me with that and then burying me in the backyard?" I asked.

He snorted. "I'm trying to figure out how to tell you something."

"I like the direct approach."

"Okay." He took a deep breath. "I think destiny sent you here for more than Nikki Dawning's sake."

"I'm here to gather information on Yvonne and Robert, too."

"Yeah, but it's more than that as well."

"Okay then. What's it about?"

His dark eyes bored into mine. "We knew each other before…all of this."

"Hah, funny," I replied.

"It's not a joke. You were young and don't remember, but we met years ago."

The spoon I was holding slipped from my fingers and clattered to the table. I felt the blood drain from my face.

"The last time I saw you," he continued, "You were

about four. I left you at a state hospital in Vegas."

I blinked and tried to take his words in.

He put his hands up and looked apologetic. "It wasn't my idea. I was just doing what I was told."

"Go on," I managed to whisper.

"At the airport, I told you your dad was in and out of my life. That's because he was my dad's best friend. When the Laurel massacre happened, your mother and father came to him for help. They were desperate to hide you, and the best place they could think to do it was with humans. You probably guessed that much."

"Ian said he thought that's what happened. I wasn't sure."

He nodded. "Now you can be sure. They needed to move fast because Sebastian had people following them. There were a couple places they could have left you, but I heard your mom say she wanted you in Vegas. It was a bigger city with lots of in-and-out travelers, which she hoped would make it harder for anyone to find you. But they couldn't take you there themselves. Sebastian's people were too close and they worried they would lead them right to you. My mom was furious when your parents asked my dad to take you, but he agreed to it. He said he had to do it because your mom saved me."

I breathed out a long breath. "Were you one of the fourteen children taken from the clans?" I asked.

"Yes."

"So, my mother rescued both you and Ian."

"I was a bit older than him, but yes, she saved us both."

I ran my hand over my eyes. My mother had freed fourteen stolen children before Sebastian killed her. Now I'd met two of them. I had to accept that if destiny was real, all of it probably happened for a reason.

"When I left you at the hospital, I was young and my vibration barely registered," he continued. "That made me perfect to take you into the city. My dad gave me some tools for protection, put us on a bus at the edge of town, told me where to go and then what to do when I got there. I was old enough to do what I was told but not old enough to understand why I was doing it."

From the expression on his face, I could tell he was haunted by what he'd done. He might not have understood it then, but he'd had plenty of time to figure it out since. Whatever his faults, he'd been too young for the kind of responsibility he'd been given that day.

An understanding dawned. Maybe he was uncomfortable having me around because I reminded him of what he'd had to do.

I reached out to touch his hand. "I don't blame you," I said.

His chest rose and fell, like he'd been holding his breath for a long time and could finally let it go.

"I've replayed that day over and over in my mind," he said quietly. "You were scared and held on to me when I tried to leave. I gave you a candy bar to get you to stop crying. It was already half eaten, but it was all I had. Feeling like the worst person ever, I hid and watched until a nurse finally figured out you were alone and took you away."

The picture his words painted was vivid and painful. It was a struggle to hold it together, but I needed to know more.

"What was it like for my parents?" I asked. "How did they react when they left me?"

He seemed surprised that I'd asked. "They were devastated. They loved you."

I'd hoped that was the case, but doubt plagued me sometimes. I'd worried that they may have left me because I was slowing them down or that I hadn't been a big deal to them.

My eyes clouded over and a few silent tears rolled down my cheeks. I'd finally gotten the answer to one of the biggest questions I'd ever had.

Theron brought me a kitchen towel to dry my face. I found it funny and started to laugh-cry.

He seemed incredibly confused. "Do you need to lie down or something?" he asked.

That made me laugh even harder.

Probably thinking I was losing my mind, he said, "I should wait until tomorrow to tell you the rest."

I wanted to learn as much as I could, so I got control of myself, sniffed, and wiped my tears away. "I'm okay," I said. "You can tell me now."

"You said something about the Laurel genealogy book last night," he began. "I'd had it with me for years. Your parents left it and some other stuff at my house. My mom was hell-bent on destroying everything that could tie you to us, but I stole the book when she wasn't looking. I kept it hidden for years."

"Why?" I asked. "It's a Laurel volume, not a Falco record."

"This is going to sound nuts, but a voice told me to take it. Every time I was tempted to get rid of it, the same voice would say not to. It was like some invisible woman was standing right next to me and telling me to do stuff."

I considered for a moment. "It might have been my dead mother. She talks to me, too."

He huffed. "You're a whole lot crazier than me."

I wasn't, though. I'd tell him more about communicating with the dead at a different time, but at that point, I had more questions.

"How did you get the book to me?" I asked. "How did you even know where to find me?"

"I always knew where you were. I tracked you through the social services database, then through school records, and more recently your tax returns."

"But the guy who left the book for me was human."

Theron nodded. "He was an old roommate from college."

I nodded finally understanding the mystery.

"This has been freaking me out for years," he said. "So many times I wanted to forget about you and let things be, but that woman's voice would start in on me again. *Find Alison, check on Alison*, she would say." He looked haggard as he spoke. "At times, she got frantic. Once, she started screaming at me. She kept saying something was wrong. That you were in danger. The only thing I could think to do was search the records of your foster family. I found some buried reports citing abuse. I fixed it so you got transferred out of that house right away, and she left me alone for a while after that."

"It was the Franklin family, wasn't it?" I asked.

"Yes."

"That place was scary."

"I had you placed with the McKyes next," he said. "At least that seems to have worked out well."

Theron had gone through a lot on my behalf, and though he probably wouldn't admit it, hearing my mother's voice had terrified him. No wonder he'd been such a jerk to me. Not only did he feel guilty every time he looked at me, he associated me with something that had scared and freaked him out growing up.

"Thank you, Theron," I said.

"For what?"

"For a lot of things, but most of all for getting me to the McKyes."

He smiled with a gentleness I'd never seen in him before. "Considering I gave you a half-eaten candy bar before abandoning you, it was the least I could do."

Chapter Thirteen

I went to my room, closed the door, and then leaned against it. I'd done my best to ease the guilt Theron felt for leaving me at the hospital. Dealing with my own emotions was going to be more difficult. Gratitude, grief, joy, and remorse spun like a hurricane through my mind. Trying to decide which to surrender to first was exhausting.

A few tears escaped before I could stop them, but I wiped them away and straightened my shoulders. I was already angry whenever a Truss was around. Dwelling on the fact that they'd caused my parents to leave me, as well as murdered my clan, would make it even more difficult to control myself.

I would save my pity party until I got home. Having made my mind up about it, I got ready for bed, crawled under the covers, and FaceTimed Ian.

When he came on, he was smiling the way only he could. He was wearing a light green pullover that clung to the muscles in his upper arms and made his eyes look lighter. The small worry line near his right eyebrow deepened and then relaxed as he watched me on his screen. "How did it go at the Ledges?" he asked.

"For once, I think destiny was on my side," I replied. "I found Phoebe and got her to agree to meeting up with me tomorrow."

"Amazing work."

"It went well. Maybe a little too well."

"What does that mean?"

"Just that it came surprisingly easy. I keep feeling like it's going to blow up in my face at some point."

"Think positive. I always do."

"You are a shining light," I joked. "What did you do today?"

"I had breakfast at a little diner in town, talked to Stacy for about three hours, had lunch at the diner, and talked to Stacy some more. She keeps at the same topic like a dog with a bone. Her favorite thing to discuss is Theron. She's told me all about the programs he's coded and the paintings he's done. She started in on his cooking about an hour ago. I had no idea he cooked, but according to Stacy he's the next MasterChef."

"He is pretty good at it," I said.

"Whatever. The point is after she briefs me on what a wonderful guy he is, she starts pumping me for information about him. Anything she doesn't already know, I can't tell her, so I'm constantly trying to come up with ways to change the subject."

"I would thoughtmake her into silence if I could."

"Just one of many reasons I miss you."

"I miss you, too," I said truthfully.

That brightened his eyes. "I was thinking you could come down and have breakfast with me. As long as I don't go up there to you, I think it's safe enough. We'd have to eat at the diner though. Stacy only has ramen noodles in the house."

"Okay, but it can't be tomorrow. I'm planning to go into the Ledges early. I want to look around the lodge and get a feel for how it's laid out."

"Maybe the day after," he suggested.

He stretched and put his arm behind his head. I blinked and I tried not to drool. Ian seemed to know how he it affected me and gave me a cocky smile.

I rolled my eyes. "You are so full of yourself."

"Why? Because I'm naturally tempting? I'm just being me. I don't get embarrassed because I think you have the most beautiful eyes I've ever seen and the softest neck I've ever kissed. I accept things as they are."

Feeling a little jealous, I asked, "How many necks have you kissed?"

"A few," he responded, like he was having the time of his life.

"I think we should say good-night now."

"You're no fun. Theron must be sucking all the positive

energy up. I'll call you tomorrow."

We said good-bye, and I turned the lamp on the night-stand off.

Hurricane emotions had worn me out. I fell asleep almost instantly.

*I*t sounded like Theron was being assaulted in the living room the next morning. Loud banging and curses traveled down the hall into my room. I turned onto my stomach and put a pillow over my head. But it wasn't thick enough to quiet the noise.

Planning how I was going to kill him, I pushed the covers off and rubbed my cold nose. Then I stomped across the room and threw the door open. I took one step out and bumped into him. He was as surprised to see me as I was to see his purple-and-green checked shirt.

"Good morning, Sunshine," I said as sarcastically as I could. "Did you kill him?"

"Did I kill *who*?"

"The intruder you've been fighting with for the last ten minutes?"

He just stood there looking confused.

"The noise. The banging," I continued. He still looked clueless. "Never mind. Move so I can go to the little girls' room."

I pushed at him, but he didn't shift. I pushed harder and

got the same result.

"Here," he said, handing me a bundle of yet more flannel material. "They're pajama pants," he explained. "They may be a little long, but they'll be warmer than whatever it is you're wearing now."

"Are you trying to convert me into a flannel-wearing lumberjack like you?"

"I'm not a lumberjack. And I'm not trying to convert you into anything. I'm trying to help you keep your legs from turning blue."

"Well…that's actually very nice of you," I said, taking them from him. "I'm sorry I planned your murder."

"Huh?"

His gaze wandered to my bare legs for like the third time since I'd opened the door. A slow smile spread across my lips. "Oh, I get it," I said. "You're a leg guy, aren't you, Theron?"

He narrowed his eyes at me.

"Theron has a weakness," I teased in a singsong voice.

He turned away. "If I did, your personality ruined it for me."

He'd chuckled at me the day before. I got to giggle at him all the way to the bathroom.

After getting ready for another day on the slopes, I went in search of that wonderful box of sugary cereal, but I couldn't find it.

Theron had moved his banging and cursing to the porch, so I wrapped a blanket around myself and went to ask him where he kept it.

He had cans of food sorted out on the stairs and was putting them into a hiking pack.

"What are you doing?" I asked. "Preparing to feed the all the wildlife within a mile?"

"Preparing to take food to a friend."

"Does Stacy know about this friend? Ian says she's in looooove with you."

He looked up at me with annoyance written all over his face.

"It's okay," I teased. "If you're going to hike with cans of beans and corn to your other girlfriend's place, I won't tell."

"For your information, my friend's name is Frank Shoemaker."

"She sounds pretty."

"He's an eighty-nine-year-old war veteran who's snowed in." He strapped snowshoes on his feet, and then said, "Hand me that pack, will you?"

I picked it up, but it was so heavy I almost tipped over. He hefted it like it weighed nothing and put his arms through the straps. Then he adjusted the weight and put a pair of sunglasses on.

I could see why Stacy was into him. It was an impressive show, and snow gear plus sunglasses suited him.

"Text me if you run into problems today," he said, turning away.

He got to the edge of the trees before I remembered why I'd come out in the first place. "Where's the cereal?" I yelled.

"Shelf above the refrigerator," he yelled back. "Leave

some for me."

"No promises," I replied.

I ate three bowls of Theron's cereal and checked the time. I still had a while.

I felt like reading, but the only book I had with me was the dewing history book in my backpack. It was better than nothing, so I went to my room, got it and hustled back to my chair by the fire.

After opening the book on my lap, I turned to the map of Atlantis and looked at all the cities with clan names. There was one name I didn't recognize, Arx. Under the word the artist had drawn several white-pillared buildings that reminded me of Greek temples.

I turned to the next page, which was all writing, and searched for a word that looked like Arx. Near the bottom of the page, I found one and concentrated on translating what was being said about it. It seemed the Arx was some kind of fortress or castle. The author went on to write things about the solstices and equinoxes.

I turned a couple more pages to another drawing. This one showed the moon eclipsing the sun. A young man and woman dressed in light blue stood at the top of a set of stairs leading into one of the white-pillared buildings. Their faces had been rubbed out, so I couldn't see their features clearly. But there was a brooch on the left side of the woman's chest. The man was wearing a similar type of thing as a buckle on his belt.

The pieces looked to be made of gold and had a design on them I recognized. The vining wreath with a few small flowers opening up on it was the Laurel signet or stamp.

The couple must have been Laurels, and whatever they were doing was important. More interested in my history than ever before, I touched their blurred-out faces and felt a kind of pull. Instead of creeping me out, it comforted me.

Closing the book, I decided Katherine was right. I should start learning more about my clan.

Chapter Fourteen

$\mathcal{I}$ arrived at the Ledges early. Like the exterior, the interior space was designed to look rustic. It worked pretty well except for the uniformed staff behind varnished wood countertops at the check-in.

I smiled at a nice-looking guy helping an older couple at the service desk. He smiled back and winked at me. A little weird, but okay.

Like Theron said, the shops and boutiques were on the main level. I wasn't interested in shopping, though. I wanted to find the elevators so I could go up and get a look at the conference rooms. I figured if there were so many Truss around, they'd likely use one of them for a meeting.

I found the elevators but was disappointed. They were key-card controlled. Without a room reservation, I wasn't going to be able to go up. At least not on my own.

I moved on to the shops. There was quite a variety. A store that sold stationery and clocks right next to one that sold ergonomic neck rolls. I knew where to go if I got the urge to write to someone's grandparents and developed a stiff neck.

Seeing some interesting lotions, I went into the spa to have a look. A woman in a lab coat approached me. "You have beautiful skin," she said. "Such a lovely olive complexion."

I looked behind me to see who she was talking to and then remembered the pills I'd been taking to make me look tan. I touched my chin self-consciously. "Thank you."

"We have a seaweed scrub especially for skin like yours. I can put you down for a facial this afternoon."

A facial sounded great, but I wasn't sure how my fake skin color would react to a seaweed scrub. "I have plans for the day," I replied. "I'll keep it in mind for later, though."

She handed me a card. "Ask for me if you decide to come in."

I put the card in my pocket and headed toward a souvenir shop. I'd just gone inside when I felt two male dewing coming toward me. Through the store window, I watched them pass.

I had another choice before me. Follow them and risk heating up or stay in the shop and look at beanies with "the Ledges" embroidered on them.

Feeling brave, I left the shop and followed some distance behind the men.

From the back they looked similar. They were about the same height, which was an inch or so shorter than me, they had matching shades of dishwater-blonde hair, and they were wearing identical white button-up shirts.

I tailed them to a bistro where they sat down at a table.

Doing a quick rewind to view even my smallest reaction to them, I was pleased. The anger was still there, and the heat was, too, but it hadn't gotten out of control. I did a few breathing exercises, waited for my temperature to normalize, and then went inside.

A waitress was still putting menus on the tables. "Sit where you'd like," she said to me. "I'll be right with you."

I chose a place a couple of tables away from the dewing guys and pretended to read my menu while observing them. It looked like they were in their mid-twenties, but that didn't mean much. They could have been fifty for all I knew.

The similarities I'd noted between them ended at the neck. One of them had a round head with round features. The other had a longish face with a pointy chin and slits for eyes. He reminded me of a fox. The kind that liked to kill chickens.

The round-faced guy tossed a questioning glance my way. I directed my eyes toward the menu again and pretended to be fascinated with the food choices.

Things were pretty uninteresting for a while. They ordered food, I ordered food. They ate food, I ate food. Things changed when the round-faced man left and fox man got a call.

Looking at the caller ID, he tensed up. Then he grumbled

something and answered. I understood a few words here and there, but for a time, nothing stood out. Then I heard, *You can't do that.* Then a pause followed by, *You're dealing with two lives.* Another pause and, *Just don't do anything we'll both regret.*

He hung up, left some money on the table, and stomped out. Whatever the call was about, he was clearly upset. I sipped my orange juice and replayed his words in my mind. *You're dealing with two lives.* He could have been talking about his sick goldfish, but instinct told me he was talking about something else. Something a lot more serious.

The guy was super creepy, but I'd be on alert for opportunities to find out more about him.

Finishing up breakfast, I paid my bill and doubled back to get my snowboard. As I approached the help desk an idea dawned, and I headed for the guy who'd winked at me.

"Can I help you?" he asked with a flirtatious grin.

I crossed my arms and leaned forward on the high counter. I gave him my best *you're so cute* smile and said, "I lost my key card. Can I get another?"

"Absolutely," he drawled. "Just put your finger on the scanner, and it will pull up your room number."

My smile turned plastic. The freaking scanners were everywhere. "It will only take a second," he assured me.

A second or not, I wasn't going to do it. *No need for the scan. She's in room 320,* I mentally suggested.

He accepted my thought. "Just a moment," he said, before going into the back room. When he came out, he handed me a card and looked me over. "Can I get you anything else?"

"Nope," I replied, catching the scent of his musky cologne.

While I tried not to gag, he said, "I'm here until two if you need anything else."

Just having him breathe on me made me feel gross. I wanted to ask for a bath in Purell, but I replied, "I'll let you know."

Phoebe arrived at the chairlift just after I did.

"Sorry I'm late," she said loudly. "My mom sat me down for a lecture this morning."

"I hate those."

"This is an important week," she said, mimicking someone I assumed was her mother. "Cross your ankles when you sit, pull your hair back like I've asked a hundred times, and find some clothes that fit. Don't talk so loud, don't interrupt people, and keep your inappropriate opinions to yourself."

I laughed. "I've heard that one before."

"Did it change anything for you?" she asked with disgust. "It didn't for me. I sit the way that feels comfortable. I like my hair down and my clothes loose. As far as the rest of it is concerned, my dad taught me to think for myself and speak my mind. It's too late to change all that."

"I hear you," I said.

She squared her shoulders, like she wanted to get rid of something clingy. "Anyway, I brought this back," she said.

She held my washed and stain-free scarf out to me. I was careful not to touch her as I took it.

"How's your side?"

"I woke up all better. I'm going to do a run. You can come if you want."

Destiny was smiling on me again. "Yeah, sure," I replied.

When we took our places in line, she got a text. "Crap," she said, reading it.

"What's wrong?"

"Jacob told my mom I interrupted one of his business calls this morning. She wants to skin me alive." She rolled her eyes. "My family's business is being restructured and no one can agree on how to do things."

The business restructuring she mentioned was probably clan-related stuff. She was steering the conversation exactly where I wanted it to go, but once again, it seemed to be going too smoothly. Destiny didn't like me that much.

"Our family business has pretty much been run into the ground," she continued. "My dad had real problems with…the last CEO and how he managed things. My mom worshipped the guy. She and too many others in the family want to go on like nothing has changed."

"You sound pretty passionate about it."

"I am. My dad taught me to care and educate myself on things that truly matter."

"And you think it would be bad to keep doing business like before?"

"Absolutely. It would be like pushing the self-destruct button on…the company. I don't know all the ins and outs, but I do know we have to reevaluate how we've done things in the past or the entire thing is going to collapse in on us."

"You're what…seventeen?" I asked. "You talk like a

thirty-year-old."

She shrugged. "It doesn't matter how I talk, no one listens to me."

I made a sympathetic sound.

She'd just given me a very important piece of information. Her mother and father, though hoping to get the clanship, didn't agree on how to move forward with it. One of them liked Sebastian's way of doing things, and the other didn't. That might make for instability if they became chiefs.

We moved up a few positions, and I felt another Truss in the area. I breathed deep and visualized a dozen brownies. This time, I barely heated at all.

Phoebe waved to a short round man who came gliding our way. He had a head of fluffy white hair, his cheeks were rosy in the cold, and his baby-blue eyes sparkled with good humor.

"There's my favorite niece," he said, giving Phoebe a hug.

She kissed the miniature Santa Claus's cheek.

Smiling, he turned to me. "Who's your friend?"

"This is Ali. She helped me out yesterday."

I watched nervously for a sign that the man might recognize me, but couldn't detect anything.

"I'm Thomas," he said. "Nice to meet you."

I shook his hand and Phoebe said, "I thought Aunt Shannon had forbidden you to ski this trip."

"We came to a mutual understanding. I get to ski from one until four o'clock, and she gets to control the TV station in the evenings." He laughed cheerfully. "She gets to control the TV anyway, so I'm getting the better end of the deal."

"How is she?" Phoebe asked with concern in her tone. "I haven't seen her yet."

"She's staying close to the phone. Lisa is due to have the baby any day now." He turned to address me. "This will be our first grandchild."

"Oh, congratulations," I replied.

He shifted his weight from one ski to the other. "Well, I'll leave you girls to enjoy the day. If I don't start at the back of the line, people might riot."

He patted Phoebe's back and nodded at me before moving away.

"He seems nice," I remarked.

"He is nice, but he can get odd sometimes. He's obsessed with some kind of laboratory science. My dad nicknamed him the Nutty Professor. When he's got something going, he can get so caught up in it that he doesn't remember his own name."

The way she described him reminded me of Lillian. Too bad Uncle Thomas was already likenessed to someone. If he hadn't been Truss, he and Lillian might have made an interesting pair.

Phoebe and I did two runs. We talked on the rides up and laughed on the way down. She had opinions about everything from what music I should listen to, Fall Out Boy and Panic! at the Disco, to what the US involvement in the Middle East should be. There was nothing fake about Phoebe. What you saw was what you got. She had a big nose, a loud voice, and an active mind. She was okay with all three.

The sad thing was that we could have been friends if I hadn't been sent to betray her.

We were heading to the lodge to get some hot chocolate when she said, "I'm actually glad my creep brother cut me off yesterday."

"Why?"

"Because if he hadn't, I wouldn't have ended up bleeding all over and you wouldn't have stopped to help me." Her phone beeped with another text. "Crap," she muttered. "My mom needs me."

I looked at the darkening sky. "I should probably head home anyway. I'll be here again tomorrow if you want to hang out."

"I'd like to," she replied, "but I'll be busy most of the day. I'm supposed to help my mom set up for a dinner she's hosting…" She paused. I could almost see the wheels turning in her head. "You should come with me."

Stunned, I asked, "What?"

"You should come to the dinner. It's a family thing, so it will be dead boring, but the food will be good. If I have someone to talk to, I might not fall asleep in my salad."

The spy inside me cheered, but I kept my outside reaction as mild as I could. "Would your parents mind?"

"The serving staff will be hu— They won't mind."

I understood the stumble in her words. If human servers were around, nothing about the Truss clanship would be mentioned. Still, I'd get to observe her parents.

Not wanting to appear too eager, I replied, "I don't know…the road back to my grandmother's is dangerous when it's dark."

"You can stay the night," she suggested. "I have my own room and an extra bed."

Mental high five. "Okay, but I'd have to leave early."

"No problem. I'll clear everything with my mom and text you."

I put my number in her phone, and we went in opposite directions.

"Hey, Ali," she called from a distance. "It's kind of formal. Do you have a dress?"

I'd make one out of Theron's flannel shirt if I had to.

"I'll find something," I replied, waving good-bye.

Chapter Fifteen

Theron was sitting cross-legged on the floor when I got back. He had three laptops set up in front of him, and they were all running programs.

"What are you doing?" I asked.

"Violating my suspension and the laws of three different countries," he replied.

I took my coat and boots off. "Why?"

"I told you I'd take care of the surveillance cameras at the Ledges, and that's what I'm doing. I was able to get a facial recognition program running about three hours ago. From now on, it will scrub you out whenever you show up on the feed."

"The security gate won't be a problem anymore?"

"You catch on quickly, grasshopper," he replied.

"But why are you taking the risk? You know you'll get in trouble if you're caught messing with tech."

"Two reasons. The first is that accessing the camera feed makes it easier for me to keep tabs on you, and the second is that I'm pissed at Spencer for putting us in this situation."

I smiled because he'd used the word "us." What had been my job was his now, too.

Sitting in the chair behind him, I watched him work from one computer to the next. "Do those little things have enough juice to break the laws of three different countries?"

"Stacy tricked these out. They're nowhere near as powerful as what I'm used to, but she's pretty good with illegal upgrades."

When one of the laptops flashed, his fingers started to fly over the keys.

He seemed changed. The previous undercurrent of tension about him was gone. He looked different, too. There was a smile of genuine joy on his lips. For the first time since meeting him, I was seeing him really relaxed. It was quite a transformation.

One of the computer screens started scrolling numbers. "What's that?" I asked.

"I just breached Greystone Bank's firewall."

"Great. Am I going to be considered guilty by association? Because I don't want to go to prison."

"Don't worry. There's only one other person who can back-trace my programs, and I made sure she's busy with other problems today."

"You did something horrible to her, didn't you?"

"I filled the operating system she supervises with about a trillion Trojans, and some Ukrainian hackers I know are exploiting five of the ten worms I planted. So yeah, you can say I did something horrible to her."

"What happens if you get caught?"

"She won't see what I'm doing."

"If you say so."

"She's on my list," he said, narrowing his eyes. "When I get out of this corner of hell, I'm going to make Ashlee Stentorian pay for snitching on me to Spencer."

He said her name with both irritation and a little admiration. "Stentorian clan, huh?" I nudged him with my foot. "Is she cute?"

"I've never seen her. I run across her digital signature often enough, but she's an abide-by-the-law type. Not interested."

"What are you looking for right now?"

"Anything and everything related to the Truss. I've already found some interesting things." He glanced at me. "Spencer is an idiot. He should have had me working this angle from the start. I can find out what color underwear they're wearing when I do this stuff."

"If you're saying I'm no longer needed, I'll gladly fly home."

He shook his head. "You're still necessary. We need to cover both angles, the things technology can tell us and the things personal interaction can reveal."

A graphic popped up on one of the screens. Theron typed something and numerical digits started scrolling again.

"Breaking the law looks good on you."

"Women find me superhot when I'm committing felonies."

I pushed his shoulder.

"I'll be able to dig a lot deeper when I get my own equipment," he continued. "I had a friend break into my apartment in New York. He's overnighting a bunch of stuff to me."

"Interesting group of friends you have. Hacker and thieves."

His brown eyes sparkled. "We're part of a loosely organized but highly skilled criminal network."

Noticing the sharp scent of cooking tomatoes and cheese coming from the kitchen, I asked, "Are you making dinner again?"

"Yep. We're having lasagna tonight."

"It's not vegan, is it?" I asked, scrunching my nose. "I've had some really bad experiences with vegan lasagna."

"What's lasagna without cheese and sausage?"

"I think I love you." I sighed.

"You should play harder to get. If it only takes meat and cheese, you're going to get into a lot of trouble."

"I have other criteria, too," I replied, heading into the kitchen. "Like shoes. I only fall in love with guys who wear nice shoes."

Opening cupboards, I looked for Theron's plates and glasses. I found some mismatched stuff and set the table. Then I got things out of the refrigerator to put a salad together.

The timer on the oven went off. "Playtime is over, Theron. Come and eat."

I put some lasagna on my plate and stared lovingly at it. "I miss meat and dairy so much I have dreams about it," I said.

He laughed as he sat next to me. It wasn't the laugh of sarcasm that usually came from him. This time it was playful. Working with tech had done wonders for him.

"Do you want to hear about my awesome day?" I asked.

He nodded, so I gave him a rundown, keeping the really good stuff till last.

"Phoebe invited me to dinner tomorrow night," I said. "All the Truss are going to be there. She termed it a family reunion, and she keeps talking about the family business. I'm pretty sure it's all code for clan business."

He looked troubled. "Are you going to go?"

"You better believe it. She invited me to stay the night, too."

"Spending the night isn't a good idea."

"Why not? I came here to find Nikki and to get a feel for Phoebe's parents. The best way to do that is to spend as much time with them as I can."

"It's supposed to storm tomorrow night, which will make it difficult to get to you if you need me."

"We'll have to risk it. I can't pass up this opportunity."

He watched me take a bite of lasagna. "Short of locking you in a closet, there's no way I can keep you from doing it, is there?"

"You could try the closet thing, but I'd thoughtmake

you into letting me out. You'll just have to submit to my will. I do have a small problem, though. The dinner is formal, and I don't have a dress. Do you think your friend Stacy would lend me something?"

A strange look crossed his face. "Ah…I don't think you wear the same size. There's a clothing store in town. They might have something."

"Ian wants me to go down for breakfast tomorrow. I'll have a look around then."

"Sounds good. I need to pick up my equipment anyway."

I hadn't extended an invitation for him to come along, but driving separately didn't really make sense.

"What did your criminal activity reveal today?" I asked.

"I found out Phoebe's parents are struggling financially."

"I don't think so. They've got to be paying three grand per night to stay with the rich and famous."

"Credit cards are amazing things," he replied.

"Does Spencer know?"

"I doubt it. I had to go through layers of information to put the numbers together. As I said before, Spencer is an idiot."

"You really don't like him."

"I really don't," he confirmed.

I might have felt the same way had Spencer gotten me sanctioned from the thing I loved most in the world. "What else did you find out?" I asked.

"That there are a lot fewer Truss than we thought. Before Sebastian took over they were more than eight hundred strong. They were the largest clan, actually. Now there are less than seven hundred of them. That's a huge loss over just a century."

"You've got to let Spencer in on this information."

"Not yet," he replied, shaking his head. "When I tell him, he'll shut me down, and I need a few more days with my tech."

I nodded. Theron was helping me, and I didn't want him to get shut down, either.

He watched me put a third helping of lasagna on my plate. "How much food can you hold?" he asked.

"A lot. Which reminds me, what are you planning for Thanksgiving dinner…Grandma?"

"Grandma?"

"I told Phoebe I'm spending Thanksgiving with my grandmother…that's you."

He pulled a face. "Who says I'm planning to cook for Thanksgiving?"

"When I got the salad stuff out of the fridge, I saw the turkey."

"Maybe I'm cooking it for myself."

"Nope. You're cooking it for both of us, because you want to show off. And I'm happy because in a small way, it will be like a real Thanksgiving."

He spun his spoon a couple of times. "It's interesting how you process things," he said. "We go along with human holidays, but it's to fit in among them. We have our own celebrations, so Thanksgiving and Christmas don't mean much to us. It's different for you, and that might never change."

I let out a long breath. "You're the first to get that," I said. "Everyone expects my humanness to fade away. They don't believe that parts of me are hardwired now. I'm never going to be all dewing, but I'll never be human, either. It's not a fun position to be in."

"I think there's something else up with you," he said thoughtfully. "Leaving your human family seems like a decision to you. We see it as destiny. Making the decision to leave them is harder than accepting it as fate."

It was an accurate and rather profound observation. The only way he could have come to that conclusion was if he'd gone through something similar. "Did you choose to leave someone?" I asked.

"Sometimes I see it that way," he replied, looking sad. "Destiny took someone from me, and I'm having a hard time accepting it. A girl I was in love with likenessed to my brother earlier this year."

"Whoa," I muttered.

"I used a different four-letter word," he said, "but yeah. Usually when likeness divides a couple, the third wheel, which in this case is me, just lets go and moves on. I've always had a bad relationship with destiny, and I'm still struggling with the moving on part."

"That's… I'm so sorry."

He shrugged. "It isn't a surprise. I usually get the short end of the stick."

"What does that mean?"

For a moment, I saw how deeply hurt he was. "It means I'm like your father. I can't join a human's mind to do anything. I thought you would have picked up on that by now. A vibration as slow as mine is a telltale sign."

"Katherine told me that happens sometimes," I replied. "It doesn't seem like that big of a deal since we hardly use our joinings anyway.

He snorted. "They may not get used much, but being a healer, a reader, a sensation maker, or having any other type of joining is like a badge of honor. I don't have a badge at all. Our kind has overcome a lot of lesser emotions, but snobbishness isn't one of them. Whether they choose to acknowledge it or not, we aren't respected like the others. "

"That's why you mentioned my father when we first met," I deduced.

"I guess so. In a twisted way, I wanted to know if Spencer had thought enough of him to go to the trouble of telling you his name."

Seeing how seriously Theron was affected by not having a joining, I was curious how my father had dealt with it. Maybe the same way. I would never know.

"When destiny likenessed Amy to my brother," he continued, "it was like I was getting screwed all over again. I lost it a little. Actually, I lost it a lot. I did some reckless things."

"That's when you hacked into the NSA."

"I've been hacking into government systems for years, but only when I was asked to. Believe me, Spencer and the other clan chiefs have been plenty grateful for the information I've given them in the past. All that gratitude went flying out the window when I—"

"Went off the reservation," I finished.

"Right. Take it as a warning. I get self-destructive when destiny takes a crap on me."

He shifted position and twirled his spoon some more.

"You're not as big and bad as you pretend, Theron Falco. You're just messed up…like me."

"Maybe we should form that support group you talked about. The one for freaks."

I grabbed my glass of water and lifted it. "Here's to the freaks," I said.

Theron clinked his cup to mine. "Yay us."

Chapter Sixteen

The next day, the roads were a mess as we headed down the mountain. The plow hadn't cleared them, so a dusting of snow covered patches of ice. The back end of the Land Rover slipped a couple of times, but like before, Theron handled it fine.

He'd been in an uncharacteristically good mood that morning and hadn't said anything insulting to me since I woke up. I was super excited to see Ian, so we made a pretty happy pair.

When we hit another patch of ice, my stomach flip-flopped. "I can't understand why people live up here," I said.

"Some like the solitude. Frank only leaves the mountain on Easter Saturday, and he wouldn't have it any other way."

"It takes all kinds, I suppose."

Theron looked at me. "Yes, it does. Even ones like you."

"Your rudeness is showing again." I smiled. "Fortunately for you, I've grown used to it."

Betsy's Diner was off the main road. It was a cute little place. Natural light spilled in through the windows, and the butter-yellow tablecloths had arrangements of fake daffodils in plastic vases on them. The only downside was the smell of burned grease in the air.

It was a seat-yourself situation, so Theron took a booth in the corner. As I scooted across the vinyl-covered bench, my pants stuck to something sticky. He noticed me pause and the look of dread on my face. "It's probably syrup," he guessed. "Betsy's is famous for pancakes."

"Hasn't Betsy heard of a washrag?"

"I don't know. Betsy has been dead for twenty years. Her granddaughter, Patricia, runs this place now. If you want, you can leave a comment about it on the bill. I wouldn't mention it before your get your food, though. Patricia might spit in your eggs."

"That's a serious health code violation."

Theron shrugged. "How often do you think a health inspector makes it up here?"

It was a good point.

I watched out the window for a sign that Ian coming and noticed the foot traffic was heavy. People on both sides of the road waved at each other and yelled things that brought smiles to the others' faces.

"How many people live in this town?" I asked.

"About a thousand. There are others in the outlying

areas, and of course those living on the mountain."

His tone was warm, almost affectionate. "You like it here," I said. "You just don't like being told you can't leave."

"I have a lot of good memories from my time in Greenvale. I used to spend summers here with my grandparents. It was always a relief to get away from the disappointment in my mother's eyes when she looked at me."

He unwrapped his silverware, spun his fork a couple of times, and took his jacket off. Nearly blinded, I put my hands up to shield my eyes.

"Uh, that shirt," I said.

Looking down at himself, he asked, "What do you have against my clothes?"

"All your shirts are flannel and checked. Today's choice is green and yellow. The contrast is burning my eyes. Add some suspenders, and you could double for the Brawny paper towel guy...on drugs."

He pulled a face at me as our waitress sauntered up with cups of ice in hand and a welcome-to-Betsy's smile. She had bright red hair and big brown eyes. "Hey, gorgeous," she said, tapping Theron on the shoulder.

"Hey, Livy," he responded. "Do you like my shirt?"

She shuddered. "I'll take the fifth on that." She put a cup in front of each of us. "I thought you'd be gone by now, Theron. You never stay this far into the winter. It's always back to the city and your classes before the first snow flies."

"I'm taking a break from the world for a while. I'm wintering over."

"Since when have you ever wanted a break from

anything?" she commented. "You're never still long enough to take one."

He shrugged, probably because he couldn't dispute what she said.

"If you're staying, be sure to check in here every now and again. You could die on that mountain and no one would find you until spring."

"Don't worry about me, Livy. I can take care of myself. How are things with Skip?"

"Good." Her eyes lit up. "He's on a long haul right now, but if the weather holds, he'll be home for Thanksgiving."

"Skip is Livy's husband," Theron explained to me. "We were all friends growing up. Skip drives a supply truck for a lumber company."

Livy gave me a good once-over. "Is this your new girl, Theron? She's pretty."

My eyes widened. "No," I said firmly. "I'm not his girl. I'm his cousin."

"Interesting, his aura is a dark green. Yours is a light blue. Cousins usually have differing shades of the same color."

"Livy is a spiritualist," Theron clarified.

"When people hear spiritualist they automatically think I'm nuts," she said, shaking her head. "But I see what I see, and I don't apologize for it."

After patting Theron's shoulder again, she walked away with a sway of her hips. Judging by the glances she got from the old men drinking coffee at the bar, she was going to make very good tips that morning.

"Is she for real?" I asked. "Does she see energy?"

"I think so. How she interprets what she sees is up for debate."

"Even *we* don't see our energy."

Theron cleared his throat and got very interested in his fingernails. "We see it under certain circumstances," he said.

Remembering the intense energy I experienced the two times Ian had joined his mind to mine, I got his drift. There were occasions when "seeing fireworks" was more than an expression.

I felt Ian coming and turned to the door.

"The Golden One arrives," Theron muttered.

"How do you know that nickname?" I asked.

"I heard Brandy call him that a few times."

The moment Ian's fingers touched the door, I was on my feet and running. Throwing my arms around him, I hid my face against his neck and breathed him in. His chest rumbled as he laughed.

"I guess I don't have to ask if you missed me," he said.

Pulling back enough to see my face, he ran his finger along my cheek. "You look so different. Still beautiful, but different." Then whispered in my ear, "Why is Theron here?"

"He needs to get some stuff from Stacy," I whispered back.

He didn't look very pleased about it, but he took my hand and headed to our table anyway.

"Hey," he said to Theron, sliding into the corner of the bench and putting his arm over my shoulders. "How's it going? Are you bored to death?"

With an edge to his voice, Theron responded, "That's exactly what your dad wants, right?"

The two of them locked eyes, and I could almost feel Theron's resentment and anger in the air.

"Alison warned me you were pissed," Ian said.

"I am," Theron replied. "Considering how I've helped your dad in the past, he could have kept his mouth shut when I messed up. He owed me that."

"He owes you on a personal level," Ian admitted, "but he couldn't turn a blind eye to the position you put the rest of us in. What you did was years ahead of the system-hacking humans can do. If you'd gotten caught, you would have been in the spotlight for all the wrong reasons."

"There was a point-zero-zero-one percent chance I'd get caught."

Ian was starting to tense up, too. I put my hand on his knee to remind him where we were. He sat back in the bench and looked steadily at Theron with an expression I'd seen on Katherine's face. He'd learned something about the importance of diplomacy from her. Just one of many reasons he was going to make an amazing clan chief.

"I'm not saying I would have done the same thing," he said calmly. "But my dad did what he thought was right for the clans. And believe it or not, he cares about you."

After a moment, Theron's rigid shoulders relaxed. "You see it that way," he grumbled, "but I don't. Because I'm hungry, I'll let it go."

Feeling like a storm had passed, I rubbed my hands together. "What's good to eat here?"

"The steak and eggs," Theron and Ian said at the same time.

I hummed in delight. "I think Betsy's might be my personal gateway to heaven."

Livy came back to take our orders, and seeing Ian, she said, "Hello, stranger. What has it been...ten hours since I saw you last?"

"I can't take anymore Top Ramen," Ian said. "I'd starve if it weren't for this place."

Livy nodded toward me. "Now this one has a bright aura," she said. "It's almost white. I've never seen one like it before."

Ian gave her a sassy smile. "That's because I'm one of a kind."

Across the table Theron rolled his eyes. "If you didn't have some of the best surfing on the Australian coast, I wouldn't admit that I know you."

We placed our orders and then got down to discussing business. "Have your parents heard anything more about Nikki?" I asked.

"Nothing so far," Ian replied.

"No more body parts in the mail?" Theron asked.

"Nope," he said. "The Dawnings are desperate for news, though. They know you're here doing what you can. They appreciate that, but they're suffering."

"I might learn something soon," I commented. "There have been some positive developments."

I caught Ian up on what happed with Phoebe the previous day.

"Phoebe even invited her to a family dinner at the Ledges," Theron added.

"All the Truss should be there," I said. "She invited me to stay the night, too."

Ian didn't look happy about it.

"I already told her I didn't think staying overnight was a good idea," Theron commented. "She said she's doing it anyway."

"He threatened to lock me in a closet," I said.

"Did he threaten to sedate you and your thoughtmaking mind? Because that might actually work," Ian grumbled.

"I'll be fine."

An uncomfortable silence followed.

"Got anything else to talk about?" Theron asked. "Because it's starting to get awkward around here."

"Actually, I do." Ian said, turning to me. "My dad's cousin moved to Vegas. He and his wife bought a house in your development. He's a plastic surgeon like your dad and is looking to join a practice. Your dad is looking for a partner, right?"

"Yes," I replied.

Smiling, he continued, "My parents are working on a long-term type of protection for the McKyes. Victor's wife likes the gym, and his son is the same age as Alex. They should fit in nicely as friends who share common interests, and they'll keep a watchful eye on your family. Which hopefully will put your mind at ease, so you can concentrate on other things."

I was completely, utterly, truly grateful. "It sounds

perfect," I said. "I can't think of anything better."

He nodded, clearly happy to have made me happy.

After that, the boys started talking about surfing. I was good at most sports but had no interest in swimming with sharks.

A bit bored, I decided to practice an advanced version of thoughtmaking called cloaking. It was like starting a chain reaction through a group of dewing. All of our minds ran two distinct trains of thought at the same time. Though we weren't consciously aware of the second one, it flowed among us as a shared consciousness. I was one of the very few who could sense it and manipulate it.

Gathering all of my energy together, I connected to Ian. Finding the shared consciousness deep in his mind, I formed the thought, *Put my spoon in my glass.* Then I painstakingly wrapped the two thoughts together.

Letting go, I prepared myself for the rebound of energy that would come back at me. When it hit, my ears zinged, my head hurt, my stomach muscles tightened, and it felt like I might puke. But I held it together.

Acting in unison, the boys picked up their spoons and put them in their glasses of water.

Smiling at my success, I interrupted them just long enough to say, "I'm going to try and find a dress now. I'll meet you back here when I'm done."

Chapter Seventeen

The clothing store was down the street, and the wind blew snow in my face as I hurried along the sidewalk. I was wiping snowflakes off my eyelashes when I went inside.

A quick glance around told me the selection would be slim. There were as many craft supplies as there were clothes in the place.

Holiday music played loudly over the sound system, while a saleswoman came my way. "Can I help you find something?" she asked.

"I need some kind of evening dress," I replied, trying to sound hopeful.

She actually laughed at me. "No one has come in asking for an evening dress…ever. The best I can offer is something casual, and we're down to just a few of those."

"I'll look at anything," I said.

I followed her to a round rack tucked into the back corner of the store where she started going through the dresses. She picked three options and then pointed to the fitting room.

"One of these might work," she said, handing them over. "They're going to be shorter on you than they would be on most girls, but give them a try. I'll let you know what I think."

I hadn't asked for her opinion, but she wasn't trying to be pushy. She was trying to be helpful. I figured it wouldn't hurt to hear what she thought about the choices.

The first dress was pretty on the top, but the skirt was too short. "Good for a casual party with friends, but shows too much leg for a dinner party," my helpful sales assistant remarked.

The second dress was too big. She scrunched her nose. "That one is too baggy."

Trying not to despair, I tried the third. It was a red sleeveless sheath with a sweetheart neckline. When I showed her, she nodded. "It's nice."

"You think?" I asked. "It's freezing, and this dress doesn't have sleeves."

She hustled off and came back with a black scarf. It was wide when she opened it and draped it over my shoulders. "Perfect," she said with another nod.

I left the store half an hour later with a new dress, a scarf, some shoes I could just barely squeeze into, and a nice clutch.

The boys were leaning with their backs on Theron's Land Rover when I found them. They didn't seem to mind the icy temperature and the wind like I did.

My feet crunched the snow as I approached.

"Man, that weirds me out," Theron said glancing at me. "I never know when she's coming."

Ian smiled. "I know." He looked at my bag. "You found something?"

"It's not great," I replied, opening the passenger side door to put my things on the front seat, "but it's more appropriate than anything else I've got."

A purple car turned into the lot and honked. Theron headed straight for it when it parked. A short round woman with hair dyed lavender bounded out and hugged him around the middle.

"Stacy," he said. "I was just headed over your way."

"It's good I saw you here, then." She giggled. "I have your things in the trunk of my car."

"I'll get them," Theron said.

Stacy put her hands on her rather wide hips. "Introduce me to your friend first."

"Okay," he replied. "This is my cousin, Ali."

Without warning, Stacy embraced me around the middle like she'd done to Theron. Her head hit me right under the chin. No wonder Theron's expression had been strange when I asked if Stacy had a dress I could borrow. We were definitely not the same size.

"You're Theron's cousin and Ian's girlfriend," she said, looking up at me. "I've heard so much about you."

"I've heard great things about you, too," I replied, surprised Ian told her I was his girlfriend. That wasn't a part of the backstory we made up.

Theron checked his watch. "I've got to get back to the cabin. If you pop the trunk, Stacy, I'll move my stuff."

"Sure thing," she replied.

I needed to keep Ian occupied while he moved his boxes of computer stuff. "Are you going to give me a Stacy hug, too?" I asked.

"How about a nice normal hug," he replied.

I rested my chin on his shoulder when he put his arms around me.

"You okay?" he asked.

In spite of my determination to do the job ahead of me, I was nervous about staying the night at the Ledges. I figured I'd be fine, but in a way, it would be like sleeping with wolves.

"I'm just tired," I replied. "Theron gets up early and he makes so much noise I can't sleep in."

"Has he been nicer to you?"

"Sort of. I'm coming to understand him better, so he's easier to tolerate. I still want to go home, though. Four more days and then this will all be over. Then I can get back to being normal. Whatever that is."

He ran his hand down my back and I closed my eyes. I really was tired. "I shouldn't be hugging you like this," I said. "I'm just... I don't know exactly."

"Don't ruin it, Alison. Just let it happen."

"Do I usually ruin things?"

He smiled and hugged me tighter. "A lot of the time, but I'm willing to work on it with you."

In that moment, I was super glad he liked a challenge… and that he liked me.

He moved back a little so he could reach into his pocket for something. "This is for you," he said handing me a small box. "It's a birthday present."

Confused, I tried to hand it back. "My birthday is in January."

"You celebrate your birthday in January because that's the day social services took you in, but according to the Laurel book, you were born on November twenty-sixth."

I had to process that for a moment. "I saw the date written under my name," I said, "but it didn't make any sense to me."

"That's because you're practically illiterate when it comes to how we date things. You're going to ruin this, too, if you don't stop talking. Just open your present."

I did as he asked and my breath caught. Inside was a pale blue sapphire suspended from a silver chain.

"What do you think?" he asked.

"I think it's amazing but I can't take it."

He took the necklace out of the box and undid the latch.

"Remember when Brandy teased about leaving me an inheritance?" he asked. "Well, she wasn't teasing after all. I paid for half of the necklace with her money and half of it with mine. You can think of it as a birthday gift from both of us."

It was the kind of gesture Brandy would have approved of. "Okay," I said. "Thank you."

He kissed me lightly on the nose. "See? You didn't ruin

it this time. Miracles are possible."

Theron closed Stacy's trunk with a *bang*. "We need to take off, Ali," he said.

"Happy birthday," Ian whispered in my ear.

On the drive back, Theron pointed to my necklace. "It's nice," he said.

"It's a birthday present. I turn eighteen tomorrow."

"I know."

"How do you know?" I asked. "I just found out."

"I had the Laurel book for years, remember?"

"Oh, right."

We were quiet for a bit, and then he said, "You know Ian is in love with you, don't you?"

I let out a long breath. "I wish he wasn't. Falling in love is a waste of time. You should know that better than anyone."

"Even a cynic like me knows that love is never a waste of time. Are you in love with him, too?"

"I could be if I let myself."

He raised an eyebrow. "What do you mean, if you let yourself?"

"It means I can't be in love with Ian because he's going to likeness with someone else and I'll lose him. I've experienced that kind of loss too many times already. I won't willingly let it happen again. Besides, if it's Ian I lose, I think it might kill a piece of my soul."

Theron tapped the steering wheel. "Maybe you won't lose him. Maybe he's destined to likeness with you."

I watched as snowflakes fell from the sky. "Destiny has made it very clear to me that he won't."

Chapter Eighteen

I laid out all the things I needed to pack to stay the night at the Ledges and went looking for Theron. I hoped he had something I could use because I wasn't going to take my mom's suitcase to a place where millionaires vacationed.

I couldn't find him in the house, so I pulled my parka off the hook and went outside. He was splitting wood in the back. Leaning my shoulder against the cabin, I watched for a minute. He wasn't wearing a coat, just his ugly flannel shirt rolled up to the elbows. The muscles in his back flexed and released with each swing he took. I smiled, enjoying the show. It would certainly have been inspiring if a girl were in the mood to appreciate it.

"I knew you moonlighted as a lumberjack," I said.

He startled and turned to look at me with annoyance.

"Are you trying to kill me? You could have given me a freaking heart attack. Stop sneaking up on me like that."

"Sorry," I said.

He squinted. "No…you're not. And just for that, you get to split the next piece."

I took a step back. "No thanks."

"Yep," he said, coming to grab my arm.

"Stop manhandling me," I complained as he dragged me to the stump where a short log sat on end.

"I'm afraid you'll run if I don't." He put the ax in my hand. "All set. Show me what you've got."

"I don't want to. I like my kneecaps where they are. I might miss and chop into one of them."

"Don't be a baby. Now raise the ax high."

He pantomimed how I should do it, and I copied him. At least, I thought I did.

"Not that high," he grumbled. "You aren't going to throw it at something."

I lowered the ax a little but apparently not enough, because Theron made an exasperated sound and angled my arms differently. "Okay, just sort of let the weight pull the head of the ax down."

I wiggled away from him. "I got it. You might want to take a few steps back in case this goes horribly wrong."

He did, and I chopped the wood right down the middle.

"It's not that hard, right?" he asked smiling. "You can take over for me now."

"I'd rather clean the bathroom."

"How about you just help me carry the wood in. Hold

your arms out," he instructed. I did, and he started loading them with split wood. He kept going until I could barely see over the top.

"That's enough," I laughed. "I can't hold anymore."

He loaded about twice as much into his own arms and we headed back inside.

"Will you lend me a bag to put some clothes in?" I asked.

"I'll have to charge you a fee."

"Can I pay you later? I'm low on cash. Ali McCain can afford lift tickets at the Ledges because the Thanes sponsor her. Alison McKye can barely afford her own car insurance. She's broke."

He knelt in front of the fireplace to stack the wood. "Jillian Laurel, however, has a pretty big estate to draw from."

"Nope. She's broke, too."

He stopped stacking to look over at me. "Spencer didn't tell you about that, either? Everything the Laurels had is yours now. You're the clan's sole inheritor."

I honestly thought I'd heard him wrong. "What?"

"You're the last member of the Laurel clan. All the assets and investments they left behind go to you. You're filthy rich." He read the disbelief in my expression, patted my knee, and continued. "You're going to be the Laurel clan chief, too. That might take even more time to wrap your mind around."

I choked out a laugh. "Now I know you're lying."

"Nope. Twelve thousand years ago it was decided that each clan would appoint a chief. Regardless of how big the clan was, they had an equal say in decisions the counsel made. It's worked that way ever since. Tradition is almost sacred to us. Twelve thousand years of clan equality won't change because the Laurels are down a few members."

"There aren't a few of us. There's only me."

"The tradition will hold," he assured me.

The idea was so overwhelming I lost the ability to speak. So I sat there while he went to his room.

If what he told me was true, I couldn't imagine why no one had told me before. I wasn't just confused, I was angry confused. The Thanes knew I was stressed about money. I'd been thinking that when I left the McKyes I wouldn't have much to live on. I'd been saving for a long time, but it hadn't built up to much. If I'd known I didn't need to worry about my finances, I would have slept a lot better.

They hadn't told me about the clan chief thing, either. It wasn't like that would just slip their mind.

I was still processing when Theron brought me a generic-looking duffel bag. "Will this work?" he asked.

"It's perfect," I replied.

I packed my overnight stuff and then got to work on myself. Since giving up my vow of invisibility, I'd become a regular user of mascara and lip gloss. I'd even used a black eye pencil once. A formal dinner event seemed worthy of the pencil, so I sat on my bed with a compact mirror two inches from my eye and did my best to spread an even line across my eyelid.

I focused on my hair next, pulling it into a high twist in the back. I secured it with some bobby pins my mom had thoughtfully stashed in my makeup kit. Then I wrapped the new scarf around my shoulders and checked myself in the mirror above the dresser. I looked nice, but the prettiest thing on me was the sapphire necklace. It sat in the hollow of my throat like a soft kiss. Feeling a little braver with that small part of Ian on my skin. I grabbed the clutch I bought to go with my dress and left the room.

Theron was busy setting up his new and improved computer system. When I stood in front of him and did a circle to show my dress, his eyes widened a little. "How do I look?" I asked. "No snarky comments."

"Not too bad," he replied.

"Don't go overboard on the compliments."

"You look great," he amended. "Do you have your phone?"

I held up the clutch. "Yes, right in here. I may need some help with the duffel bag. These shoes weren't made for walking in the snow, and I'll need both hands for balance."

He slung the bag over his shoulder and followed me out the door. I managed the steps fine, but looking at the slick packed snow between me and my car was scary. I could almost see myself face-planting in my new dress.

I took two steps and felt myself going down. Theron steadied me and helped me cross the snow.

"Times have changed," I commented. "The first time I slipped in this driveway you almost laughed."

"You've grown on me since then," he replied. "Kind of like a fungus."

I giggled. "You are the opposite of charming."

He gave me an evil smile and opened the door of my car. "Last chance to change your mind about staying the night up there like a person who should be medicated," he said.

I opened my door and got into the car. I'm going."

"Text me if even the slightest thing seems off," he said before I started the engine.

Chapter Nineteen

*P*hoebe was already waiting in the lobby. Like me, she'd lined her eyes and used mascara, but her fuzzy brown hair was coming out of the bun she'd forced it into, and her dress hung off her like a sack. Still, it was her unfortunate nose that stole the show.

"Hey," she said, turning a wave into a bigger gesture than it needed to be.

I couldn't help but laugh a little. Phoebe was Phoebe. If she was going to wave, she was going to make it count.

I went to her side. "Is this okay?" I asked, looking at down at my dress. "It isn't formal, but it was the best I could manage on short notice."

She tipped her head to the side and looked up at me. "Yep. Simple suits you best, I think. That's quite a rock you're wearing."

"It's a birthday gift."

"Really. When is your birthday?"

"Tomorrow."

She bounced up and down a little and looped her arm through mine. "We'll order cake for breakfast."

"Um, cake for breakfast on Thanksgiving day. I don't think it could get better."

"Agreed," she said. "Are you ready to meet my family?"

I hoped I was. There were going to be a whole lot of Truss around, but I'd come up with some additional strategies I thought might help with the anger. My backup plan was to run.

"Don't worry," she said, giving my arm a squeeze. "They're all old and boring. I wish you could be here for the dinner we're having Saturday night. That one is going to go on forever. Without someone to talk to, I might slip into a coma. It's for family only, though, so I have to tough it out."

She'd given me more information to pass along.

"Why so many get-togethers?" I asked.

"Financial stuff, mostly. The last CEO was…I'm trying to think how to put it…a mental case. I'm curious how he blew through so much of our money in so short a time. The family is trying to decide what to do about it. We could merge with…some other companies and maybe get a loan that would tide us over for a bit, but that would mean giving up some freedoms."

The mental case had been Sebastian, and that she had seen him for what he was made me like her even more. I was willing to bet an important organ that the merger she mentioned was a reference to coming back to the clans.

"If was up to me, I'd take the merger," she said. "It would be better for everyone that way."

Phoebe got her key card out and swiped it. The elevator door opened and we stepped inside.

"Hold the door, please," a female voice said.

I stopped it from closing, and a woman whose face I'd seen on dozens of magazines and in several movies bustled in.

"Thanks," she said, a little breathless.

Starstruck, all I could manage was a nod. Phoebe wasn't fazed at all. "I saw your last movie," she said.

The woman smiled graciously and said, "Thank you for saying so."

"I didn't say I liked it," Phoebe replied. "Don't get me wrong. I'm not knocking your acting. You made the most you could out of that awful script."

The movie star couldn't decide what to react to, Phoebe's poor opinion of the film or the praise of her work.

Fortunately, the ride to the second floor was quick. "You should do a film with Allen Purdy," Phoebe said, stepping out of the elevator. "It might save your career."

The door closed on the woman's shocked face. It looked like Phoebe wasn't going to hold back her opinions that night. Which meant, things might turn out good...or very, very bad, depending on the topic of conversation.

"Time to face the music," she said unfazed. "The room is this way."

As I expected, my anger started building the closer we got to the Truss. I initiated plan A and visualized myself walking into the room and smiling calmly at the faces of my family's murderers.

That didn't work very well, so I moved on to plan B. Pulling up mental images of all the famous paintings I wanted to see at the Louvre, I ran through a slow slideshow of them in my mind.

That did the trick, and my anger subsided until my body temperature regulated to the level of a high fever.

Phoebe was right about her family being old. I did a quick calculation and figured the average age was probably around two hundred seventy or seventy, whichever species definition you chose to go with. There was an eerie feel to the place. There was no laughter and no loud conversations like you'd expect at a family reunion. Only old people involved with their own thoughts.

"See what I mean?" Phoebe whispered to me. "It's like they're all taking Valium."

I choked down a laugh as we made our way to the hors d'oeuvres table.

There was a lot to choose from. I busied myself putting things on my plate while Phoebe hemmed and hawed over the stuffed mushrooms and mini quiches. Finally, she picked something and pointed to one of the tables. "We're there," she said.

I sat by my place card and looked around.

The conference room was an interesting space. Animal heads hung high on each of the walls. Buffalo, elk, and deer looked down on us with glass eyes. Stuffed ducks in various poses had been arranged on the mantel over a fireplace at one end of the room. There were glass cases on each side of it with animal skins in them.

It definitely was not a PETA-approved room.

As I opened my napkin and laid it on my lap, I checked around to see if anyone was particularly interested in me. The makeover Katherine had provided seemed to have worked. No one gave me a second glance, so I relaxed a little. That's exactly how I wanted it.

"Wow, that's a lot of hors d'oeuvres," Phoebe whispered.

"When faced with difficult food choices, my policy is to take one of each," I explained. "It's more a matter of curiosity than anything else. I want to know what tastes the best."

She giggled. "I like that idea. I think I'll adopt your philosophy."

We ate and talked quietly about snowboarding and our classes at school. We made pretty much the only noise in the room, until a familiar dewing approached. "How are my girls?" Uncle Thomas asked with sparkling eyes.

Calling me one of *his girls* should have felt strange, but it didn't. I'd been thinking of him as *Uncle* Thomas since we were introduced.

"Phoebe, you look beautiful," he said, sliding into his chair.

"Thank you," she replied. "You're a great liar."

Uncle Thomas kissed her cheek and shifted position.

"Where's Aunt Shannon?" she asked.

"Making arrangements to fly home," he said with a worried frown. "Lisa has gone into labor. Shannon wants to be there to help with the baby."

Phoebe patted his hand. "I'm sure everything will work out fine."

He returned to his cheery self pretty quickly. "What's to eat?" he asked.

"Try the crab cakes," I suggested. "They're the best of everything."

He bobbed his head up and down, in agreement. "Be right back," he said.

I bit into a mini Parmesan roll and happened to glance at the doorway. A woman in a long black gown with jewels on her fingers and diamonds sparkling at her ears stood there. Her nose was just like Phoebe's.

"That's my mom," Phoebe said, nodding toward her. "She likes to make an entrance."

Yvonne paused long enough to draw as much attention to herself as she could, then she promenaded into the room. In spite of her large nose, or perhaps because of it, she looked formidable. I kept at the Parmesan roll and watched as she stopped at each of the tables and greeted people. She smiled with just the right amount of warmth, leaned in as she spoke, and laughed quietly.

Her social grace reminded me of Brandy. Which made me think she was probably a drawer like Brady had been.

Drawers joined humans' minds and made themselves seem irresistible. The human developed a type of obsession with them and would do just about anything to please them.

When Yvonne came to our table, I felt a tightening in my head as she joined my mind. I could have stopped her, but that would have ruined my cover, so I let her poke her way between my thoughts until she mesmerized me. My instinct had been right. She was definitely a drawer. Up close, Yvonne's earrings were a bit too showy. I doubted they were real.

"Ali, right?" she asked. I could tell she was unimpressed with my dress, but her eyes lingered on the gem in the hollow of my neck.

She was eying my necklace like a snake about ready to swallow a mouse. I knew then that she liked to steal things. Under the influence of her joining, a human would give her anything she asked for. I wondered how many of the rings on her fingers were stolen.

Fortunately for me, she wasn't brazen enough to take my necklace in front of so many people.

"How are you enjoying the evening?" she asked, releasing my mind.

"The food's good," Phoebe chimed in. "The rest is so-so."

Yvonne gave her daughter a scathing look. "I expect you to be on your best behavior tonight. Keep your voice down."

"Yes, ma'am," Phoebe replied with an exaggerated smile. "What's on the schedule tonight?"

"Some friendly small talk," Yvonne replied. "Then some introductions." She surveyed the room like a predator. "Oh look," she cooed. "Thaddeus and Jasmine have arrived. I should go say hello. I hope you have a lovely evening with us, Ali."

"And she's off to kiss more butt," Phoebe muttered as her mother walked away. "I know that's rude, but I don't have a lot of patience for this kind of stuff. I get that from my dad."

I wanted to ask where her father was, but Uncle Thomas came back to our table and had a lot to say.

"Tell me about the colleges you have applied to," he prompted Phoebe.

That started a long conversation about the pros and cons of West Coast schools versus East Coast schools. It only stopped when Yvonne stood at the front of the room and called for everyone's attention.

"Welcome to our first gathering in this important week," she said. "It's so nice to be with all of you again. Since this evening is a chance for us to catch up and share news about our families, I thought I'd start off with a happy announcement. My son, Jacob, has recently been married. I'd like to introduce you to his bride."

The fox-man from the bistro came walking in. He was holding the hand of a petite girl. Her shoulders were bent and she walked with jerky steps. Her vibration was so weak I didn't recognize it at first. When I did, I almost choked on a stuffed mushroom.

I'd known her when her reddish blond hair was lush and beautiful. Now it hung lifeless and dull around her shoulders. When she lifted her eyes to look around, they were hazy and roamed the room without focus.

Jacob was holding on to her left hand, so I couldn't see her fingers, but there was no doubt in my mind…she was Nikki Dawning, and she looked drugged to within an inch of her life.

Chapter Twenty

"Nikki is the newest addition to our family," Yvonne said.

The others in the room hadn't known Nikki when she was beautiful, so they couldn't make the comparison. The way her eyes wandered the crowd could have been attributed to nerves. I knew better. She was definitely drugged.

When she looked my way, I froze like a deer in headlights. She was out of it, but if she recognized me and said something, I'd be in trouble. I needed to get out of there quick.

"Is there a restroom nearby?" I whispered to Phoebe.

"Down the hall to the right," she whispered back.

I slid out of my chair, took a few quick steps to get behind the serving staff lining the back of the room, and hustled out the door. Thankful that I'd thought to get a key card the day before, I took it out of my clutch, ran to the elevators, and swiped it. The doors opened at the same moment I got a text from Theron.

Get out of there, it said. *Something is wrong.*

I texted back, *Nikki is here. I'm on the way out.*

As usual, the man at the gatehouse waved for me to stop so I could get my imaginary phone. *Open the damn gate,* I put into his mind. He did it, and I sped through.

I hoped Theron's tech was working, because the feed was going to show me bolting out of the Ledges like a maniac. I stopped on the side of the road long enough to text Phoebe and lie about going home because of a headache.

My whole body was shaking, and not just because of the treacherous drive.

I'd been told to listen for mention of Nikki. I was supposed to report if I overheard something that might lead to finding her. I hadn't expected her to walk into the same room as me. From the beginning, I'd known spying on the Truss was dangerous. If they found out I was spying on them, there would be unpleasant consequences. Seeing Nikki as a shadow of herself made the danger all the more real to me. If they could do that to her, they could do worse to me.

I formulated a plan. I'd get back to Theron's, make a call to Katherine, and then get a ticket to fly home.

I'd found Nikki and gathered some information that suggested Yvonne and Robert would make an unstable clan chief combination. I could report that Yvonne was a kleptomaniac, never a good quality in a leader, and last but not least, Yvonne was a Sebastian worshipper.

I'd done my job and wanted to go home, but I had the sneaking suspicion they'd want me to stay.

Theron was waiting for me when I drove through the trees and parked my car. He came down the steps at a jog and scooped me up. When he set me on my feet inside the cabin, I was shaking uncontrollably.

Grabbing the handy-dandy quilt off the back of the chair, he pulled it over my shoulders and wrapped his arms around me in a straitjacket-like hug.

"Tell me about it," he said.

"You wouldn't believe how she looked, Theron. She was so drugged she could barely stand. And she's likenessed to Jacob," I said with disgust.

"Yvonne and Robert's son?"

"Yes."

I could tell by the way his body tensed that really disturbed him. "We'd better go over everything," he said, helping me to a chair. "Start from the beginning."

It took me a few seconds to remember where the beginning was. Then it came to me. "I saw Jacob two days ago at a bistro. I didn't know it was him at the time, but I overheard him say, 'You're dealing with two lives.' Now I think he was talking about himself and Nikki. He obviously knows the bad condition she's in. If appearances are anything to go by, she might actually die. And if she does, he will, too. Why would he let that happen?"

"Who knows what likeness means to the Truss anymore? Assuming the physical connecting is still there, Jacob has probably been weakened by her state."

He hadn't looked sick, but then I had no reference point to compare him to.

"Jacob seems like he's in his mid-twenties. I have no idea how old he really is, but Nikki is seventeen. The age difference alone is disgusting."

"Nikki is young to have likenessed," he agreed. "It rarely happens before we're twenty. But age and time are different for us. Some likeness pairs are fifty years apart in age."

"Yuck."

"I agree, but it's a fact."

I put my head in my hands. "I don't understand why she's being treated like this."

"If they're keeping her drugged up the way you say, she must pose some kind of threat to someone. Your guess is as good as mine what that threat might be."

"This entire thing is so messed up. The last time I saw her, she was bold and beautiful. All of that was gone tonight. We have to get her out of there."

"Don't worry. Spencer will turn the matter over to the Dawnings now. They'll take care of it. Your part is done."

I shook my head. "I thought so, too…for about half a second. Phoebe said there's another meeting Saturday night. I think the Truss at the Ledges are the Elders Spencer and Katherine told me about. What if Yvonne wants to get appointed clan chief this weekend?"

"That's an issue for the clan chiefs to deal with. Not you. There's nothing you can do about it if Yvonne calls for a vote."

"That's not really true," I said, putting my head in my hands. "I'm a bit more advanced than most thoughtmakers. I can cloak thoughts."

"Wow," he said. "Ian told me you were good, but I never suspected you were that good."

"I just want to go home," I said wearily. "I want to be done with the Truss. I never want to see or even think about them again, except for maybe Phoebe. But deep down I know it isn't finished yet."

"You should probably get the hard part out of the way," he suggested. "Call Spencer and Katherine."

"I will. I just need a minute to get myself together first." Remembering Theron had texted me when I was in the elevator, I asked, "How did you know I was in trouble tonight?

"That voice…yelled it at me."

I laughed a little.

"Don't laugh. I already feel like I'm losing my mind."

I could have told him he might be able to open a pathway to the dead like I could, but if hearing my mother's voice freaked him out, that revelation might have given him a stroke.

"By the way," I said, "where did you learn to hug? You almost squeezed the life out of me."

"I'll tell you, but you won't like it."

I gave him a *go ahead* look.

"Animal Planet," he replied. "You know how they put straitjackets on dogs to keep them from going nuts during fireworks and storms?"

"Yeah."

"I figured if that kind of thing worked on dogs, it would probably work on you."

I chuckled. "I should be insulted, but I'm just…glad you're around to hug me when I need it."

"I do what I can," he said, picking up his trusty quarter and tossing it in the air. "You better call the wonder team now."

I got voicemail for both Spencer and Katherine, so I tried Ian. He picked up, and I told him what happened.

"This is really big," he said. "I'll keep calling my parents."

"Hang on," Theron interjected. "Put him on speaker, will you?"

I did and he continued, "Tell your parents I accessed the Truss financials, travel records, and some other things. They'll be interested in the information I uncovered. I'm sure your dad will be thrilled to report I broke my suspension."

"Ian," I chimed in. "Theron only messed around with tech to help me. He wouldn't have done it otherwise."

"I know. I'll remind my dad of that and be in touch."

I ended the call and laid my phone on the arm of the chair. "You still think Spencer and Katherine are going to ask you to stay up here?" Theron asked.

"Yes, I do."

"Want some advice?"

"Sure, why not?"

"Check yourself into a mental hospital for even considering it."

I gave him my sweetest smile. "Maybe they'd let us

share a room, since we both hear voices from beyond the beyond."

He fake-laughed and changed the channel on the TV.

We ate leftover lasagna, watched more History channel, a documentary on William the Conqueror this time, and still Ian didn't call.

Theron looked me over as the credits rolled. "You should go to bed," he said. "Waiting up won't make them call any faster."

It was a good suggestion, so I dragged my tired self to my room, took the red dress off, and rolled into a ball under the covers.

Sleep came easily. I had a dream that I was back at Fillmore High. The halls were crowded with kids trying to get to their next classes, and through the throng, Nikki came toward me. She was wearing the familiar sneer on her face. When she got close enough, she grabbed my arm. Her grip was so tight it stung.

"I can't find my next class," she said. "I don't know where to go. You have to help me, Alison."

The dream version of me tried to loosen her grip on my arm and replied, "I don't know where your next class is either."

Her eyes widened. "If you don't help me, he'll kill me."

I snorted. "Who will kill you? Your teacher?"

She said something I couldn't quite make out and then transformed into the sickly, bent girl I'd seen at dinner. She mouthed *help me* then faded away.

I woke in a cold sweat and kicked the blankets off. It

was just a nightmare, but I couldn't help wondering if my subconscious was trying to tell me something.

A little freaked out and not wanting to be alone, I went back to the living room.

Theron was sitting in his chair, staring into the flames of the fireplace. He had a pad of paper on his knee and a pencil in his fingers. "I can hear you breathing," he said. "Might as well come in and sit down."

"Okay," I replied softly.

"Did I wake you up?" he asked. "I tried to be quiet."

"No. I had a nightmare. I could use some company for a few minutes. Is that okay?"

"Yeah," he replied.

"Did Spencer call back?"

"No, but Ian did. He told his parents everything. They're thinking it through and will call us back when they decide what step to take next."

"Great. I love living in suspense."

He started twirling the pencil he was holding.

"What are you drawing?" I asked.

He moved his project so I couldn't see it. "It's personal."

I wasn't upset that he'd warned me off. Sometime since meeting him, I'd gotten used to how he worked. When he was in the mood to talk about something, he had a lot to say. When he wasn't in the mood, he made it clear. There was no guessing with Theron.

"What time is it?" I asked.

"Almost two a.m."

"I'm officially eighteen. I should probably feel great

about it, but I'm just another year closer to leaving my life in Vegas."

"Do you know where you'll go when you do leave for good?"

"Lillian, my boss, offered me a room at her new place. It's in Sweden, so at least I wouldn't be as tempted to sneak back and check on my family. What about you? Where will you go when your suspension ends?"

"I should go back to Columbia and finish my art degree, but I think I'll travel instead. For the first time in my life… or maybe the second, I feel like being entirely irresponsible. Maybe I'll swing by Lillian's place and say hi."

"I'd like that," I said.

He stood up and stretched. "I'll plan on it then. I should get some sleep or I might mess up the turkey tomorrow. Will you be okay out here on your own?"

"Probably. If I get scared, I'll wake you up."

"Thanks for the warning. I'll be sure to lock my door."

Chapter Twenty-One

"Good morning, Sunshine," I said when I went into the kitchen the next morning.

Theron turned around. He had a towel over his shoulder and a kitchen knife in his hand. "What's with you and 'good morning, Sunshine'?" he asked. "Can't you just say good morning, like a normal person?"

"I call you Sunshine because of your sunny disposition."

He raised an eyebrow at me. "For a somewhat intelligent person, you have a remarkably distorted view of reality."

"Maybe I see things that others don't," I countered. "No word from the wonder team yet?"

"Not yet."

I scooted up to look over his shoulder. "What are you doing?" I asked.

"Packing up Thanksgiving dinner. We're going to Stacy's house to cook it."

"You didn't tell me that was the plan."

"That's because I decided it about an hour ago." He got the cranberries out of the fridge. "I checked the weather report. The roads should be clear for a while."

"Not that I'm not thrilled to get out of here, but why the change?"

"Because we'll go stir-crazy sitting and waiting for Spencer and Katherine to call. Get your stuff. I'll be finished with this in ten minutes."

I hummed a little on the way to my room. I was going to see Ian again. Happy Thanksgiving to me.

We didn't say much on the drive to town. Theron kept on the main road past Betsy's and parked the Land Rover in front of a cute little house a couple blocks down. There was a snowman in the front yard. The poor guy was wearing a purple scarf and a heliotrope-colored hat. One of his coal eyes had popped out, but rocks poked into his face in the shape of a smile made him look happy anyway.

Stacy and Ian were waiting for us at the front door. Ian came down the steps looking casually hot in a dark gray sweater and jeans. He winked as he passed me on the way to help Theron carry stuff in.

Stacy waved me forward, so I went up the steps to meet her. She gave me one of her infamous "Stacy hugs," led me into her living room, and opened a coat closet. "You can put your jacket here, if you'd like," she said.

I picked a hanger to use and looked at the space around

us. It was clean but as haphazard-looking as the snowman. Computer equipment and tools were spread over every horizontal surface. Cords and wires cluttered the floor.

"I'm sorry about the mess," she said. "I'd like to say I'm in the middle of a life-changing project, but it always looks like this. I run a computer repair business. This room is my front office and workspace. Follow me close and I'll get you through the chaos. Careful not to trip on anything and kill yourself."

She guided me along an uncluttered but narrow path to her kitchen, which was pristine. There were no electronic odds and ends to be seen anywhere.

Theron knocked at the back door.

"That's our chef," Stacy said, going to open it.

Theron came in with his arms full of bags. Ian followed with more bags and the cooler.

"Just put everything on the counter," Theron said. "I'll unpack it."

Ian did as he was asked and then came to sit next to me. "Happy birthday," he whispered.

"Thanks," I whispered back.

Though it was partially hidden by the collar of my shirt, he picked up the sapphire. "I'm glad you wore it."

My skin tingled where his fingers touched my skin, and I smiled, thinking I might never take it off.

"I didn't know you liked to cook," Ian said to Theron. "Stacy says you're really good at it."

"He is," I agreed.

"Stop talking and come help me get this meal ready," he

grumbled.

Ian got up. "I'm glad to see you've gotten more polite," he said.

Theron put his hands on the counter and let his head drop to his chest. "Sorry," he said quietly. "This thing with the Ledges is stressing me out. I'll try to do better."

Ian thumped him on the back. "It's okay. I feel the same way."

He pulled it together and asked, "Will you put the potatoes in the oven, Stacy? Ian, you can peel the apples for the pie, and Alison, you can finish the bread."

He got out a covered bowl and handed it to me. "This is the dough. It has to be kneaded one more time before it bakes."

He got some flour out of one of his handy-dandy containers, sprinkled it on the counter, and then put a ball of rubber-looking dough on it. He demonstrated how to push and roll the dough to knead it and turned me loose.

It went fine until the gooey dough started to stick to my fingers. "Theron, something's wrong," I said, lifting my hands so he could see them.

Ian gave a short laugh. "You need to put more flour on the dough every once in a while, so it won't stick to you."

"Oh," I said, shaking my hands to loosen some of the sticky stuff.

"You're never going to get it off that way," Ian said.

He took my hands and started stripping the goo off of my fingers one by one. It created an intimate awareness between us. Without thinking about it, I moved toward him. Our faces were close, and his breath brushed across my cheek. I lifted my chin to kiss him and caught Stacy and Theron watching us.

"Well, that was disturbing," Theron said. "I may never see bread the same way again."

We worked together until Theron said everything was done and then sat at the table while Stacy bustled around getting drinks.

She reminded me of the snowman in the yard, a little messy but cheerful.

"I have orange or grape soda," she said. "What do you want?"

We all chose grape, and she brought them to the table.

"I just got the new *Tomb Flyer* game," she said, sitting down. "I haven't opened it yet, but you guys can do the honor later. It's sitting on the PS4 right now."

Ian and Theron shared a look. "I won't tell if you don't," Ian said.

"How about now?" Theron asked.

"Knock yourselves out," she replied.

Theron grabbed his soda. "Her gaming systems are set up in the den," he said.

"Don't spill on my stuff," Stacy called after them as they hustled out of the room.

"Theron is happier than I've seen him in a long time," she said, twisting her can back and forth. "Having you around must be good for him."

"How can you tell he's happy?" I asked, sarcastically. "He seems the opposite of happy most of the time."

We shared a smile. "He's gone through a lot this year," she continued. "He broke up with his girlfriend a couple months ago. It's been hard on him."

I nodded. "He mentioned that."

"I never thought they'd work out," she continued. "Amy wasn't as committed as Theron was. It was almost like she thought she was better than him. I think he suspected it, but was too in love with her to give up. When she broke it off, it really shook him up."

Learning that Amy may not have been as in love with Theron as he was with her made my heart break a little more for him.

"What was he like before her?" I asked.

"He joked around and laughed more. He's always had a serious side, though. I appreciate that about him. He thinks before he speaks, so you know he means it. He's not showy like your boyfriend, but he's steady."

"You like him, don't you?" I asked.

She chuckled. "He doesn't see me the same way I see him, so it doesn't matter. He'll move on from Amy and find someone else. It's just a matter of time."

I took a drink of sweet grapy soda. Stacy and I had more in common than she knew.

Ian and Theron weren't gone long. They came back looking disappointed.

"One of your friends wants to game with you," Theron said. "If you don't get online, he's going to tell BlueDog45 where you hid the treasure in *Fantasy Marathon*."

Stacy's eyes got so big they almost bulged out. "He

wouldn't," she muttered.

"He seemed pretty serious about it," Ian replied.

Truly upset, she looked at me. "I'm so sorry to just leave you here, but this is an emergency."

My brother was a gamer, too, and though probably not as hard-core into fantasy games as she was, he'd freak if someone told where his treasure was stashed.

"It's okay," I said. "I understand."

She was gone in seconds. Which was good because my phone rang and the caller ID read Katherine. I turned it so the boys could see.

"Let's go for a ride," Theron suggested.

The phone continued to ring until all three of us were in the Land Rover. I answered and put it on speaker.

"Happy birthday, Alison," Katherine said.

"Thanks," I replied. Then, wanting to get down to business, I asked, "When are Bruce and Amelia coming to get Nikki?"

"We haven't told them," Spencer replied.

"They should know as soon as possible."

"We're going to wait a little longer."

Frustrated, I said, "I thought helping Bruce and Amelia was what this was about."

"There's a bigger issue now," Katherine replied. "Six more Truss couples are scheduled to fly in today. We confirmed they are Elders. Yvonne is going to call for a vote on the clan chief this weekend."

Theron had driven a couple blocks from Stacy's. He pulled off to the side of the road. "Just like you thought," he muttered.

"What?" Spencer asked.

"Nothing," I said. "What does that have to do with telling the Dawnings where their daughter is?"

"We can't scare the Truss right now," Spencer continued. "The Elders are already reluctant to come back to the clans. If the Dawnings know they have Nikki, they'll storm the place. That would offend the Elders, making them even more likely to support a leader who thinks coming back to us isn't a good idea."

"So you're going to leave her there while Yvonne and Robert get the clanship?"

"No. In fact, they aren't even being considered. Robert died two months ago. We just found out earlier today."

I let out a breath. So that was why he hadn't been at the Truss dinner. Phoebe had only mentioned her father twice. What a horrible thing for her. She'd lost the father she'd been close to, and even if her mother was a thief, Phoebe was going to lose her as well.

"We think Yvonne is campaigning for someone else," Katherine said. "The most logical guess would be her son, but he seems to be an unlikely candidate. He's young and undistinguished. In fact, he's barely ever set foot outside of Virginia. If it's him, we have no idea what his plans for the future of the clan might be. He never worked for Sebastian, but he may have the same ideology as he did."

"But it could be someone else altogether," Spencer added. "We don't know anything about the candidate yet. We need to stop the Elders from voting before we find out more."

"You mean *I* need to stop the Truss Elders from voting," I said, clipping out the words.

"Yes," Katherine replied.

My stomach churned, and my chest tightened. And there it was. My suspicions were confirmed. The danger level had gone up another notch.

Ian's brows were drawn together. Theron's brows were drawn together. Mine were probably drawn together, too. None of us were happy with the situation.

I sighed. "What do you want me to do?"

"First, we need you to talk to Nikki directly," Spencer said. "We need to know who took her."

I laughed disbelievingly. "Talking to Nikki would be like asking the grim reaper for a haircut. She never liked me. She'll go straight to Jacob or whoever and tell them who I am."

"She's got to be hurting and scared," Katherine continued. "You're a familiar face. You can offer her hope. Tell her you'll let her parents know where she is. You won't be lying, and it's probably an opportunity she won't pass up."

Theron shook his head. "If Nikki is as drugged up as Alison thinks, she may not be able to answer any of your questions."

"Is that you, Theron?" Spencer said.

"Yes. Ian is here, too," I added. "I put you on speaker. Theron's right about the drugs. I might not get anything of value from her."

"Still, will you try?" Katherine asked. "It would help us

figure out who the candidate is."

Frustrated, irritated, and agitated, I ran my fingers through my hair and winced when I pulled at a tangled piece. "I have the feeling that's not all you want me to do," I said.

"We want you to get into the meeting on Saturday and thoughtmake the Elders into a disagreement," Spencer admitted. "Something big enough that some of them get offended and leave. We need to get them to postpone whatever decision Yvonne wants them to make, so we can evaluate things."

"Why don't you just swoop in and stop the meeting yourself?" Theron asked.

Spencer huffed into the phone. "I'll say it once more. We don't want to put the Elders on the defensive right now because we don't want another Sebastian situation. We want the Truss to come back to the clans. They're already reluctant to do so, and if we make them angry, they're more likely to appoint a clan chief who doesn't want to work with us at all."

I squeezed my eyes closed, glad I didn't get headaches. If I did, I'd probably be having a migraine from all the pressure I was feeling.

"Thoughtmaking other dewing is difficult," I said. "It saps my energy and the rebound hurts. I'll have to cloak a thought just to get into the meeting. Then to create the kind of chaos you're asking for, I'll have to cloak a lot more of them. If I manage it, I may not be able to walk out on my own."

"And if she passes out in the room during their meeting, they'll figure out quickly she's been spying on them and get rid of her," Theron said.

"You mean kill me," I corrected him.

"I'm trying to be more polite," he said through his teeth.

Ian had had enough. "This is a complete load of crap," he said. "You're asking too much of her. There has to be another way to deal with this."

"That's a little hypocritical isn't it, son?" Spencer interjected. "Remember why you went looking for Alison in the first place. You wanted her to risk her life in a fight with Sebastian."

"She had something to gain then," he bit back. "She was trying to protect her family. Who is she protecting this time?"

"All of us," Katherine replied. "The Truss need a chief we can trust. Someone we can work with. Someone who wants peace."

I knew Ian understood her reasoning, but I could still hear the frustration in his voice. "You're sending her in alone," he continued. "Brandy and I were with her last time."

"She won't be alone. Theron is there."

Ian mumbled something I couldn't make out.

"I won't be able to disrupt the Elders and hide Theron's vibration, too," I said. "He'll have to wait outside the building until I'm done."

"We know we're asking for a lot," Katherine said. "We know it's dangerous. I selfishly want you, Ian, and Theron to get as far away from the Truss as you can. Unfortunately, this is not about what I want. It's about the greater good."

I loved Katherine, but at that moment, I wanted to shove the greater good down her throat.

"When it comes to the meeting," Spencer cut in, "we'll need a real-time relay of what happens. Can you rig up a video device to do that, Theron?"

"I can," he answered in a voice full of sarcasm. "But it would be breaking my suspension."

"From the information you emailed me last night, I gather you've already done that."

"After all the times I've helped you with my criminal skills, this is the thanks I get."

"I turned you in for several reasons," Spencer said. "One of them was to protect you from yourself. You were out of control."

"You could have talked to me about it. Instead you handed it over to Gage. You know he never liked me. He gave me twice the time up here than is required by tradition."

"You needed an opportunity to cool down," Spencer insisted. "Maybe Gage was a little harsh on your sentence, but it's only one year out of three hundred. Take the time to get yourself straightened out. You're amazingly talented at just about everything you try, and most of the time you have good sense. You needed a reminder to use it."

Theron snorted.

"Will you make a device or not?" Spencer pressed.

"Yeah, I'll put some tech together, but I want to be clear about this. I'm not doing it for you. I'm doing it for Alison. A video feed will help me know if she's in trouble and needs my help."

"I figured that's how it would be," Spencer replied. "Thank you."

"Will you send the feed to me, too?" Ian asked.

"Yeah," Theron agreed.

"So, that's the long and short of it," Spencer said. "Alison, will you do what we've requested?"

"What about Nikki?"

"When the meeting is stopped, we'll get her out."

It was hard to decide. The plan involved Theron, too. We'd both be stepping into something more dangerous than we'd originally agreed to. It was as unfair to him as it was to me.

"What do you think?" I asked him.

It was quiet until my deceased mother said, *Do it for the greater good.*

Theron's eyes flickered to me. Of course he'd heard it, too, and like all the other times, it was messing him up. It was kind of funny to see a guy as big as Theron nod his head like a scared child.

"Yes, we'll do it," I replied.

Chapter Twenty-Two

Stacy was the only one of us who really enjoyed the Thanksgiving meal. Ian, Theron, and I sat at the table in various states of anxiety. We only picked at our food.

As she finished her second piece of pie, she said, "The clouds are rolling in."

Theron looked out the kitchen window. "You're right," he said. "Ali and I better get on the road. It could be a bad one tonight. I'll go start the car."

"Thanks for everything," I said to Stacy.

"Sure. It's nice having people in the house. I hope you'll come down again."

"Me, too," I said, meaning it.

"I'll walk you out," Ian said, grabbing my hand as I headed through the mess to get my jacket.

Out of everyone's eyeshot, he pulled me to a stop and kissed my neck.

"You really shouldn't do that," I said. "It's only going to make things harder in the end."

He turned me around to face him. "I don't understand. Why would any of this be harder in the end? You know how I feel about you. And I'm not stupid, I know how you feel about me."

I shook my head. "You don't understand."

"Then tell me."

I thought about it, but knowing the how the explanation would hurt him, I couldn't. Not with everything else I had to deal with.

"We need to talk," I said. "Just not until we get back to Vegas."

He crossed his arms over his chest as he looked at me. "Okay, I'll wait. But speaking of Vegas, I seriously think you should just pack your things and let me buy you a ticket to fly back."

"I'm tempted to take you up on that, but I can't."

I didn't tell him that part of the reason was because of what my dead mother said.

He let out a breath. "Fine. But can you come down for breakfast tomorrow morning…by yourself?"

"It's going to snow tonight. The roads will be bad."

"Let Theron drive you then," he relented. "But make sure he knows you need some time alone with me."

"I will."

The drive back to the cabin was quiet. Theron and I had

our own worries to think about.

I was starting to get angry with Spencer and Katherine. I could kind of understand why they hadn't told me I had Falco relatives. But there was no reason for them to keep my supposed inheritance and being a clan chief from me. I loved Spencer and Katherine, but not knowing those things left me in a vulnerable position. I was easier to manipulate in that state. I was starting to wonder if that's what they'd been doing all along.

They'd asked a lot of me over the past four days. I'd agreed to it because I wanted what was best for humankind as well as the dewing, but I was starting to feel like a weapon they could point and shoot at a target.

Feeling like my mind was twisting up in knots, I closed my eyes and tried to sleep the rest of the way to the cabin.

It was dark when we got back. Theron flipped the light switch, and the lamp in the window came on.

Running a hand through his spiky hair, he said, "Today is your birthday but it feels more like a funeral."

"How about for the rest of the night we don't talk about anything related to what's going on at the Ledges," I suggested with a sigh.

He laughed a little. "Do you think that's really possible?"

"We can try."

"Okay," he agreed. "I have something for you. Go sit at the table and close your eyes."

Suspicious, I narrowed my eyes. "Why?" I asked.

"Just do it, please."

I did what he asked and heard him moving around the

kitchen. Then he set something in front of me.

"Okay, you can look now."

I peeked open an eye and saw a cupcake with pink frosting and silver sprinkles on a plate patterned with balloons. It looked like it had been made for an eight-year-old. I loved it. There was one candle burning on top.

"Go ahead, blow it out," he urged.

"Will you sing to me first?"

"Not in a million years. Hurry—make your wish before candle wax gets on your frosting."

My wish was pretty simple. I wanted to go home. I blew the candle out and said, "That was very sweet of you."

"That's me…sweet." He handed me an envelope. "This is for you, too."

I hesitated before taking it. "You didn't fill this with bugs, did you?" I asked.

"You're so suspicious all the time. It's a birthday present. Open it."

"You didn't have to get me…"

My words died away as I pulled three sketches out.

The first was of a woman with long pale hair. Her eyes were large and her face heart-shaped. It was done simply, but I could tell she was beautiful. There was a man standing next to her. The two of them were looking down on a child.

I exhaled the breath I'd been holding. "Are these people who I think they are?" I whispered.

"They're your parents," he replied.

My eyes filled with tears, but I blinked them back so I could see clearly.

"Look at the next one," he suggested.

The second sketch showed the woman on her knees. She was hugging the child tight. Theron had drawn a mixture of love and anguish in her expression. "Oh my gosh," I muttered.

I turned to the third sketch. It was of the man. He'd picked the child up. Her head lay against his chest, his chin lowered to rest on top of it. There was no mistaking how precious she was to him.

"You asked how your parents felt about leaving you," he said. "These are from my memory that day. This is how it was for them."

I couldn't hold the tears back anymore. They came gushing out.

"Don't cry," Theron said, grabbing my hand. "You weren't supposed to be sad. I wanted to make you happy."

Managing somehow to get control over my emotions, I said, "I am happy. I'm very happy. You were working on these last night. You have amazing talent."

He shrugged. We both knew the gift had nothing to do with his ability and everything to do with the subject matter.

I looked at the drawing that showed my parents together. "She was pretty, wasn't she?" I asked.

He nodded. "Like you."

"She looks miniature next to him."

"Your father was around six five, I think. Once, when he visited my dad, I asked if he was a giant. He said yes. I thought it was the coolest thing. You must get your Amazonian height from our side."

I looked into Theron's eyes and repeated, "Our side… It's nice to have a side."

Maybe he blushed a little, I don't know. "I wanted to do them in color," he said, "but I didn't have time. I'll do another set and send them to you later."

"If you never get around to it, I don't care. These are perfect."

I leaned over and hugged him tight. He hugged me back.

"You'd hug anyone, wouldn't you?" he said.

"I went a long time without hugging," I replied. "I'm making up for lost time."

Chapter Twenty-Three

*T*heron and I left early for Greenvale the next morning. More of his stuff had arrived from New York, and he wanted to get it from Stacy, so he'd happily…almost…agreed to drive me down.

Betsy's had just opened when we got there. Ian already had a table. "You charmed Livy into letting you in before officially opening, didn't you?" I asked.

He winked at me. "I'm here so much she's come to think of me as a part of the furniture."

"Or a backup if things don't work out with Skip," Theron said.

"I'm taken. My heart belongs to a dark-haired, gray-eyed girl with a great right hook."

I smiled as we slid into our bench seats. "She sounds

amazing," I said.

Betsy's started filling fast. We placed our orders and listened to the buzz of talk around us. Ian tried to start a conversation about surfing, but it didn't work. Our minds were busy mulling over more important matters.

We were halfway through breakfast when Theron got a text on his ancient phone.

"Stacy needs me," he said. "I should head over."

"We'll follow you," Ian said.

When Ian and I pulled up to Stacy's, I noticed the poor snowman had lost his other coal eye.

"I need to help her with a system...thing," Theron said as we got out. "I promise it's nothing big, and if it was, it couldn't be traced back to us."

Ian laughed. "Control your criminal instincts, man," he said.

"Technically, what we're doing isn't illegal in China."

"Whatever. I'm pretending you didn't say anything about it," Ian replied as we climbed the stairs.

Stacy was sitting in the middle of the mess in her living room. She had three computers set up the same way Ian had them at the cabin. "Hi, Ali," she said, without looking up. "It's good to see you...well not see you, but you know... hear you. I'm going to be in the middle of this for a while. Feel free to make yourself a cup of tea in the kitchen."

Just the thought of tea made my stomach turn.

"What's wrong with your face?" Theron asked. "You look like she offered you a cup of dirt."

"She doesn't like tea," Ian supplied.

"There's cider mix in the tin above the stove," she said. "Have one of those."

"That's okay," I replied. "I'm going to put the coal back in your snowman's eye sockets."

"Thanks," she replied with her fingers moving fast over her keyboard.

It took me a while to locate the missing pieces of coal. When I finally did, Ian had started carrying boxes to Theron's car.

"Do you need help?" I asked.

"Nope. One more trip and I'll have it done."

I dug the holes a little deeper for Mr. Snowman's eyes and put the black blobs in it. Then I straightened his hat.

"He looks a lot better," Ian observed after putting the last box in the back of Theron's Land Rover.

I hid a smile as he closed the door. He had no idea he'd just helped Theron break more laws.

The snow was deep a few feet away, so I walked over and lay down in it. Moving my arms and legs, I started to make a snow angel.

Ian lay down next to me and did the same thing.

"When was the last time you did this?" I asked.

"Um…I think I was six."

"I can imagine you at six," I said. "A little blond-haired boy with too much energy to contain. You probably climbed the walls and made your mom want to pull her hair out."

He looked over at me. "Maybe, but you would have loved me."

I scooted over to fresh snow to make another snow

angel. "What have you and Theron been doing in your spare time?" he asked.

"Talking and watching TV. I looked through the dewing history book the other day, though."

Surprised, he looked over at me. "What did you think?

"It's pretty interesting," I admitted. "I'm going to go through it some more when we get home."

"That's progress," he said. "You want to sit in my car and warm up a little?"

I had worked on the snowman without gloves, and my hands were freezing. "Definitely," I replied.

We got in and Ian turned the car engine on. "It should only take a minute for the air to heat up," he said.

I put my head in my hands. "The last five days feel more like fifteen," I grumbled.

He kneaded the tight muscles on my shoulders. With my eyes still closed, I sat up. It didn't surprise me to feel his lips on my own. The kisses moved from my mouth, to the side of neck, and then to the hollow where the sapphire still rested.

Sighing, I gave in and moved so I could kiss him back.

"The windows are going to fog up," I whispered.

"I don't care…when are you going to leave?"

"Soon. I'm supposed to meet Phoebe for a late lunch."

He brushed a piece of hair away from my face. "That's not what I mean. When are you going to leave Vegas and come with me?"

"I never told you I was going with you."

"You should," he urged. "My parents have protection living in your neighborhood. My uncle will make sure your family is safe. You don't have to worry about them."

I sat back. "I can't go yet…I'm not ready."

"How long are you going to put yourself through this?" he asked. "You have to leave them. Knowing that is a weight you carry. If I've noticed, I'm willing to bet your parents have, too."

I'd come to a similar conclusion. That didn't mean the solution was to go.

"Imagine you were in my place," I said. "Imagine you had to leave your parents. How would you feel about it?"

"It would hurt," he said. "I would be sad, but if destiny put me in your position…if I was living a life that interfered with who I was meant to be, I would leave.

I was so angry I couldn't look at him.

"When this thing with the Truss is finished, come with me," he pushed. He lifted my hands to kiss the insides of my wrists. "You were planning to move to Alaska the day I told you who I was. I promise you'll like where I live better."

"I want more memories with my family," I replied. Remembering how Theron understood my reasoning, I continued, "I know wanting to stay with them is a human desire, but that's part of who I am. I've believed in making decisions all my life and right now I'm deciding to have more time with the McKyes."

"You have perfect recall. You can pull up a million memories and experience them like they're happening for real."

He was right, but I wanted absolutely as many pictures in my mind as possible. It made me angry that he still didn't get that. After opening my door, I got out. He was at my side before I'd taken two steps.

"I didn't mean to make you mad," he said. "But be honest with yourself. It's torture to live the way you are. It's better for everyone if you just move on."

That did it. I clenched my hands into fists and asked, "What do you really want, Ian? What do you think will happen if I go with you? Let's get it all out in the open."

He put his hands on my shoulders and squeezed gently. "I think I've made it obvious what I want. I want destiny to pair us."

It was going to hurt, but I had to get the truth out. "We will *never* likeness, Ian."

"You can't know that."

I swallowed the lump in my throat. "The night we fought Sebastian, it happened. But the destiny you feel so strongly about didn't let it stick."

His hands dropped to his sides. "What are you talking about?"

"When Sebastian was seconds away from crushing your mind, I accepted everything about being dewing. I accepted because...I loved you. It started out as a thought I was going to put into Sebastian's mind to trick him into believing I belonged to someone else. But it became something different. My energy was yours and yours was mine. The beginning of likeness. We were two parts of the same person...and then we separated again."

It was like I'd punched him in the stomach. "It couldn't have happened. I would remember."

"You were pretty close to dead at the time," I said. "At first, I didn't understand what had happened. With Brandy dead and you dying, it was too much to take in. Days later, when I could sit down and think things through, I realized what had happened."

Ian took half a step back. "I don't believe it. You imagined it."

"It's the truth," I insisted. "The last thing I want is to hurt you, but we have to face the truth. There is too much human going on in my mind. I will never likeness…to anyone."

"It was just the wrong time," he insisted. "The wrong place and the wrong time."

"No," I said firmly. "We were connected one second and we were separate the next. I can't go with you because I'll come to love you even more. Then when you find the one you're meant to be with, you'll leave me. I can't…I just can't watch that happen. I don't think I can survive that kind of loss again."

He cupped my face in his hands. "Maybe things will change when you *admit* who you really are. The rest will fall into place."

I moved his hands away. "I want that to be true, but it isn't."

I could see the pain in his eyes, and it killed me that I'd caused it.

Theron walked around the side of the house. "Time to leave," he said.

I leaned forward and kissed Ian's cheek. "I'm sorry," I whispered.

As Theron drove us out of town, I asked, "How much of that did you overhear?"

He glanced at me. "Enough."

"Thanks."

"For what?"

"For not asking questions."

"I'm fighting my own demons, remember?" he replied quietly.

Chapter Twenty-Four

Theron cut the engine in front of his cabin, but neither of us got out.

"I hacked the Ledges' guest registry," he said, "Yvonne rented all of the rooms the Truss are staying in under her own name. The cabins, too. I can't tell you where Jacob is staying or where he's keeping Nikki."

"I'll have to track her vibration, which means I'm going to have to wander around the guest floors all afternoon."

"Pretty much," he agreed.

"Ugh. I can hardly think straight right now. All I can see is Ian, and the way I hurt him."

"It's going to be difficult between you two for a while," he said, "but he'll rebound. Ian won't stop being your friend. It's not his MO. Right now, you have to compartmentalize your feelings. You agreed you'd talk to Nikki today. That has to be your focus."

He was right. I took a deep breath and pushed my hair back. "How good are you in a bar fight?"

He gave me a blank stare.

"I need to lose some excess energy," I said, getting out of the car. "And you're the only one around."

If I asked him to spar with me, he'd say no. We'd have to go a few rounds about how it wasn't right to hit a girl. I didn't have the patience for that. When he got out of the car, I grabbed his hand and dragged him into the deeper snow.

Facing him, I said, "Sorry."

Then I threw an uppercut to his jaw.

"Ahhh," he said, holding his face and bending at the waist. "What was that for?"

"I need this," I said. "It will help me focus. I can take as good as I give, so don't be shy. Just don't hit me in the face. I have to meet Phoebe at the lodge."

"You just hit *me* in the face."

"Block me next time."

I threw a left, and he stopped it. He wasn't expecting the right kick I nailed on his upper thigh. Just as I hoped, it really pissed him off. After that, it was on.

We punched, ducked, kicked, and dodged. It was clear Theron could beat the crap out of me if he wanted, but I trusted he wouldn't. He needed a good fight as much as I did.

I compared his style to Ian's. He was less skilled and slower, but his reach was longer and the force behind it was pretty amazing. The rage in him I'd caught glimpses of in our time together was closer to the surface than ever before. It didn't scare me, but it made me think Spencer was right. Theron needed time to resolve his anger. Otherwise, someone really was going to get hurt.

When I had enough, I signaled time-out.

"Ian's a good teacher," Theron said, breathing hard. "You're not bad."

We headed to the house and I chucked him with my arm. "Why do we train to fight?" I asked. "If we're supposed to be so evolved and peace-loving, why do we all learn to rage against the machine?"

"I would have thought you'd have asked Ian that question a long time ago," he replied.

"There are a lot of questions I've put off, but I'm asking now."

"It's complicated," he said, opening the door so I could go inside. "Somewhere along the chain of evolution we learned what we could do to each other with our energy. At the same time, we developed a deeper respect for life. Especially our own. Maybe in the beginning we did fight to kill, but by the time our kind relocated to Atlantis we only fought for fun. It was a lot like how the Greeks boxed and wrestled for sport. There were matches and games between clans on the solstices and equinoxes."

We sat down and he continued. "There were clear rules. The fights would always stop before anyone's mind was crushed. The ending was symbolic. The winner would turn his or her opponent's head. Not hard enough to break the neck…but close. Breaking the spine is the hardest injury for us to come back from."

"When did it change back to fighting to the death?"

"During the war between Tenebrosus and the Rorelent. Tenebrosus and his followers stopped pretending. We have long memories, and since then, learning to fight has been an important step in growing up."

"When did you learn?" I asked.

"Early. Your dad was the first to teach me. I've always appreciated that. He was a good guy."

I nodded, but there was a knot in the pit in my stomach. I really wished I'd known him.

After we thawed out a bit, I went to change and get ready to meet Phoebe. Theron was waiting for me by the front door when I was ready to go.

"This is for you," he said, putting an envelope in my hand. "Well, technically it's for Jacob, but you're supposed to give it to him."

I opened the envelope and pulled a card out. It had a picture of a daisy on the front and inside it said, "Congratulations on your big day."

"What's it for?"

"It's a 'happy to hear about your wedding' sort of thing. I put a tracking chip under the daisy. Sign it, get it into Jacob's hands, and we'll hope it ends up wherever Nikki is."

"Smart. Thanks."

He nodded and followed me to my car. "Don't take too many chances up there," he said.

I was hopped up on anxiety, but did my best to hide it. "I'll be careful," I replied.

Chapter Twenty-Five

I met Phoebe in front of the restaurant. It might have been nerves, but for once, I didn't want to eat.

"They won't open until two," she said, looking disappointed. "Sorry I asked you to come up so early."

"That's only fifteen minutes away," I replied. "We can look through the shops if you want to."

Her fuzzy hair bobbed up and down as she nodded. "Let's go through the souvenir store first. They have some hilarious stuff."

I agreed and we headed in that direction.

"I was hoping to see your brother today," I commented as we walked. "I feel bad that I had to leave the dinner before I could introduce myself the other night."

It was a lame reason for wanting to see Jacob, but she

didn't seem to think I was a creeper, so that was good.

"I'll text him and see if he can meet us at the restaurant."

We went into one of the souvenir shops. It was typical of what you'd find on any vacation. There were a lot of overpriced knickknacks and tchotchkes to look at. In the back, we found a really interesting selection of hats, most of which were completely inappropriate for a ski vacation.

"Hey, come here," I said, pulling a wide-brimmed sunhat from the top shelf. I put it on her and pulled the sides down a little. "You look like you should be on a beach in Florida."

She found a mirror and turned side to side in front of it. "It makes my nose look smaller. I'd get plastic surgery, but…"

She didn't finish. She didn't need to. I knew her nose would just regenerate in its original shape.

"Who buys these things?" I asked, pulling down a Russian military hat.

"People like my mom. She can't resist gaudy stuff like this."

"Come to think of it, my mom would probably buy some, too."

We wandered down more aisles until I found a shelf of snow globes. "I need to get one of these," I said.

"Why? They're as bad as the hats."

"Which makes them perfect. I promised my little brother I'd bring one back for him. Help me find the most obnoxious one they've got."

We started looking through them. "How about this?" she asked, handing me one with a snowman inside. He was wearing sunglasses and a flowered shirt as he skied down a steep hillside on a snowboard. I tipped the globe to start the snowflakes swirling and noticed a turn-key on the base. After twisting it a couple of times an off-key version of "Margaritaville" began to play.

"Perfect," I said.

I paid for the globe and we moved on to the next shop. It happened to be an art dealer's store. The overhead light was dim so that the lights pointing at the pieces stood out better. A saleswoman on the phone gave us a polite nod and motioned for us to have a look around.

At the far side of the store, handblown glass vases and bowls were arranged on pedestals. Light refracted off them in rainbows of color. Phoebe followed me over to them. "Which is your favorite?" she asked.

"That one," I replied, pointing toward a yellow-gold vase. The neck of the vase had been stretched and bent, like the stem of a flower. "If I ever become wealthy, I'm going to get something just like it."

It was a jolt to my system when I remembered what Theron said about me having an estate. Spending my dead relatives' money seemed cold, though.

"Which is your favorite?" I asked.

"One of the paintings, actually. Come see."

I tagged along behind her, enjoying the art we passed.

Thank you, Mr. Dawson at Fillmore High, for expanding my universe to include paintings and sculpture, I thought.

Phoebe stopped in front of the last painting on the wall. It was done in the impressionist style, so the lines weren't clearly defined, but the effect was great. It made the scene seem brighter. The artist had painted a boy sitting on a hillside. His elbows were propped on his knees, and he was leaning forward with his chin on his hands. It gave me the impression he was deep in thought. From the long green grasses and wildflowers that carpeted the valley below him, it was probably late spring. Without seeing it anywhere in the painting, I knew the sun was bright overhead and that there was a breeze blowing.

"It's amazing, isn't it?" Phoebe asked.

"It really is," I agreed.

Bending closer, I searched for the artist's signature. "T. Falco" was scribbled in the corner.

Theron had painted it; he was better than good, he was genius.

I could have looked at the painting all day, but Phoebe sighed and said, "I guess the restaurant is open now. Jacob is probably waiting for us."

He was sitting at a table in the center of the room. He raised a glass of water to his lips as we approached. I noticed that his hand trembled when he put it down. There were shadows under his eyes, too. He looked like a fox who didn't feel well. I wondered if he was suffering the effects of Nikki's drugs. The idea made me a little happy.

Leaning back in his chair, he ran a lazy hand across his chest and looked me up and down. He was revolting, but flirting with him might help me in the long run.

"You're Ali," he surmised. "I've seen you around, I think."

I pulled a lock of hair over my shoulder as I sat down, keeping eye contact with him the entire time. "I think we had breakfast at the same place a few days ago," I said, "and I was at your family's dinner the other night."

"Oh, that's right. I remember now."

"I didn't stay long enough to introduce myself. I would have congratulated you."

He waved a hand. "My mom turned our…marriage into the event of the evening, but she just wanted to liven up the party."

"It didn't work very well," Phoebe muttered.

Jacob's eyes focused in on her. "What was that?"

"Nobody really cares who's married to whom," she said. "Everyone is here for something more important."

"Yeah," he said. "I'm part of that, too."

Phoebe rolled her eyes. "I know, and it scares the crap out of me."

Her brother glared at her.

Hoping to prevent a sibling quarrel, I said, "Your wife is…pretty."

Jacob waved dismissively once more. "I'm more interested in talking about you. Where are you from, Ali?"

"Arizona."

"Never been there. I like trees and shade, not sun and sand."

He asked about twenty more questions, each time telling me something about himself. If I read him right, he had an enormous ego. Something else I could take advantage of if I had to.

I laughed at his jokes and acted like I was charmed by the attention he paid me. It could have gone on forever, but thankfully he got a text. "Business," he said after reading it. "I have to go. It's been great talking to you, Ali."

I only remembered the envelope when he got up to leave. After pulling it out of my pocket, I handed it to him. "Ah…this is sort of an apology for missing your big announcement the other night," I said. "Will you make sure your wife sees it?"

I put the thought *Give it to Nikki* into his mind, hoping it would last long enough for him to actually get to her.

"Sure," he replied.

"And that piece of work is my brother," Phoebe said as he walked away. "He thinks he's bound for greatness. Too bad he's about as dumb as a box of rocks."

"He seems okay to me," I lied.

"It's all an act. The one thing Jacob is good at is following directions. He hasn't had a *good* original idea pass through his head since…well, since ever. I love him, but I don't like him. He nailed a dead rat to my bedroom door once. He thought it was a great joke. It's hard to like someone who does that kind of thing."

Spencer and Katherine hadn't been particularly concerned about Jacob. They should have been. Like Yvonne, he loved attention. He was in love with himself, too. The rat incident indicated he had a sadistic side. He had a lot in common with Sebastian.

Maybe he was the candidate Yvonne was trying to get appointed after all, but I still needed to confirm some stuff with Nikki. Then I'd return and report my findings.

While we ate, Uncle Thomas came by.

"Hi, girls," he said.

"Has the baby come?" Phoebe asked.

"Yep. Nine pounds eight ounces. Healthy as a horse."

"You have more time to ski, then," I said to him.

The smile he gave me was bright but gradually faded. Maybe he was worried about his daughter. "Uh, I forgot my wallet upstairs," he said. "I better get it. Food is not free."

Phoebe kissed his cheek, and he left.

It was snowing when we caught the ski lift. There weren't as many people out, so we had a lot of room to ourselves on the way down. More room meant more fun. I was excited to do another run, but my phone vibrated in my pocket.

"Where's the restroom?" I asked Nikki. She pointed to a little building. "I'll be right back," I told her.

The moment the door closed behind me, I read the text Theron had sent.

The tracker has been at cabin M5 for the last half hour. Nikki might be there.

I'll check it out, I returned.

Come straight back afterward. If you aren't here in an hour, I'm coming after you.

Chapter Twenty-Six

$\mathcal{I}$ pulled a reproduction of the map I'd looked at out of my memory bank and confirmed that cabin M5 was within walking distance of the lodge.

"Sorry to do this," I said to Phoebe, "but I'm not feeling good again. I just can't seem to adjust to the altitude."

She squeezed my arm. "No problem. Go home and get some rest. It looks like it's going to start storming anyway. Text me later. Let me know how you're feeling."

"Okay," I replied.

I went to my car to wait a while. I wanted to give Phoebe plenty of time to get inside. Then I'd double back toward the walking trail that would lead me to the cabin.

After getting in, I started the car's engine and turned up the heat.

I felt like a terrible person. In addition to being riddled with guilt for what I'd said to Ian about the impossibility of us likenessing, I felt bad about what I'd done to Phoebe. I'd had a good reason for doing it, but I'd used her. She was loud, brash, and opinionated, but she was also genuine and concerned about me. I liked her, but I'd disappear after Saturday, and she'd never see me again. I hoped she'd never find out who I really was and what I'd been sent to the Ledges to do.

I waited about ten minutes and then started walking to cabin M5.

The air felt ten degrees colder than it had when I left the chairlift. The snow was coming down heavier, too. Phoebe's prediction was right—it was going to storm. Wrapping my arms around myself, I moved faster.

I knocked at the cabin with Nikki's weak vibration inside, but she wouldn't answer. I tried three times before finally feeling for her mind and thoughtmaking her to come open it. Still, she only cracked it enough for me to see one of her eyes peering out at me.

"Who are you?" she asked, opening the door a little bit wider.

I expected some sign of recognition from her, but there was nothing. Just a blank look. "I'm a friend," I replied. "Can I come in?"

She undid the chain on the door, and it glided open. I followed her into a dark room. All of the curtains were closed and the lights were off. It smelled bad, too, like vomit and sweat.

I assumed she was going to sit in one of the chairs, but

she dropped to the floor like a rag doll and started rocking back and forth. I felt like I was in some low-budget horror movie where the heroine gets possessed.

So I could look her in the eyes, I sat on the floor as well.

Looking her hands over, I confirmed she was missing the middle and ring finger on the left one. I hadn't seen it the night of the dinner because Jacob had been holding that hand.

"Nikki. Do you know who I am?" I asked.

"No," she replied in a voice that cracked.

"My name is Alison. We went to school together in Las Vegas."

She looked at me, but there was still no recognition in her gaze. Agitated, she started rocking faster.

"I'm here to help you," I assured her.

She closed her eyes as though she didn't want to hear me.

Desperate to get her attention, I pulled Alex's snow globe out of the inner pocket of my parka. "This is for you," I said, turning it so the little flakes would float in the water.

She watched until it settled.

I put the globe next to her and tried again. "Nikki, I'm Alison. From Las Vegas. I'm here to help you."

The next time she looked at me, there was some life in her eyes. "Alison," she repeated. "From Vegas. I want to go home."

"I'm going to help you get home, but you have to help me first. I need to know why you're with the Truss."

"Jacob," she replied simply.

"When did you meet him?"

She turned the globe so the snow would fall and

shrugged. "He says I'm insurance."

"Was it Jacob who took you away from Vegas?"

She sighed. "No."

I was getting nowhere but I had to keep trying. "Who cut your fingers?" I asked as patiently as I could.

"He was so mad," she muttered. "I killed his project."

"One of Jacob's projects?"

"No."

She dropped the globe on the carpet like the small weight was too much for her to hold any longer. I picked it up and shook it for her. "I need to know who's drugging you, Nikki. It's important."

"I have to have shots…every day… Maxwell says I have to have the shots."

My heart thudded. I'd heard of a Maxwell, and if he was involved in the Ledges mess, we were really in trouble.

"Maxwell Truss told you that?" I asked to confirm.

She nodded.

"Where is he?"

"Here," she replied. Then she looked up at me with the eyes of a child. "I want to go home now."

That's when I was sure the Nikki I'd hated, the girl who'd helped Sebastian find me and my family, was gone forever. I saw her in a new and very sad light. Even if we managed to get her away from the Truss, she would never be that girl again.

"I'm going to get you home," I said. "Don't tell anyone I came here today. If you tell, they'll stop me from helping you. Do you understand?"

"Yes," she replied.

I turned the key on the bottom of the globe so the music would play and put it next to her.

Tears welled in her eyes as she looked at it. "He'll take it. He'll take it away."

"I'll hide it for you," I said, putting it in a drawer in the TV stand.

She went back to rocking, like she'd forgotten I was even there.

I let myself out just in time. Jacob's vibration was coming my way. My heart pounded as I darted off the trail and waded through deeper snow. He passed me without looking.

Finally getting back to my car, I breathed a sigh of relief. I had news to report. It was bad…but it was news.

I'd made it about halfway to Theron's cabin when the car's wheels started to slip at regular intervals. I did my best to stay alert. But I couldn't stop thinking about Maxwell.

He was Sebastian's cousin and trusted assistant. The two of them had spent years working together. I assumed Maxwell was a true believer in his policies and ideas. Spencer and Katherine had tried to dig up information on him, but had come up empty-handed. With all the chaos after Sebastian died, I think they hoped he'd been killed or gone rogue and would never be heard from again.

If Maxwell was bidding to be appointed clan chief, and he got it, he'd never agree to work with the clans, and we'd end up in the same uncertain and dangerous position we'd been in for decades.

My tires squealed when the car lost traction. I managed

to correct the slide and keep on the road, but the tires lost their grip again. The back end slipped around so I was heading down the hill sideways. I cranked the wheel to the other side. That didn't help. The back end skidded once more and I was going backward.

Having zero control, I accepted that gravity was going to pull me off the road. I was either going to roll down the ravine on one side or slam into the trees on the other. Gritting my teeth and gripping the steering wheel, I voted for the trees. But destiny made it the ravine.

The car crashed through a snowdrift and flipped end-over-end. I'm pretty sure I lost consciousness, because I couldn't remember actually coming to a stop. When I opened my eyes, I was hanging upside down from the seat belt surrounded by air bags and white powder.

Excruciating pain came from my shoulder. Needing to get the pressure off it, I unlatched the seat belt and fell.

Lying there freezing, bruised, bleeding, and probably with a dislocated shoulder, I tried to decide what to do next. Theron would be on his way up to get me soon, but it was snowing so heavily my tire tracks would likely be hidden.

Figuring movement was better than simply sitting there and getting hypothermia, I crawled one-handed out the shattered driver's side window. After getting to my feet, I started walking. I didn't look up at the hillside. Seeing how far I had to go would overwhelm me.

I stumbled a lot and fell once or twice but managed to make it to the top just as a set of headlights appeared from around a corner. I sat down in the middle of the road when

I realized it was Theron.

He pulled up next to me and helped me into the Land Rover. Then he got back in and carefully turned us around.

"Theron," I said in a weird haze. "I think my shoulder is dislocated."

"I figured that by the way it's hanging."

"I talked to Nikki."

"I really don't care. Don't say anything else until I get you home and warmed up."

I was too tired to argue.

When we got inside the cabin, Theron made me sit on the table and angled my arm so he could put it back in the socket.

"This happened to me once," he said. "I watched the doctor put it back in place. I'm pretty sure I can do it for you."

"Pretty sure?" I whispered.

"Very sure," he amended. "It's going to hurt, but it will feel a lot better when I'm finished."

I nodded and then screamed as he pushed and maneuvered my arm back into the shoulder socket. I heard a *pop* when it slid back in place.

"Now it's time for a shower," he said. "I'll turn the water on and bring you some clothes. You're going to have to do the rest."

"I can manage, but Theron…"

"What?"

"Spencer is going to kill me. I wrecked the car."

"He won't kill you," Theron replied, "because I'm planning to kill him first."

Chapter Twenty-Seven

$\mathcal{I}$woke up to an ache in my shoulder, but it was nothing compared to how it had hurt before Theron fixed it. Turning the lamp on, I checked the time. It was nine o'clock. I hadn't slept for that long. Gingerly, I moved the covers off me and got out of bed.

Looking down at myself, I groaned. I'd relented and was wearing the flannel pajama pants Theron had lent me. He'd made me wear the matching shirt, too. I looked like a giant blanket.

I grabbed a second pair of socks to put on over the ones I was already wearing, and padded my way down the hall in search of food.

Theron was sitting at the table holding the world's smallest screwdriver. I watched as he turned it in the world's tiniest…something I couldn't identify.

"What are you making?" I asked.

Startled, he dropped the tool.

"How's your shoulder feeling?" he asked.

"Sore, but I'll live. What are you making?" I asked again.

"A button-cam to feed video of the Truss meeting to Spencer."

"That's good, because I have the feeling things are going to get ugly. Maxwell Truss is at the Ledges, and he's the one who has been drugging Nikki."

"Should I know who Maxwell Truss is?"

"He's Sebastian's cousin, and there's little doubt that given the chance, he'll run the clan exactly the same way his predecessor did."

He got up. "This just keeps getting better and better," he said.

"Where are you going?" I asked.

"To get your phone. You need to make a call."

It ended up being another conference call with Katherine, Spencer, Ian, Theron, and me. I gave them a word-for-word recounting of the conversation I'd had with Nikki and then waited for their reaction.

Katherine made a distressed noise, Spencer grumbled, and Ian said nothing at all.

"Maxwell will be at that meeting tomorrow," Katherine said. "The question is, what do we do about it?"

"Why should anything change?" I asked. "I'll disrupt the vote like I agreed to do."

"That would only stall him," Spencer said. "He'll probably

try again, and we won't know when or where. He's contained up there. It's an opportunity for us to put an end to him."

Theron blanched. "You're talking about killing him?" he said.

"Sebastian killed more of our kind than you want to know," he replied. "We have to prevent Maxwell from doing the same thing."

"You promised to keep me out of it, remember?" I said.

"You took care of Sebastian for us," Spencer said. "We'll try a different way this time."

"We need to discuss this with the other chiefs," Katherine said. "It will take a while to get everyone on a conference call. There's nothing any one of you can do tonight, so everyone get some rest. We'll call back in the morning with some plan of action."

They hung up and Theron stared at me. "Obviously, there are things I don't know," he said. "What did you do to Sebastian?"

"It's complicated," I replied, squeezing my eyes closed and rubbing my temples.

"It wasn't Spencer who killed him. It was you, wasn't it?"

I didn't say anything.

"But how? You can't fight with mind energy. How did you do it?

"Do you trust me?" I asked.

He thought about it. "Yes, I do."

"Then trust I'll tell you someday, but not now."

He nodded once.

My phone rang. "It's Ian," I said with my heart in my throat.

"I've got stuff to do," Theron replied. "Give him my condolences. His dad is an even bigger ass than I thought."

He went to his room, and I accepted the FaceTime request. Ian's image appeared.

"Are you okay?" he asked tensely. "Your face is scratched up."

I was happy he couldn't see the rest of me. I was covered in little cuts and bruises from the wreck. "I wiped out a couple times today. It's nothing."

He looked skeptical but didn't push for details. "Don't worry about my parents and their plan for Maxwell. You've done enough for the greater good."

"I think I've reached my fifty-year limit," I agreed. "I won't do any more than disrupt the meeting. They'll have to figure the rest of it out on their own."

"Be ready. They might push you."

"They can push all they want. I only take orders from my dead mother."

His brows drew together. "What?"

"Nothing, sorry."

He smiled his long, lazy smile, and his shoulders relaxed. "You're so weird," he said.

I returned his smile. He was back to teasing me, and it was a huge relief. I'd hurt him, but Theron was right, he'd bounce back. What our relationship would be afterward, I couldn't say.

"Nice jammies," he commented.

"Thank you. I think I'll re-cover a sofa with them later."

He chuckled and then grew serious. "I'm sorry for pressuring you to leave your family this morning."

I took a big breath. "I'm sorry, too. I should have told you what happened months ago, but I was afraid we couldn't be friends after I did."

"Alison," he said gently. "I will always be your friend. No matter what. But do you remember that thing you said to me today? That thing about loving me?"

As if my greatest secret had been revealed, I swallowed and managed to say, "Yeah."

"Say, hypothetically, that I loved you back. How would you feel about that?"

I picked at edge of the quilt around me. "It doesn't make any difference."

"Here's another hypothetical," he said patiently. "If there were no such thing as destiny, and we were free to choose who we'd be with, would you choose me?"

"Yes, but that's a hypothetical."

He started to laugh at me. "Sometimes I don't know why I like you so much. Aside from the fact that you're beautiful, brave, and you constantly surprise me by saying yes when most people would say no…and then saying no when most would say yes, you frustrate the heck out of me. That said, I need you in my life. You're the landmark I keep coming back to, and when we're together, I think everything is going to be okay. I see a change in you when I'm around, too. Whatever it is between us, it works. You can't deny that."

He was right. I couldn't.

"I accept what you told me about the night we fought Sebastian," he continued. "Everything...except that there's no hope for us. Your thoughts may run different than ours now, but ultimately you are one of us. Everything I'm capable of, you are, too. I won't push you to leave your family again. And I won't push for more than what we have now...well, maybe I will occasionally...but I'm not giving up hope that we will be together. Not until I know for myself there's no hope left. So what do you think about that?"

The way he said it made me smile. "Why are you always so sure you're right about things?"

"Because I usually am. I don't want to make things more painful for you. I wouldn't keep trying if I thought it would turn out badly for us."

He believed what he was saying. I wanted to believe it, too.

"I can tell you're tired," he said. "So take your ugly pajamas and go back to bed. We'll talk tomorrow, okay?"

"Tomorrow," I agreed.

When I put my phone down, the lights flickered off and then on a couple of times. Theron came out of his room and started going through the camping equipment piled high in the corner.

"What's with the lights?" I asked.

"I'm betting the power is going to go out, and my generator is broken. This place is cold enough when the heat *is* working. It's going to be icy without it. We'd better sleep by the fireplace tonight or we risk freezing to death in our sleep. Somewhere in this mess I've got cold-weather sleeping bags and a camping mattress."

The lights flickered again and then went out for good.

"Crap," Theron muttered as he kept digging.

"Nikki looked worse today than when I first saw her," I commented. "I don't know how much longer she can last."

Theron threw a sleeping bag out of the pile. "She'll be back with her parents soon."

"It feels like Spencer and Katherine are playing with her life. I told her I'd help her get home. I hate waiting to make that happen."

He turned a look on me. "Jacob needs to keep her alive for his own health. So stop worrying about her dying."

He threw out a deflated air mattress.

"Jacob isn't in charge. Phoebe says he's only good at following orders."

"Look, I want to help her, too, but we can't do it tonight. And if I can't find the other sleeping bag, we're going to have to share. We're both big people. It would not be comfortable."

"Fine," I replied. "I'll just sit here with my mouth shut."

"I can't imagine anything better," he said.

He did find the sleeping bag, and when we had everything set up in front of the fire, I snuggled into it.

"You know, all I ever wanted was a normal life," I said. "I got this instead."

"What? Sleeping on the floor?"

"No. Contemplating death and murder."

He punched his pillow a few times and lay down. "Spencer has that effect on people."

"I'd just like to wake up in the morning and be certain who I am, not anxious for my family, and not worried about what I'm going to have to do to keep them safe."

He turned on his side to look at me. "I'm not usually the introspective type," he said, "but I get the feeling you don't think about what makes *you* happy very often. Maybe you should give that a try. If you didn't have any worries, what would you *want* to do tomorrow, or next week…or next year?"

Other than what book I wanted to read next, I made plans based on what was necessary, not what I wanted. I almost didn't know where to start, but I let my mind wander until it focused on something. "I'd like to come back here in the spring," I said.

"Why?" he asked with disbelief.

"I like the quiet here, and I want to see this valley like you painted it."

"Oh. You saw my painting in the art studio?"

"Yep. I loved it."

There wasn't a smile on his face, but I could hear it in his voice when he replied, "You can use the cabin anytime you want. My grandparents gave it to me. I'll get you a key before you leave."

"Can I join your loosely knit, highly skilled criminal network, too?"

"Why would you want to?"

I shrugged like I didn't know. But I did. I wanted to be a part of Theron's life after the Ledges mess was cleaned up.

"I'll have to interview you first," he said. "What criminal

type skills do you have?"

"I can manipulate people's thoughts. It doesn't get more underhanded than that."

"True. I'd have to teach you some hacking, though. We do have standards."

"Okay," I agreed.

"Now stop thinking about Nikki and try to sleep."

I lay awake for a long time after he dozed off. He'd posed a good question…*what did I want to do?*

I started making a list in my head. I wanted to go to Thailand and eat real Thai food, I wanted to spend a week looking through the Louvre, I wanted to cut my hair, and I wanted to see Leonardo da Vinci's notebook. The list went on and on until I fell asleep thinking I wanted to skateboard through a mall with Alex and maybe get booked into jail by the police. He'd think that was fun.

When I woke up, Theron was making breakfast in the kitchen. "Still no power, but the stove is gas," he said, flipping a pancake. "At least we'll get a warm breakfast."

It smelled delicious. Once again, I was grateful Theron learned to cook. "What time is it?"

"Nine."

"Wow, you let me sleep in. I'll bet it's been driving you crazy to be quiet."

He smiled over at me. "Yep."

I'd promised to use thoughtmaking on him, and the time was right for it. Joining my mind to his I slipped *I should make some hash browns* between two of his thoughts.

"Do you want hash browns?" he asked, with his brows

drawn together like he didn't really understand what he was offering.

"Do you want them?"

"Not really. I don't have the stuff for them anyway. Huh…why did I offer to make them?"

"And that, my friend, is what it feels like to have a thoughtmaker in your head," I told him, giggling.

His eyes got wide. "No way."

"You owe me now," I said. "Can I see one of your paintings?"

"Go ahead, but you can only look at one. I don't like to show my stuff to anyone until I'm entirely finished with it."

I nodded, got up, and hop-stepped across the room. After picking up the nearest canvas, I took it back to the warmth of my sleeping bag.

Theron had painted a portrait of a girl. She was around twenty, her hair was honey-colored, and she had gold-brown eyes. She was looking up and to the right, with a smile that touched not just her lips but her eyes, too.

"Of course you'd pick that one," he said, bringing me a plate of pancakes and eggs.

"It's Amy, isn't it?" I asked quietly.

He nodded and took the canvas from my hand. "I painted it about six months before my brother came to visit me in New York. That's when *it* happened. I brought this here thinking I'd burn it or something. Kind of a final gesture to close that part of my past." He shook his head. "I haven't been able to do it yet."

It was such a sensitive issue for him, but I got the feeling *he* needed to talk about it. "How did *it* happen?" I pushed.

"Suddenly, is the best way to explain it. One day Amy and I were making plans to spend spring break together. The next she was packing her things and moving to California with Zack."

"Have you seen either of them since?"

"No, and I don't plan on seeing them anytime soon."

"Are you angry with them?"

"I don't know. Zack and I never got along, but I guess I'm glad he found his partner. I'm not really mad at Amy, either. I actually want her to be happy. I'm just…"

"Hurting," I finished for him. "Has she tried to contact you?"

"A couple times. When I see her name on the caller ID, I don't answer."

"You should take her call next time. Listening to what she has to say might help you feel better."

"Hum," he said. "Thanks for the advice. I'll think about it."

"I have a question for you, but you may not want to answer it," I said.

He gave me his evil smile again. "I'll tell you if I don't."

I cleared my throat. "If you could do it over again and chose not to love Amy, would you? I mean, if it meant not having your heart broken, would you change what happened between you?"

He thought about it. "I can't answer that question. I'm not sure."

"Has it gotten any easier since she left? They say time

heals all wounds and that kind of thing."

"Yes and no. I miss her less, but I don't love her less. What keeps me going is the thought that someday, I'll love someone more."

"That's poetic. Maybe you should add studying literature to your future plans."

"I'm not making future plans," he said, taking the canvas back to its place against the wall. "I'm going to live like a traveling hobo, remember?"

I lay back to stretch. "What are we going to do today? I mean, before I have to disrupt a Truss meeting and possibly be killed because I'm a spy."

"We can decide that later. I've got to go to Frank's. With the power out, he's going to need more wood for his fire."

"My shoulder is stiff but not sore anymore," I said, pulling the sleeping bag edge up to my chin. "I should probably try to rest, though."

He attempted to be quiet as he got ready to leave, but it was like a boxer performing a ballet…awkward and ultimately unsuccessful.

As much as I wanted to, I couldn't sleep after he left. I'd started to really miss home. I hadn't talked to my mom since I left, so I tried her cell phone.

"Hey, sweetheart," she answered. "How's the snowboarding?"

"Good, but there was a bad storm last night. It knocked the power out, so the lifts might be down today."

"Just stay in. Get a massage or something. You're always busy with work and school when you're here. Some time to relax will do you good."

I chuckled. "How would you know, Mom? Do you ever relax?"

"I cuddle with your dad now and again."

"Ugh. You could just have said yes and left it at that."

"Oh, Alison. I'm not stupid. I'm sure you're getting some cuddling with Ian, too. Although that's all you better be doing."

I hadn't been cuddling with Ian. I'd been sleeping on the floor next to Theron, but she didn't need to know that.

"Is Dad taking Alex golfing today?" I asked.

"No. A great family just moved in. Alex is becoming friends with the boy his age. They're going to the skateboard park and then to a movie."

I was pretty sure Alex's new friend was one of Ian's relatives.

"Does he have a sister I can bond with?"

"I know you're asking that sarcastically. You're with Ian all the time."

She was right. I was grateful all over again that he hadn't cut me out of his life.

"I'm making a special lasagna tomorrow night to welcome you back," she continued. "You can invite him over if you want to."

"I will," I replied.

"I should go, honey. I've got a yoga class in thirty minutes. Remember what I said…rest and relax."

After the call, I tried to read one of Theron's tech magazines, but gave up on page two. I ate another pancake, walked around looking at his piles of crap in the corners, and then plopped down into a chair. It was miraculous Theron was still sane. Boredom was killing me.

What would you want to do today, or next week…or next year? I asked myself.

The answer was pretty simple as far as that day was concerned. I wanted to talk to Phoebe. I wanted to see her once as a friend, not as someone sent to betray her. And I had one last opportunity to do it.

The snowplow's engine roared on the road and its blades scraped along the asphalt. The way to the Ledges would be clear. I took it as a sign to get off my butt and finally do something only I wanted to do.

I moved my arm around in a three-sixty to test for pain. It was okay. My scrapes and bruises had healed, too.

Theron kept the keys to his Land Rover on the kitchen counter. I picked them up. I wasn't going to steal his car. I just needed to borrow it. He'd be red-hot angry when he found out, but I could take the heat. At least, I hoped I could.

I texted Phoebe to ask if the lifts were working. She said yes, so I texted back that I was coming up for an early run. She messaged saying she'd meet me at the lifts in thirty minutes.

Chapter Twenty-Eight

"I only have time to do one today," I said, adjusting my board on the lift up.

"Yeah, me, too," Phoebe replied. "I'm flying home in a few hours."

"Seriously? I thought you were staying until tomorrow."

"I was supposed to, but last night I told Jacob he was an idiot and his ideas were crap. I said it kind of loud. Really loud, actually. Everyone on the third floor probably heard me."

I laughed. "Oops."

"I think my mom has finally given up on me. She rearranged my flight so I'd be out of the way."

"What are you going to do with the rest of the weekend?"

"Fill out college applications, I guess. I've been putting

it off because I can't decide if I want to stay local or go away to school." She sighed and looked off in the distance. "My dad died recently. I want to be around to support my mom, but sometimes I think she's more annoyed with me than it's worth. She prefers Jacob's company."

Now that she'd brought it up, I could offer my condolences. "I'm really sorry," I said.

She nodded. "I'm more like he was than I am like my mom. He got me, you know?"

I did know. As much as I loved my mom, my dad was easier to spend time with sometimes. He was the quiet voice of reason.

Gliding off the lift, we pulled our masks down. But someone called Phoebe's name before we could get very far. It was a middle-aged woman I'd seen at the Truss dinner. She was sitting in the snow, waving us over.

"Oh, crap," Phoebe said. "That's my aunt Bev."

"Look what I've done," Bev said. She pointed to her ankle. "Twisted the darn thing."

"Do you want me to get ski patrol to take you down?" Phoebe asked.

"They're already on the way now. Would you sit with me until they get here?"

"Ah…sure," Phoebe replied. She turned to me. "Can you wait?"

"I probably shouldn't. I have to get my…grandma's car back."

"I'll text you," she said. "We'll stay in touch."

"Yep," I lied. "I hope everything's fine with your ankle,"

I said to Bev.

I don't think she heard me. She'd already started to explain her fall to Phoebe.

I glided away to enjoy the snow for a last time.

It couldn't have been more perfect. The storm had cleared completely, leaving blue sky, sunshine, and fresh powder. I built up as much speed as I could and carved hard into the corners. Riding the edge between exhilaration and a danger, I felt Uncle Thomas ahead of me.

He was on a different line but not moving. Remembering Bev and her twisted ankle, I decided to check on him.

Just like I'd found Phoebe on the first day, he was lying on his back in the snow. The difference was the angle of his left leg. Either he was really flexible or it was broken.

I got off my board. "Is ski patrol coming?" I asked him.

He grimaced. "Yeah, someone went to get them. I suspect it will be a while, and the cold is getting to me. Can you help me sit up?

"Don't you think that will make your leg worse?"

"I'm not sure, but I can't continue lying here like this."

"Okay," I agreed.

I reached for his hand, and the moment my fingers met his, everything shifted into slow motion. A flash of sunlight reflected off something metal. Instinctively, I pulled my hand back, but it was too late. Thomas had sliced clean through my glove with a knife.

Searing pain ripped into my hand, and I stumbled back, seeing red dots of my blood color the snow.

Uncle Thomas's expression was so menacing I almost

didn't recognize him. "Go ahead," he said. "Try to thought-make me."

I didn't understand what was happening. Fighting panic, I took a step back, but he caught my good hand and twisted it until it felt like my wrist would break. I formed the thought *let her go,* and tried to join his mind. There wasn't enough energy in me to make the connection.

"You can't join while bone is regenerating," he said with an ugly smirk. "Nikki knows that better than anyone."

I looked at my blood-soaked glove. He'd cut off three of my fingers. I wanted to throw up. But survival instinct kicked in, and I lashed out at him with my booted foot. He lost his grip on me enough that I could turn away and hustle toward my board.

Phoebe's uncle had turned into a homicidal manic. He might have been old, but he wasn't slow. He got to his feet and caught me. I felt the sting as he whacked me in the back with his ski pole. All the oxygen in my lungs whooshed out and I crumpled to the ground.

Like a savior, Phoebe skied over a bump in the hill. She was alone.

"Get help!" I yelled. "He's lost his mind!"

She skidded to a stop. Behind her goggles, her eyes were wide. She looked at the blood-smeared snow and gulped.

"This girl isn't who she says she is," Thomas snarled. "She's been spying on the rest of us."

I pushed myself up and swung my good arm to hit him in the shin. He kicked me and pushed my face into the snow before I could connect.

"Stop!" I heard Phoebe cry. "What's happening?"

I tried to get leverage to get myself up again but slipped. That's when he hit me in the diaphragm with his mind energy. I pushed back against the pressure, but I didn't have the strength to hold him off for long.

I was able to slide out from under his foot, but I barely had air to speak. "Help me, Phoebe," I whispered.

"This girl is the White Laurel's daughter," he continued. "She used you to get close to us. But don't worry, I'm going to take care of her. Get back to the lodge." When she didn't go, he yelled, "Now!"

Phoebe's confusion turned to anger. Maybe she'd had enough of being told what to do, same as me. "Whoever you think she is, I won't let you kill her. I'm going to the lodge, but I'm getting security. I'm going to tell them everything."

She started to move then, but Thomas sent his energy at her. She cried out when the force of it hit her. She'd probably been taught to fight back, but she was no match for him. She fell forward.

"Damn it," Thomas muttered. "Now I'll have to deal with two of you as well as clean up this mess."

That was the last thing I remember before he choked me out.

Chapter Twenty-Nine

I woke up tied to a chair with a gag in my mouth. My head ached, my hand throbbed, and I was shaky from lack of blood and energy. Tears of pain ran down my cheeks.

Phoebe was somewhere behind me, either asleep or unconscious. Nikki was around, too. I was back in cabin M5.

The man I'd thought of as Uncle Thomas was outside pacing back and forth and talking. Since he and I were the only conscious ones, I figured he was either speaking on the phone or to his imaginary friends. The friggin' psycho.

Jolly Old Saint Nicholas had never shown any sign of recognizing me, but he'd obviously figured it out. He'd played it perfectly. What I couldn't figure out was why he'd brought me back to the cabin. If he wanted to kill me, he could have done it on the hill and buried my body in the snow. I probably wouldn't have been found 'til spring.

I did a quick flip through my memories of the Truss dinner. As far as I could tell, Thomas and Yvonne hadn't interacted at all that night, but with a new perspective, I noticed they'd shared a few looks of understanding.

From the angle of the sunlight coming through the window, I figured it was probably late morning. If I was right, Theron probably hadn't made it back from Frank's yet. Depending on how much wood he chopped, he might not realize I was gone for another hour. I'd taken the Land Rover, so he'd be on foot if he came after me. Which meant if I wanted to be around for another birthday, I was going to have to rescue myself.

Tears kept coming as I tested the strength of the rope binding my hands. It was agony, but I had to accept the pain and keep trying to get free. Rolling my wrists, I pulled. There was hope. I could feel the warmth of my blood seeping through the fibers of the rope. If it was made of the right sort of stuff, moisture might loosen it. My wrists as well as my hands were going to be shredded, but being dead would suck worse. I twisted my wrists more.

I only got to work at it for a minute or so, because I felt Jacob coming. I let my head roll forward just before he and Thomas came inside.

"Take Linton to the back room," Thomas said.

Wondering who Linton was, I opened one eye slightly and looked through my lashes. A small boy with blond hair trailed Jacob down the hall and out of sight.

Thomas pulled me by the hair to lift my head, yanked

the gag out of my mouth, and slapped me hard across the face. The sting brought more tears to my eyes. He looked like a happy elf again.

"Hello, Ali McCain," he said. "Oh, I know that's not your real name. You're Grace's daughter. You're not much like her at first glance, but the resemblance is there…in the expression. I saw it when you were having breakfast with Phoebe yesterday."

I didn't bother saying anything. Denying my identity was useless.

"The thing about looking like I do," he said, "is that people constantly underestimate me. They think I'm all smiles and laughter. What they don't realize is that I'm the smartest person in the room."

He stepped away from me. "You seem confused," he continued. "Let me explain. The family knows me as Thomas. Those outside it, particularly the clan chiefs' spies, know me as Maxwell."

I'd sort of pieced that bit together. Uncle Thomas was Maxwell, Sebastian's henchman.

"You understand now, don't you?" he asked. "When I worked for my cousin, I made contingency plans. I used the name Maxwell for all my business transactions, knowing the time might come when I would need to distance myself from Sebastian's reputation." He tapped the side of his head with his finger. "See…smarter than I look."

He said it like I should clap or something. Modesty wasn't his virtue. Which would work for me if I could keep him talking.

"So long as Sebastian kept funding my research, I didn't mind working for him. You know all about my cousin, don't you?"

"I know he was insane," I replied.

Maxwell laughed. "That's not what I was referencing, but yes. Toward the end, ambition got the best of his mind. I never liked him much, actually, but his father had been my mentor.

"We shared a passion for science and research. He didn't foresee Sebastian's mental issues when his father created him. For a long time, he thought he could fix them. But when nothing worked, he destroyed everything that might lead to creating another dewing like the boy he called his son. He thought he'd failed his work."

I kept my expression as bland as possible while I twisted the rope behind me. "What does any of this have to do with me?" I asked.

"I'm getting to that. When my mentor died, I vowed to continue his research, but the kind of science I'm talking about costs a lot of money. I had to shut everything down, but then like a gift...you walked into dinner Wednesday night."

"How am I a gift?" I asked.

"You're worth a lot of money. Enough that I can re-launch my research."

My laugh came out like a cough. "I have access to two hundred dollars taped under the dashboard of my car. You're welcome to it."

He tipped his head to the side and considered. "Has

Spencer been playing games again? Didn't he tell you how wealthy you are? It isn't very nice the way he keeps secrets, but a lot of what Spencer does isn't very nice. Like sending you here to look for Nikki. That was quite a risk."

"What did you do to Phoebe?" I asked.

"Oh, she'll be fine," he replied as Jacob came back into the room.

"She's enjoying a dose of Nikki's medication," Jacob said with a cocky smile. "When she wakes up, I'll tell her all of this was your fault." He handed my phone to Maxwell. "I broke through her password protect. You can access her contacts now."

"It's time to begin, then," Maxwell said.

I pushed back in my chair as Jacob came to me. He was pale and sweating, but in his eyes, I glimpsed what he must have looked like as a kid about to nail the rat to his sister's door. He enjoyed cruelty.

"I knew there was something off about you," he said to me. "Phoebe doesn't make friends. She scares people."

"Are you sure you aren't talking about yourself?" I asked.

He jerked me to my feet and slapped me across the face. Even broken and weak from blood loss, the fight in me wasn't gone. I pulled together enough energy to ram him with my shoulder. He reacted fast, grabbing my hair and twisting me around, forcing me to my knees. Then he hit me again. I tasted blood.

"I think that will do for now," Maxwell said. "Turn her face to me, please."

Jacob wrenched me around, and my phone flashed a few times. Then he jerked me up and sat me back on the chair. It was all I could do to keep from falling sideways onto the floor.

"I'll just send these off to Spencer," Maxwell said, typing on my phone. "I expect he'll be in touch soon."

"How long before we get the money?" Jacob asked.

"Not long. As soon as Spencer sees we're serious, he'll contact us."

If I hadn't been concentrating so hard on staying upright, I might have laughed. Spencer wouldn't transfer one penny of my inheritance to Maxwell. He'd let me die a slow and painful death and consider it a sacrifice for the greater good.

Jacob grabbed his jacket. "Nikki is building a tolerance to whatever drug you're giving her. You need to switch to something else to keep her quiet until the vote is over."

"I'll take care of it," Maxwell said. "Where are you off to?"

"My mom expects me at the lodge for an early lunch," he explained.

"Actually she's doesn't," Maxwell replied. "I told her we wouldn't be back until the meeting at seven."

Jacob's shoulders went rigid, and his face reddened. "I'm the one calling the shots here. You don't speak for me."

"Of course," Maxwell replied, putting his hands up in what appeared to be surrender.

When Jacob turned to go, Maxwell got the switchblade knife out of his pocket. Before I could warn him, Maxwell had sliced into Jacob's throat. He dropped into a pool of his own blood, but his mind was still alive. He fought to hold on, but it didn't last long. I felt the moment the energy ran dry and his vibration stopped.

The scent of his blood filled the room. My stomach heaved.

"Such a mess," Maxwell said, looking down at Jacob's body. "But knives are so effective. Much more effective than breaking someone's neck. Why we've held on to that tradition for so long, I don't know."

He went to the sink and washed his knife.

"Why did you do that?" I muttered. "He was working with you."

"I don't need him anymore. He was useful when he paired with Nikki. It presented an opportunity I couldn't pass up. But he's served his purpose. Consider it tying up loose ends."

He dried his knife and picked up my phone. I started moving the wet ropes on my wrists again.

"Why were you working with him?" I asked.

"It's a long story."

"Obviously, I've got time," I replied.

"You're a bit on the sassy side, aren't you?"

I gave him a sickeningly sweet smile.

"Very well, I'll tell you. Nikki helped Sebastian locate you. I was the go-between when they needed to communicate. I didn't like the idea of Sebastian going into Las Vegas to get you himself. I worried he wouldn't make it back out with Spencer in the area and all.

"I knew I'd need money if it went badly, so I took Nikki.

I thought ransoming her would be a good way to get cash. But when I stopped by Yvonne's to pick up the keys to my lab, Jacob was there. He and Nikki paired, and suddenly I could see another...better way to get the money. I'd simply use Jacob the same way I'd used Sebastian.

"I'd help him get the clanship, in exchange for financial support. It was disappointing when we found out that Sebastian had spent most all the clan's financial reserves."

I was starting to feel some slack in the ropes. I just needed a little bit longer.

"You're right," I said. "You are smart...and insane."

"But I'm not," he replied. "I haven't perfected the process, but like my mentor, I've created a dewing-human hybrid. Jacob arranged this family reunion at just the right time. I'm going to show my creation to the Elders tonight. When they realize there's a way to build a clan's size, they'll see me as a hero. I'll be seen as a great scientist and a savior. I've wanted that recognition for a long time.

"Too bad my wife won't be here to witness the Elders' reaction," he continued. "She hates that I spend so much time in the lab. She resents my work and never wants to know what I'm doing there. She'll appreciate it now."

The truth dawned. "The boy in the next room is your hybrid, right?"

"Yes. He had a twin, but that boy died. Neither of them turned out right. They were intellectually and physically stunted. But I'll perfect the process and when I do, Linton will have served his purpose...just like Jacob.

The implication was clear—he was going to kill the

child, too.

He checked my phone for messages. "The problem is that the clan is broke. I still need money for research, but I'll have yours soon. Everything is working out amazingly well."

The train whistle on my phone sounded.

"Will you look at that?" Maxwell said. "Spencer is trying to stall. I guess we'll have to give him some incentive to hurry."

He grabbed his knife off the counter and came toward me. It was now or never. I slid my wrists out of the knots, let him get to within arm's length, and then jumped up and knocked the knife from his hand. I followed that up by punching him in the throat. My favorite move.

While he struggled to breathe, I freed my feet from the ropes.

He made a growling noise and directed his mind energy at my kneecaps. I thought they might explode from the inside out, but I managed to kick him in the hip. He swayed but kept his footing and then hit the underside of my nose with his palm. I was weak from loss of blood and couldn't protect myself when he pushed me to the floor.

Irritated more than anything else, he wrapped his sweaty fingers around my neck and squeezed until I saw stars. While my vision narrowed and my fingers and toes started to go numb, I glimpsed a shadowed shape coming toward us.

She stepped into the light. Her hair was tangled and matted. Her clothes hung loose off her too-thin body. Her eyes were wild with hatred. She picked Maxwell's knife off the floor, and with a burst of energy that sometimes comes just before death, she sprang at him.

He rolled off me and tried to push her away. She had a half second's advantage though. That's all she needed. She threw herself forward and ran the blade deep into his eye.

Maxwell had fought Phoebe, Jacob, and me. He was tired.

As happened with Jacob, his vibration slowed and then stopped. Nikki had used the last of herself to crush his mind. Their energy died at the exact same moment, and they rolled lifelessly away from each other.

Chapter Thirty

*H*earing a noise behind me, I turned my head. Phoebe was looking at the carnage. She was on the verge of frantic, as anyone would be if they woke to such a bloodbath.

"What happened?" she asked, choking on tears.

I was holding back tears of my own and having a serious internal argument with myself about whether I should run away or stick around and do what needed to be done for the greater good.

The freaking greater good won out.

Hauling my sore and bleeding body to a stand, I limped over to her. I was still Deborah McKye's daughter, and not wanting to get my blood on the sofa, I sat on the floor next to her. Laying my hands in my lap, I looked at my wrists. The skin over them was torn and they were oozing blood. My left hand looked like it had gone through a meat grinder.

The repercussions of that loss were devastating, but I couldn't allow myself to dwell on them. I had to get the little boy in the next room away from the Truss. They couldn't know Maxwell created him. They'd try to create more. And there was a very real danger that his halfling mind was as messed up as Sebastian's had been.

"How much did you see?" I asked.

She blinked a few times, trying to get herself together. A lesser person wouldn't have managed it, but I'd guessed there was steel inside Phoebe. She proved me right.

"I saw my uncle go after you with a knife," she recounted. "I saw you get up and knock it away. Then I saw Nikki...kill him."

I reached out with my good hand and laid it on her shoulder. "Jacob is dead, too," I said softly. "Your uncle killed him."

"Why?" she asked in a quiet, quivering voice.

For a moment, I wasn't sure how much to say. In the end, my instinct was to trust her, so I told as much of the truth as I could without giving anything away about Maxwell's research with halflings and what I knew about Linton.

I only told two bald-faced lies. The first was that Jacob died trying to protect Nikki, and the second was that he must have loved her very much.

"This will devastate my mom," Phoebe said, wiping her eyes. "She'll never recover. I didn't like my brother, but he was family. When my mom goes, I'll be alone."

"I'm sorry," I said, meaning it. "I came here as a spy,

but I never wanted anyone to die. I just wanted to help the Dawnings find their daughter."

Phoebe laid her head back on the pillows. "I believe that. What happened is just…"

"Don't worry, I don't know a word to describe it either."

"Why does my head hurt so much?" she asked.

"Your uncle gave you a dose of whatever he'd been giving Nikki. Didn't you suspect she was being drugged?"

"No. I thought she was just…weird. She'd have to be to have paired with Jacob."

"Didn't you notice her missing fingers?"

"What? No. I was only really around her twice. Now that I think about it, Jacob held her hand the entire time I was with them. I just didn't see it."

Her eyes went to the gore on the floor. "What are we going to do?"

"We have to figure some things out really fast. The history between our clans and yours knowing I've been spying on them, might get me killed if I'm found here. If they kill me, they won't be able to hide it. The Thane chiefs will figure it out right away.

"You said you hoped your family's company would merge with others," I continued. "I assume that what you meant was you hoped your clan would rejoin the others. Murdering me will make that an even uglier process. I don't think you want that."

"You're right," she said. "Aside from the fact that I don't want you to be killed. It's best if I keep you out of whatever story I tell."

That's what I hoped she'd say, but there was another matter I had to deal with.

"There's something else," I said. "Maxwell brought a little boy here. A child he planned to ransom. I think I should take him with me. It will be less complicated. The Thanes will manage a way to get him back to his family."

"Take him. I won't say anything about him either." She squinted at me. "You look pretty bad. Are you sure you're going to make it out of here?"

"I have to, but I'll clean up a little first."

She teared up again. "How am I going to tell my mom Jacob is dead?"

I squeezed her arm gently with my one good hand. I had no advice to give her.

After going to one of the bedrooms, I pulled the blankets off the bed and took the sheet to where Jacob lay in his gore. I threw it over him so Phoebe wouldn't see him that way. Then I picked up my phone off the counter where Maxwell left it.

Fortunately, someone had taken my parka off when I was brought to the cabin. It was relatively free of blood, so I pulled it on to cover the mess that had soaked my shirt. After finding a bathroom, I washed my hands and face. Even blood-free, I looked like one of the MMA fighters my brother liked to watch on TV.

I didn't know what to do about my sliced hand and missing fingers. I ended up wrapping a small towel around it and tucking the ends into the sleeves of my parka.

Linton was watching *Sesame Street* in one of the back bedrooms.

He glanced at me with innocent brown eyes when I went in.

"Hi," I said softly. "I'm Alison."

He went back to watching the television.

Not really sure how to proceed, I asked, "Do you like *Sesame Street*?"

He nodded.

"Me too. Elmo is my favorite."

That got him to smile a little, and he wiggled his tiny feet.

I sat beside him. "I need you to come with me."

I could see he was unsure. "We can go to my friend's house," I said. "He has a big TV, and he'll let you watch as much *Sesame Street* as you want."

He nodded and put his hand in mine. When our skin touched, I could feel a very light vibration and a hint of something else coming from him. After scooping him up with my good arm, I carried him out.

"We have to go through a scary room," I said. "Close your eyes and don't look until I tell you, okay?"

He nodded and squeezed his eyelids tightly closed. "That's good," I said, turning his face to my neck and pushing his head to rest gently on my shoulder. "Don't look until I say so," I reminded him.

Phoebe was still on the sofa when I went back out.

"Bye, Phoebe," I said.

She sniffed. "None of the numbers you gave me are going to work after today, are they?"

"No," I admitted. "It's better for both of us that way."

I let myself out and started back toward the lodge and the Land Rover. I was in horrible pain on every level, but I couldn't put Linton down to walk. My stride was three times what his was, and I needed to get away from the Ledges as quickly as possible.

Somehow, I made it.

After buckling Linton into the backseat, I started the Land Rover and drove out of the parking lot for what I hoped was the last time. It felt like being freed from prison, but like Robert Frost's poem said, I had miles to go.

Dialing Theron on my phone, I let it go through Bluetooth and the speakers. He answered in a rush.

"Where are you?" he asked.

"On my way back. I know you're freaking out right now, but don't ask me questions. Just get everyone on a conference call and dial me back. I can only tell this story once."

When he called back, I pulled the car off the road so I wouldn't drive into the ravine while I went through everything.

"What the hell is going on?" Spencer's voice rang out.

"Maxwell is dead," I replied. "So are Jacob and Nikki."

No one said anything. They were likely a little bit shocked. By a little bit, I mean a whole freaking lot.

I told the story, but kept what I'd learned about Maxwell and creating halflings to myself. I didn't mention that I had one of them in the backseat either. I didn't trust Spencer or Katherine anymore. I wasn't going to tell them until I'd considered the ramifications.

"I think it's over," I summed up. "When the Truss find out those three killed one another, the Elders will get away from the Ledges as soon as possible."

"I don't think so," Spencer said. "I think they'll try to clean it up and hide what happened. Yvonne arranged too perfect a situation. The Elders are in the same place at the same time. Someone is sure to step into the void Jacob left. I'm almost positive that person will be appointed clan chief tonight."

If there was anything he could have said to make me feel worse, that was it.

"I know you're hurt," he said. "Maxwell's disgusting pictures more than illustrate that. I don't want to ask this of you. I wouldn't if I could think of a better way. Please, will you try to get into the Truss meeting tonight? This isn't over until the Elders go their separate ways."

I knew Spencer cared about me. He truly didn't want me to suffer anymore, but he was treating me like a weapon as I'd feared. The anger that had been building in me over the past few days started to flood over.

"I haven't asked a lot of questions about my heritage," I began. "That was wrong of me, and it's going to change, but you've kept important things from me. I want to know…am I the Laurel clan chief?"

"What?" he asked.

"Am I a clan chief?" I repeated.

"You will be, but there's a lot you need to learn."

"Does my vote count as much as any other chief's?"

"It will," he confirmed.

"Then don't try pressuring me into anything else, and if you want me to help you in the future, tell me everything up front. I'm on my way to Theron's now. The Truss meeting starts at seven. I'll be there."

I hung up, not caring that I'd been short, impolite, and offensive.

The truth was, I had no idea how I was going to stop the Truss vote. I couldn't thoughtmake with my hand cut to shreds. All my energy was redirected to heal it. Maybe I'd just light the Ledges on fire and be done with it.

One way or the other, I'd figure something out. Not because Spencer told me I had to, but because I wanted to finish what I started. I ended Sebastian to protect my family and establish peace among the clans. For the most part, I'd accomplished the first objective. The second wasn't finished, so I'd see it to the end.

Chapter Thirty-One

Theron's face was a study of disbelief as he watched me lift Linton out of the Land Rover.

"What the…? Who the..?" he stuttered.

"This is Linton," I said, hugging the small boy to me as I climbed the steps. He'd fallen asleep. Taking a seat in the rocking chair by the fire, I held him tight. Maybe because he was an orphan like me, I felt a bond with him.

"Why is he here?" Theron asked.

"Because he's a halfling," I replied. "I couldn't leave him with the Truss. They'd figure it out. I can't give him to the Thanes, either. The only place he's safe is with me."

"What are you talking about?"

"Maxwell created him," I said. "Don't bother asking me how he did it, because I have no idea. He's half human like

Sebastian was. I'm not going to tell the Thanes. Not until I'm sure it's the right thing to do."

Theron got down in front of me and put his hand on the boy's back. "He looks about five or six," he said. "His vibration should be detectable beyond touch by now."

"Maxwell said his growth is stunted and that his intellect is, too. He doesn't speak."

"If you're right about half dewing's thoughts working like an infection corrupting the rest of us, the boy has to be…contained. We can't have that spread."

"You know what they'll do to contain him, Theron. No matter that he's a child, they'll kill him. They were willing to send Ian, their own son, to his death for the greater good."

He took a long breath. "But maybe that's how it has to be," he said.

I wanted to puke. I was willing to do a lot of things, but handing over a child to be murdered wasn't one of them.

"I won't give him to them," I said firmly.

"Okay," he replied. "We'll try to figure something out."

I nodded and took a breath, relieved that he was on my side.

Compartmentalizing things had gotten me back to the cabin safely, but I was losing control. My hand hurt, my face hurt…everything hurt…and I think it started to show.

Theron gently touched the bruising on my face and checked the cut on my lip. Then he noticed the towel wrapped around my hand. A bit of blood had soaked through.

"What's this?" he asked.

I couldn't say anything because if I did, I'd start to cry.

He began to unwrap the towel, but I cried out when some of the scabs pulled away.

Linton wiggled in my arms. "Take him," I said, moving the boy forward with my good arm. "I don't want him to wake up and see this."

Theron nodded, picked him up, and carried him into his bedroom. I watched through the door as he laid Linton on the bed.

When he came back to me, he checked my hand again. I squeezed my eyes closed. Not only was I physically finished, I couldn't hold it together emotionally any longer, either. It started like a hiccup, but quickly progressed to great cries that heaved up from my soul.

Theron held my good hand and stroked my hair.

"Maxwell cut my hand to keep me from thoughtmaking," I managed to say through my tears. "He told me I couldn't join a mind while my bones were regenerating. He was right. I'm useless. Even if by some miracle I can stop the Truss tonight, I can't go home when it's over. I can't hide this kind of damage or how fast it will heal. It's finished, Theron. My time with the McKyes is finished."

He pushed my hair away from my face. "I'm sorry. I wish I could help somehow."

The uncontrollable crying started again. It must have gone on for quite a while before my mother's voice rang out louder than I'd ever heard it before. *Open the portal, Jillian.*

Theron and I glanced around, but of course no one was there.

You can do it, Jillian, the voice said sternly. *Open the portal.*

Completely freaked out, Theron muttered, "What is she talking about?"

"The portal is a kind of door. I don't understand why, but I can open it. It's like a pathway to the other side."

"You mean a pathway to dead people? I forgot you're batshit crazy."

As weak as I felt, I managed to stumble to the center of the room. Closing my eyes, I let myself remember how it happened the first time. It had started with a burning in my stomach. I pulled the pitiful amount of energy I had left together and focused it there. It took a while, but then something inside me caught fire. The flame grew slowly at first and then suddenly burst into white-hot energy. More and more of it poured through me until I felt I was going to combust.

When I opened my eyes, there was a glowing bubble of white around me.

"What's happening?" Theron whispered.

A shape appeared inside the bubble. It started to take the form of a woman. I'd seen her before…in the sketches Theron had given me. I was looking at my mother.

"My brave girl," she said, materializing in full. "Destiny has asked so much of you."

Not caring if I was batshit crazy, I grabbed for her. The contact between us wasn't flesh to flesh. It was energy to energy and searing. I couldn't maintain the hug for long, but it didn't matter. I'd felt my mother's touch.

"The portal won't stay open for long," she said. "And I

can only do this once. It's going to hurt."

She wrapped her hand of energy around my mangled one and held onto it tight. I thought my skin was boiling off my bones, but I forced myself to remain still until she let me go. When I held my hand up to look, it was whole again.

"The only gift I can give you," my mother said, "is a little more time with your human family."

I was too stunned to say or do anything more than stare at my regenerated fingers.

She turned to Theron. "We meet again," she said to him.

His face had frozen like he'd turned to marble. "Right," he muttered. "This is happening."

"I'm sorry I have to yell at you sometimes. You're just so hardheaded."

"No worries," he replied with minimal facial movement.

She smiled at him. "If you hurry, I can take the boy with me."

"Take him with you?" I asked.

"He can come through the portal with me. That way he'll never feel death. It will simply be a transition of state for him."

Theron obviously understood, because he hustled out.

I understood, too, but wasn't sure I wanted her to take Linton...to wherever she was going. "What will happen to him?" I asked.

"He will exist in another form."

"Will he be accepted? He's not really dewing."

"There are all kinds on the other side. He will be fine... he will be happy."

Theron came back carrying Linton. "How am I supposed to give him to you?" he asked. "I can't come inside the heat you're standing in. It'll kill me."

"It would kill most people," my mother agreed, "but not you. You are part of a different portal."

"This is all freaking insane," Theron muttered.

"Trust me," my mother said, extending her arms for Linton.

Theron took a leap of faith and stepped into the bubble. His skin took on the same bright glow as ours. He laid Linton across my mother's arms, but I couldn't let her take him. The little boy hadn't lived yet.

"You can't," I said.

My mother shook her head. "This is for the best."

"Not for him, it isn't. He didn't ask to be made half human, and he shouldn't have to go before he's lived some kind of life."

"I think I agree with her," Theron said quietly. "The little guy is different, but that doesn't mean he shouldn't get a chance. We don't know that he'll turn out like Sebastian. With the right kind of upbringing, maybe he won't. Alison and I can figure something out. We'll make sure he has a fighting chance at a normal life."

My mom sighed. "You need to be realistic. What kind of life could you offer him? You're hardly more than children yourselves. This boy isn't well. His mind and his body have been damaged. He has less than a year to live and probably a painful death at the end of it. Do you want that for him?"

I really didn't. "You'll take care of him?" I asked.

"I promise."

"Okay," I agreed.

Beside me, Theron nodded, too.

"The portal is closing," my mother said, turning to look deeply in my eyes. "You are the Laurel clan chief. You may see that as insignificant, since you're the only one left. But we still exist, Alison, and our future is tied to yours. Destiny hasn't decided everything. Fight for what is right. Do it for your clan."

She turned to Theron. "You found each other. That's important. Two conduits working together can be powerful. Learn to use the energy inside you, Theron. Someday, you will have to hold a portal by yourself."

With that, the light around us started to dim and we were alone in the living room again.

Chapter Thirty-Two

Theron's shoulders slumped. He ran a hand over his eyes, and asked, "You've been through that before?"

"Yes. It was a bit different this time."

He was still in the disbelief stage and in a shaky voice said, "I need to sit down."

He didn't get to, because a car came speeding up the road through the trees and into the clearing. Snow flew in all directions when the vehicle braked in front of the cabin. Ian bounded out and came running up the steps. Theron opened the door just in time for him to rush in.

"Are you all right?" he asked, grabbing me up so my feet dangled above the floor.

"I'm okay," I whispered.

It was partly true. Physically, I was whole. The pain that

had been under my bruises and cuts was gone. Emotionally, I was a mess. I'd been beaten, seen three people die violent deaths, and then witnessed my mother cross over from the dead. It was going to take some time to get my head around all of that.

He put me down, looked me over, and pointed to the blood on my sleeve where I'd tucked the towel to keep it in place. "What happened there?" he asked.

"Don't worry," I answered. "The blood isn't mine."

The shirt under my parka had started to dry and was itchy. Without thinking it through, I unzipped it to scratch my collarbone.

He froze when he saw the dried blood down my chest. "And that?" he asked.

I didn't want to tell him I'd been beaten badly enough to leave me covered in gore. He'd want to know why I'd healed so quickly, and I wasn't going to explain the portal and bubble of light thing to him. I trusted Ian, but I didn't trust his parents. He wouldn't tell them intentionally, but something might slip out if he knew.

"Three people died tonight," I reminded him. "It was a bloodbath. Don't look so surprised."

He knew I was holding back, and the silence between us got awkward.

"Who's hungry?" Theron asked.

"Not me," I said. "I need to shower and change. You and Ian can eat, though."

I felt the guys' eyes on my back as I walked out of the room.

When I'd showered and dried my hair, I called home.

My dad answered this time.

"Hey, Dad. How was the Tofurky?"

"It tasted like rubber coated in gravy. Alex and I have been eating at the country club as often as possible."

I smiled, just glad to hear his voice. "Good idea. Has Mom found your snacks under my bed?"

"No, but the dog did. He ate everything. Didn't even leave crumbs."

I heard him yawn. "Long day?" I asked.

"A long night, actually. One of my patients ended up in the emergency room last night. I went in to consult and stayed until ten this morning. I'm getting too old to run the practice on my own. I'm thinking of asking the guy who just moved in down the street if he wants to buy in."

"He's a surgeon, too?"

"According to his bio, he's a very good one."

I hoped it was Spencer's cousin he was talking about.

Dad yawned again.

"I'll let you go. When I get back, I'll help you find a new hiding place for snacks."

"Glad to have you on my side, sweetheart. You've been missed."

"I'll see you tomorrow. Mom said she's making lasagna."

"Heaven help us," he replied.

I felt a little better about life after that, but I was still exhausted. I had some free time before I needed to drive back to the awful, horrible, grotesque lodge that would probably haunt my dreams for the rest of my life. Deciding talking to the guys could wait, I got back into bed and pulled the covers over my head.

The sun had gone down when I opened my eyes. Though he hadn't knocked, I felt Ian at my door.

"You can come in," I said.

He opened the door and peeked in.

"Don't worry, you didn't wake me up."

He came and sat on the bed next to me. He smiled a little and then I noticed his posture was sort of defensive, like he expected to get slapped or something. The worry line by his eyebrow was deeper than normal, too. I wanted to rub it away.

"What's wrong?" I asked.

"You're keeping something from me again. Tell me what happened up there."

I'd hurt him and didn't want to make it worse by lying to him. Still, I wasn't ready to talk about the halflings or the portal. "I am keeping something from you," I admitted, "but it's not because I don't trust you. I just need some time to… process all that happened today."

"You're scaring me," he said. "It must be something big."

"It's…complicated, but I'm not in danger. Just give me time."

He nodded, but his posture continued to be defensive. I thought I understood why. We'd disagreed on our chances of being together, and he didn't know where the boundaries between us were anymore. It was like he worried I'd send him away. He was afraid of it. I'd never seen him like that. Not even when he fought Sebastian. He'd come to see me, knowing I might not like it and I might ask him to leave. He cared deeply enough to risk my refusal over and over until I finally gave us a chance.

"Are you cold?" I asked.

"Yes, does it ever warm up in this room?"

"Not much."

I lifted the edge of the covers so he could get in. Seeing how relieved he looked made me laugh.

"What's so funny?" he asked, pulling me into his arms.

I laid my head on his chest. "Change. Sometimes change is funny."

"What's going to change?" he asked.

"A lot of things. I'm going to start asking questions about our kind. I'm going to insist on being more involved with the clan chiefs. I'm going to get a better idea of what the future holds for me and I'm going to start planning for it."

"Those are all good things."

"You're a good thing," I replied.

Ian had fallen asleep when Theron knocked on my door. I was careful not to wake him as I got up and went into the hallway.

"We should talk," Theron whispered.

He had a hot drink waiting in the kitchen. I sat at the table and blew on the surface to cool it.

"How bad did it get up there?" he asked. "There was too much blood on your shirt to have been just from your fingers."

"I thought he was going to kill me," I admitted.

He put his head in his hands. "I let you down," he said. "I was supposed to keep you safe."

"I sneaked away without telling you. It wasn't your fault."

"I should have buried the keys to the Land Rover before I left for Frank's place."

"Everything has worked out so far. Just let it go," I said, sipping my drink.

"How much are you going to tell Ian about the halflings and the portal?" he asked.

"All of it, I guess…when I'm ready."

"I'd appreciate it if you don't mention I'm some kind of portal-person when you do. I haven't figured out how I feel about it. Anyway, I'm not like you. I probably couldn't open one of those things if I tried."

"You're a part of this," I said. "There's nowhere you can run that my mom won't find you."

Ian came out rubbing his eyes. "What are the two of you whispering about?"

"Strategy," I said. "We didn't want to wake you up."

"I assume you'll be coming along to break up the Truss meeting tonight," Theron said to Ian.

"Yep," he replied.

"No," I countered. "You can stay at Theron's, but I don't want you any closer."

Ian's eyes widened in surprise. He was used to telling me how things were going to go down or arguing with his parents about it.

"I didn't mean it to come out quite so harsh," I said, "but

I'm the one who will be doing the thoughtmaking, and I'm the one who's going to stop the meeting. I get to say how it will happen."

"You sure are bossy all of a sudden," Theron said.

I poked his arm. "And you will be staying in the car at the edge of the parking lot. I'm going in alone."

"I don't like that idea," Ian said.

"I can't make the Truss forget about Theron's vibration, get myself into the meeting, and work my magic on the Elders all at the same time. The best thing is for him to keep as far from the lodge as he can to minimize the chances they'll feel him."

"I don't like it, either, but what are you going to do when you go inside?" Theron asked.

"I have a key card to get me to the second floor. I'm sure they'll have the door guarded. I'll use mind control to get inside."

"You'll have to thoughtmake to hide your identity the entire time you're in the room, too. That will be tough."

"There's no other way."

Theron tapped his fingers on the table in a familiar cadence. "There might be. There's a holding area behind each conference room. The food is kept warm there until the staff is ready to serve. They enter through an attached door at the back. You could go in through there."

"The Truss will be extra careful tonight. They'll lock every door when the meeting starts."

"I can teach you to pick a lock," he said.

Ian shot him a look. "What other hobbies do you have,

Theron?"

"You don't want to know," he replied. "If you pick the lock, you can hide behind a curtain or something."

"Hiding behind curtains only works in cheesy mystery novels," Ian said.

"Cheesy or not, it might work," he replied.

"How do you know the setup so well?"

"I have friends in many places. Let's just say you won't be the first to use a holding area door to get into one of the rooms."

"You should be in prison," Ian remarked.

"It might work great," I said, considering it. All I really need is to feel their energy and hear what's going on. Cracking the door open might be enough."

"You'll have to use the staff elevator to get to the holding rooms," Theron said. "I'll draw you a map after I teach you to pick a lock."

After ten minutes with a padlock and some tools Theron just happened to have on hand, I had picking locks pretty well figured out.

"I guess the two of you will be leaving tonight," Theron said.

"I want to go as soon as possible," Ian confirmed.

"Well, at least the last week has been more lively than usual."

I grabbed Theron's hand. "Thank you for everything."

"I owe you some colored sketches," he replied. "And maybe a visit in Sweden."

"I'll look forward to it."

Ian's head swiveled to me and then to Theron and back again. "What are the two of you talking about?" Ian asked.

"I'll tell you later. I need to pack my things. It's almost time to go."

"Hold on," Theron said, handing something to me. "This is the button cam I made to feed video of the meeting. Pin it on your jacket."

I packed quickly and looked around the old-lady-chic room. I hoped it wasn't a good-bye forever look. I wanted to take Theron up on the offer to come back to the cabin someday.

Ian carried my ugly suitcase to his car and put it in the trunk. "When you get back, we'll drive down and get my stuff from Stacy's. If I have to I'll pay triple for airplane tickets back to Vegas, we're going to be home before sunrise tomorrow."

I kissed his cheek. "See you soon."

"Just be careful, okay?" he replied.

My stomach was churning with nervous butterflies. "I always am."

"Technically, that's not true," Theron remarked as he passed us on his way to the Land Rover. "You steal cars and drive into ravines."

"Just get in the car," I grumbled.

Chapter Thirty-Three

On the drive up, Theron not only drummed the steering wheel, he kept shifting in his seat. He was antsier than normal.

He parked the Land Rover at the farthest end of the parking lot and said, "I need your phone for a minute."

I handed it over and he typed a bunch of stuff on it. Then he turned the screen so I could see. "You only have to push this button once, and I'll come for you."

"How did you break into my phone so fast?"

"It's a trade secret. Now, go mess with people's minds."

From the feel I got in the lobby, there were a whole lot of Truss upstairs. At least twenty more than there had been the night of the dinner. Did it scare me? Yes. More minds to work meant more energy I'd have to expend.

It wasn't difficult to find the kitchen that serviced the conference rooms. Theron's map was excellent. I slipped inside when no one was looking and took a catering jacket from a rack near the door.

"Are you with team two?" a harried woman asked.

Sure, why not. "Yes, ma'am," I replied.

"The hors d'oeuvres cart is loaded. Take it up to the Aspen room."

"Yes, ma'am."

I had no idea which cart held the hors d'oeuvres. All the trays were covered, so I picked the nearest one. People were everywhere in the kitchen. All of them going in different directions at the same time. I started pushing the cart through and around them, hoping I wouldn't run over anyone.

"Hey," a man's voice called out. "Hey, you with the cart."

"Me?" I asked.

"If you're going upstairs, take these with you."

I held my arm out so he could drape some dish towels over it.

"Hurry. We're going to serve in ten minutes."

I made it a few steps and another woman stopped me. "Take this, too," she said, loading a crate of sparkling water on the bottom of the cart.

It was getting so heavy and awkward that I couldn't turn it around people.

I'd had enough when another guy tried to hang aprons over my shoulder. "Get someone else to do it," I said, sending the same thought into his mind.

I finally made it out of the throng to the elevator. Ed, who according to his name badge was food services manager, pushed the up button on the control panel.

"Are you new?" he asked.

"I started Monday."

"I do the hiring, and I don't remember you."

You remember her, I put into his mind.

I followed him into the elevator hoping no one else would talk to me.

"After you drop that off, help clear in the Maple room," he said.

I saluted him, but he didn't see because he was speed-walking down the hall toward a plaque that said TABLE LINENS.

I decided right then and there that food service people didn't get paid enough.

The Truss were in the farthest room down the hall. I pushed the cart to the plaque for the Aspen room and left it near the door. I was pretty sure someone would find it or trip over it.

The door to the holding area was unlocked, so I let myself in. The interior space was dark and quiet. Activating the flashlight app on my phone, I shone it around until I found the door into the conference room. That one was locked.

Holding my phone between my teeth, I got the pins Theron had given me from my pocket and began working them in the lock. When the latch gave, I held the handle so it wouldn't engage again. I secured my phone and the pins back inside my pocket and mentally prepared myself for what I was going to do.

Opening the door a crack, I listened.

"In spite of tragedy and loss," a female voice said, "we came here to make a decision."

I recognized the voice. It was Phoebe's. She was supposed to have left...but then her brother was supposed to be alive, too. Maybe Yvonne had been too devastated to go on with the meeting. Maybe Phoebe has stepped into the role of hostess. She'd really be hating that.

"It's up to you to decide who will lead our clan," she continued. "Over the past few days we've discussed the pros of joining with the clans as well as the cons. Joining them would mean an end to the conflict between us, and they might help rebuild our infrastructure."

Her strong, confident voice cut through the silence of the room. "It comes at a price, though. We would have to work with the others again. They hold a lot of bitterness and resentment toward us. I know many of you resent them, as well. It would take patience and perseverance, maybe decades of it, to resolve our feelings about one another.

"Of course, the biggest consideration, the one I know weighs heaviest on your minds, is that we would lose some of our autonomy. We would have to abide by what *all* the clan chiefs decide. We would be part of something bigger than just us."

I rubbed a kink out of my leg, thinking things were getting super confusing. Phoebe knew a lot about the state of her clan, but she was really laying it out there for someone who was only hostessing the meeting.

"I'm young," she continued, "but I'm Robert Truss's daughter. You knew him. You respected him. A friend asked me recently why I cared about our *family business* so much. I told her I care because my father taught me to. He taught me to look at the whole picture and not to make selfish decisions."

Her voice broke with emotion. "I love this family, but we've been selfish. Making decisions out of fear is selfish. Refusing to change out of stubbornness is selfish. Refusing to forgive is selfish.

"What you do now will affect our clan for generations. We are dewing like the other clans. We are the children of Atlantis like them. Our kind has survived this long because we've tried to work together."

It was starting to make sense to me, and I couldn't believe what was happening. Phoebe was making a bid for clan chief!

"You should know up front, if I'm appointed to lead I'll end our quarrel with the other clans. The Truss will become part of the whole again, because I know in my heart that's the right thing for us."

The applause in the room started slow at first and then got louder.

"We have one candidate present," a male voice said. The tone of his voice indicated he was in charge of whatever was going on. "We'll call for a vote of appointment now."

I was running out of time to disrupt the meeting like Spencer and Katherine wanted me to.

They didn't know anything about Phoebe, but I did. She was smart, opinionated, and had a good heart.

Most importantly, instinct told me to trust her to do the right thing. Even knowing I was a spy, she'd fought her disgusting uncle to keep him from killing me. I'd betrayed her and her clan, but she didn't want revenge. She wanted the greater good. She wanted peace.

I had a choice to make, and it was a three-way gamble. I could disrupt the meeting like I'd been asked to do, let Phoebe take her chance at getting the appointment, or help her get the appointment.

Deep down, I was sure she was right for the job. She might have had enough votes to get the appointment on her own, but I was going to help her anyway.

"Thaddeus and Jasmine, do you vote to appoint?" the man asked.

Concentrating, I felt for Jasmine's mind and then searched for the strand of shared consciousness deep within it. I formed the thoughts, *This girl will be the best clan chief for us. I vote yes* and painstakingly wrapped it around that collective strand of thought, so it would affect all the Truss in the room.

My chest caved and the air was pushed out of my lungs as the energy for my final effort left me. The force created when it came back toward me caused momentary blindness and terrible pain behind my eyes. Struggling to stay upright, I listened for the answer.

"I vote yes," a man's voice rang out.

"Yes," a woman's voice followed.

"Charles and Lydia, how do you vote?" they guy in charge asked.

Over and over, the votes came back as yes until he said, "It's unanimous. Phoebe Truss has been appointed clan chief."

Loud applause broke out.

I breathed a sigh of relief. My cloaking had worked. I carefully let the door close between me and the celebration in the next room.

I sat still in the dark for a few moments, allowing myself to recover some strength. Then I pulled myself up to the counter and waited for my head to clear. Hoping destiny was on my side, I walked slowly out of the room.

I'd made my first executive decision as a clan chief, and I didn't regret it.

Chapter Thirty-Four

I was in the back corner of the Shadow Box looking for something to give Alex for Christmas when the chime above the door sounded.

"The moment you've been waiting for has arrived, Lillian," Ian announced. "I'm here to flatter and entertain you. Maybe I'll dance with you, too."

"Do you want a book thrown at you?" she replied.

I chuckled. One day he was going to get a real emotional rise out of her. I hoped it would be a positive one, and she wouldn't actually hit him with something.

"I'm looking for a supercute, supersmart, super-tall girl," he said. "I heard you had one. Would you point me in the right direction, please?"

"I'm in the humor section," I replied.

He came around the corner, strutting like he was the king of the world. His eyes lit up when he saw me, and before I could prevent it, he pulled me to him and started spinning me and then leading me in a waltz.

"What are you doing?" I wheezed.

"Shhh…try not to ruin it," he replied, starting to hum "Deck the Halls."

When he was nearly too dizzy to stand anymore, he let me go and leaned against a bookshelf.

"What's up with you?" I asked, trying to catch my breath.

"It's December twenty-third and school is out. Everyone should be dancing, even Lillian, though she'd let hell freeze over first."

"I didn't know Christmas was such a big deal for you. Theron said human holidays don't mean that much to dewing."

"This year, I have someone to give a gift to, and she's not my first cousin or sister-in-law. I'm planning to celebrate my brains out. What are you doing back here in the deepest, darkest corner of the store?"

"Trying to find a gift for Alex. I'm pretty sure he's regifting me the snow globe I brought back from the airport when we left Colorado."

Ian pulled out a book called *Farts*. "How about this one?" he asked.

I shook my head. "He'd enjoy it too much. I'm hoping to find something a little less his style." I ran my hand down the shelf until my eyes fell on one I thought would work, *Cat Expressions: What Your Cat Is Saying to You.* I flipped a few pages. It was basically a picture book of sweet, fuzzy cats in various poses. It was exactly the kind of thing my brother would be embarrassed to own.

"Found it," I said, handing the book over for Ian to see.

"Do you want him to get beat up at school?" he asked.

"That would be a bonus."

Ian draped his arm over my shoulder as we walked to the front, where Lillian was typing on her computer. She looked fierce with the Santa Claus pen I'd given her tucked behind her ear.

"Will you lock up?" she asked. "I'm bidding on a very interesting horticulture book from the eighteen hundreds."

"If that's interesting to you," Ian remarked, "you don't get out much."

"I don't."

Ian rummaged through the selection of candy on the counter while I turned the sign in the window to Closed.

Mr. Brown, the soon-to-be-former owner of the Tiny Cup Teashop, was locking his door for the last time. He patted the handle once or twice, then turned and walked away under the streetlights.

It made me sad. The Shadow Box would suffer the same fate, and I still hadn't adjusted to the idea.

"What's wrong?" Ian asked.

"It's hard to watch so many of the shops close up."

"Businesses are like people," Lillian replied. "They get old and die."

"That's a cheery way of looking at things," Ian muttered.

I went around the counter to count out the register.

"You're still coming to the compound tonight, right?" Ian asked me.

I nodded. "I need to swing by my house first to wrap this book for Alex. Then I'll head over."

"Connor invited half the school to come over, and just a heads-up, my parents are back, too."

I paused in the middle of counting the fives. "I thought they weren't coming back until the first of the year."

"You've known them long enough to understand their plans are always changing."

He was right. But the idea of seeing them again made me nervous. The last time we'd talked it hadn't gone so well. Spencer had been furious with me for allowing Phoebe to get appointed clan chief. Katherine wasn't so much angry as she was confused by what I'd done. I'd been mad at both of them for keeping so many secrets.

The last thing I'd said before leaving their house was that I wanted it all in writing. From my position as a clan chief, to finances, to any extended family I might have in other clans… I demanded it all be written down.

Katherine had emailed me the next day, apologizing for how things happened and promising when they got back from their business trip, they'd go over everything with me.

I wanted to be forgiving, but the wound was still fresh. Seeing them that night might be too soon.

Ian took my hand. "It will be okay. They feel bad about how they acted. And anyway, I'll have your back."

"Thanks. I'll be nice to them so you won't get grounded."

"Funny, McKye. Funny."

I started counting money again.

"You're invited to dinner at my house tonight," Ian said to Lillian.

"Um-hum," she replied.

"My dad and I will swing by next week and move the exercise equipment out of your back room," he continued. "We're going to set it up somewhere in the compound so Alison can continue training without being in your way."

"Um-hum," Lillian muttered.

"We can load any boxes you need moved while we're here."

"Um-hum."

"I think I'll do a naked tap dance on the counter."

"Um-hum."

"How does she tune me out like that?" he asked.

"It's one of her many talents."

With his elbows on the counter, he looked up at me. "Do you want to see me do a naked tap dance, Alison?"

I put a rubber band around the tens. "No, but thanks for the offer."

"You're missing out. I just came by to tell Lillian she's invited to dinner. I've got to head out. Dad and I are going to get a tree."

He left humming "Joy to the World."

Lillian closed her laptop.

"Did you get the book you wanted?" I asked.

"Not this time."

I wrapped a band around the last of the bills and put everything in the bank bag. "Sometimes I think it's the thrill of the hunt you like, not so much the books."

"No. It's the books."

"You heard Ian say you were invited to dinner, right?"

"I can't go. I'll be packing. I'm leaving for Ystad tomorrow morning. I'm going to look at my new house. I signed the official paper of ownership yesterday."

"You bought a house without seeing it?"

"It seemed nice online. It has enough bedrooms, and it's close to the sea. That's all I care about."

"Do you have a picture I can look at?"

She pulled a real estate photo up on her phone. I'd been expecting a cottage type of house, but what she'd bought was more like a villa. There were gold wheat fields in the background with gray seagulls flying above, just like she wanted.

"Who else have you invited to stay with you?" I asked. "The place looks enormous."

"I figured you might come, and if you did, Ian would visit. He can only stay for three days, though."

Three days was quite a generous allotment of time for Lillian. "I'll make sure he understands," I promised her.

She took the bank bag from me and put it in her gigantic purse while I went to hang my work apron on its hook.

"Oh," she said, pulling something out of her purse. "I got this for you. It's a Christmas present."

It was wrapped in plastic shopping bag.

"You didn't need to get me anything," I said.

"I know."

I opened the bag and found one of her precious old

books. It looked a lot like the Thane history I'd almost gone blind trying to read over the past few weeks. I turned to the first page and saw a vine and flowering wreath on it, the signet of my clan.

"I found it among some other things at an auction," she explained. "I don't know how it escaped getting burned. The seller said he picked it up in France last year. He thought it was a fairy-tale book, but it's a story about your clan. Now that you're interested in learning about our kind, I thought you might like to have it."

I turned some more of the pages. "It's lovely, but it's written in French."

"That's a good reason to learn to speak French."

"Fair point," I replied.

"You should get going," she said. "It's going to snow."

I doubted it. There were clouds in the sky, but it rarely snowed in Vegas.

"I know what I'm talking about," she insisted. "I've lived two hundred eighty-two years. I feel it in my bones."

I gave her a quick kiss on the cheek, which she probably didn't like, grabbed my jacket, and said, "Merry Christmas, Lillian. I hope you love your new house."

Chapter Thirty-Five

My house smelled like pine trees and gingerbread. Mom was in the kitchen, mixing something I didn't want to know about.

"Hey, you," she said. "How was work?"

"Good. I mostly helped Lillian sort through things for a clearance sale."

She wiped her hands on a towel and pulled a tray out of the oven. The cookies on it were burned.

"Where did you say she was moving to?" she asked.

I hadn't said, and I didn't want to, in case she went looking for Lillian to question her when I had to disappear. *That's not important* I put into her mind.

She moved on to a different subject. "There's more mail on your desk for you. You've got quite a stack of college applications building up."

She handed me one of the burned cookies. It was hard and bitter. I chewed and swallowed anyway. "I'll sort through some of it before I go over to Ian's house."

She nodded. "You can take some cookies over when you go."

"I'll try not to forget," I lied.

Mom was right. The desk in my room was piled with envelopes. I'd been putting off the inevitable, but the time had come to sort through my mess.

My method was simple. I kept applications for schools east of the Mississippi River and threw the rest away. I hated it, but the fact remained I needed physical distance from the McKyes. Fortunately, I'd get to come back for holidays and breaks. I'd be able to call, text, and Skype, too. I planned to make the most of all those things.

After filling my trash can with the rejected applications, I wrapped the book I'd bought for my brother and took it downstairs. When I put it under the tree, I saw his gift for me. He hadn't put it in a box or anything. He'd just put some wrapping paper around it and taped it down in a few places.

The shape was a clear giveaway that it was the snow globe I'd given him with two penguins on springs that wiggled back and forth when you shook it.

Looking at it made me sad. Snow globes would probably always stir up memories of the last time I'd seen Nikki. The end of her life had been awful. No one deserved what she'd gone through. I'd once considered her my mortal enemy, but she'd saved my life when no one else was around to help.

Whether she understood she was helping me or not, it didn't matter. I was grateful.

I talked to her parents when I got back, but I didn't tell them how her beauty had faded or how her mind had gone and would never have come back. Some things they just didn't need to hear.

It was a tragic ending, but at least I was able to give them some closure. They could be sure Nikki wasn't suffering anymore. How they forgave destiny for what she'd gone through I didn't know, but they were moving on more quickly than a human family would.

That's how it was for my kind. Don't mourn what you can't change…unless you're Theron or me.

I packed up my gifts for my school friends, Connor, Felicity, and Ian and headed for my car again. I'd almost made it out the door when my mom caught me. "Don't forget the cookies," she said, handing me a plate of them with an envelope on top. "And here's another letter that came in the mail. Be back by eleven. We've got a lot of last-minute shopping to finish tomorrow."

Holding my bag of gifts and the cookies in one hand, I stuffed the letter in my pocket with the other.

"I'll be back by curfew," I promised.

I was in my car ready to back out of the garage when I got a text from Theron. *In town. Meet me at Pet's Pancake House* it said.

The joy I felt at the idea of seeing him surprised me. We hadn't communicated since Ian and I left the cabin. I thought about him a lot, though.

I texted him back. *Be there in ten minutes.*

The pancake house was crowded, but it wasn't hard to find him. His slow, steady vibration was easy enough to follow.

"You really like to eat at classy places, don't you?" I asked, sitting across from him in a booth.

"Ahhh...how I've missed the way it makes my skin crawl when you sneak up on me," he said with a big smile. "Get over here."

We stood up and hugged each other. "Okay, that's enough," he said, sitting back down.

I did the same, and my pants stuck to the vinyl again. "Man, I hate syrup," I grumbled.

He just laughed.

"What are you doing here? I thought you were on house arrest until the end of the summer."

"Spencer got me out early. It seems His Royal Highness believes I've come to my senses enough not to be a danger to society. He called in a favor and Gage reduced my sentence."

"Have you come to your senses?"

"I'll always be a danger to society," he said with a mischievous look. "But I finally burned the painting of Amy. That's progress, right? I might even call my brother on Christmas morning. I've never done that before."

"I'm happy for you," I said, reaching out to squeeze his hand. "How's everyone in Greenvale?"

"Stacy is busier than ever. She got the freelance work she wanted, and the repairs keep coming in. She's thinking of renting a shop to work from. Her house would be less dangerous that way."

"And Livy?"

"She's great. She and Skip are expecting a baby now. They are disgustingly happy all the time."

"What about Frank?"

Theron cleared his throat before he spoke. "He died…a little over two weeks ago. I went to take some groceries in and found him in his armchair. I didn't realize he was gone at first. I thought he was sleeping."

"I'm so sorry. I know you had a real soft spot for the old guy."

"It's not as sad as I thought it would be. He was happy right up to the end. We'd had a good laugh together the day before. He went the way he wanted to…on the mountain."

I nodded. Lillian wanted to go on her own terms, too.

"I guess you'll get officially titled Laurel clan chief soon," he continued.

"I guess so. Katherine sent me a few emails about it, but we haven't talked in person since just after I got back."

"That bad, huh?"

I nodded. "It wasn't pretty. From what she's written since, I guess the confirmation ceremony will happen next October. I'd like to fly under the radar a bit longer, but if I'm going to make decisions like a clan chief, I better get declared. I was going to get in touch with you about it. I'm supposed to have two witnesses there. I was hoping you'd be one of them?"

He smiled big. "Sure."

"You can't wear flannel, though."

He opened his jacket so I could see his shirt. It was a dark sweater. "You're branching out." I laughed.

"The ceremonies take place in Spain," he said. "They have nude beaches there. Maybe I'll wear nothing at all and work on my tan."

"What's with all the guys in my life threatening to take their clothes off? Ian offered to do a naked tap dance at the Shadow Box earlier today."

"You're just a lucky girl," he said, unwrapping his silverware.

"I'll introduce you to Phoebe. She'll be going through her confirmation at the same time."

"That's got to be a little weird, right? I mean, you weren't honest with her. Won't she hold you at least partially responsible for what happened to her brother?"

"We've kept in touch, and she honestly doesn't. She understands that I was trying to help Nikki. If anything, she's ashamed. Not of something she did, but of her uncle and her brother. She's amazing in a lot of ways. I think she's one of the few people in the world who instinctively see the big picture, even when things are painful."

"How's Yvonne doing?"

"She's been bedridden since finding out about Jacob. She's still alive, but who knows for how much longer."

When a waitress brought plates to us, he said, "I ordered for you because I was super hungry. Don't be mad."

I looked at my food. "You got extra sausage for me, so I'm not."

"Have you told Ian about Linton or the portal?"

"Not yet, but I'm going to within the next couple of days. Have you heard anything from my ghost mother lately?"

"No, and I'm grateful every second she leaves me in peace. I suspect she's not done with me, though. She'll be in touch if you need me. Try not to need me, okay?"

"I'll do my best."

Theron finished and pushed his plate to the edge of the table. Then he spun his knife on the table. I put my hand over it.

"No more fidgeting," I said. "What life-altering event is on your mind?"

"I just want to say thank you."

"For what?"

"I'm not sure exactly," he said, spinning his fork instead. "All I know is that I felt like absolute crap when I first met you, and by the time you left, I didn't anymore. I felt... hopeful for the first time since Amy."

I slapped his hand to stop him from spinning the silverware. "So, you're saying my natural charms worked a magical change on you."

"I wouldn't call what comes out of your mouth charming, but yeah. You helped pull me out of a dark place."

"I should thank you, too. I've been able to talk to you about some stuff I don't think anyone else would understand."

"You did the same for me. Remember at the cabin when you asked me that question?"

"Which one? I asked you a lot of questions."

"The one about if I had a choice, would I choose not to be with Amy because of how it felt when she left?"

"Yeah, I remember."

"Well, I've thought a lot about it and the answer is no. As much as it hurts, I wouldn't give up the good times we had together. I'll always remember them."

I looked in his eyes and saw truth. "Thanks for the answer."

We finished up, and he walked me to my car.

Before I got in, he handed me a key. It was big and old-fashioned looking.

"This is to the cabin," he said. "It's really just a gesture. You could open a window and climb through if you wanted. There aren't locks on any of them. Feel free to use the place whenever you want. Just knock first in case I'm lying around in my underwear."

I smiled. "If they're flannel, I'd like to see."

"Someone somewhere in the universe thinks that's funny, but I don't. Just so you know, you've been tentatively accepted as a member of my highly skilled, loosely knit criminal network."

"Really?"

"I'm having a card made for you," he joked. "Text me the details about your coronation. I'm going to travel in South America for a while, but I'll make certain to be there for the big day."

Chapter Thirty-Six

Ian and Spencer were putting up their tree when I went into the living room. It seemed they'd had trouble choosing between big and bigger, so they opted for biggest. The tree was over twelve feet tall.

"How are you going to decorate the top of that?" I asked, craning back to see.

"We've got a plan," Ian assured me while helping his dad adjust the tree's angle.

Across the room, Katherine was going through boxes. She'd ordered a ton of stuff while she was away. It had arrived in shipping boxes during the past few days. Ian had refused to open any of them until she got back.

"Hi, Alison," she said sweetly.

Somehow she still managed to look elegant with her

sleeves pushed up and her hair held in a bun by a pencil while she sat among cardboard and foam packing peanuts.

The intercom buzzed, and Spencer left Ian holding the tree to answer it. The weight of it slowly began pushing him to the ground.

I hurried to help.

"It looks like your friend with the fake hair is coming through the gate," Spencer said.

"That's Connor. His hair isn't fake. There's just a lot of gel in it."

"Prepare to be talked to death," I warned.

Katherine pulled a garland out of one of the boxes. "Where am I going to put this?" she muttered.

I didn't bother answering. Part of the fun of decorating was figuring out where to put things.

Spencer took the weight of the tree so it wasn't crushing me, and I moved out from under it.

"Let's just bolt it to the floor," Ian suggested. "We're never going to get it to stand straight if we don't."

"We'll get it," Spencer encouraged him.

The doorbell rang, and I was the only one with a free hand to get it. "Would you mind?" Katherine asked me.

"No problem," I replied.

When I opened the door, ten kids from school were standing on the steps. "I brought some friends," Connor said.

"I see that. Head to the back of the hall, everybody. The others are in the room to the left."

Felicity was one of the last to come in. Little red bells tinkled on the elf socks she was wearing with her skirt. "You look cute," I said.

"Thanks," Connor replied, straightening his shirt.

Felicity and I giggled as we went into the room of chaos. "Where would you like me to put these gifts?" she asked Katherine.

"On the dining room table will be fine for now, sweetheart," Katherine replied. She held up a snowman candle. "Did I really buy this?" she asked herself.

Everyone congregated around the table, shaking boxes and chatting. I said hi to Melissa, who introduced me to her new boyfriend. He wore black eyeliner and had tattoos up to his chin. He seemed pretty nice.

Connor was talking to Spencer. "My grandma in Wisconsin had a tree that big once," he said. "I don't know how she got it in the house. She only has two doors. It's a small house. The garage is big, though. She parks a motor home in it. Anyway, my cousin's dog peed on that tree. It smelled in her house for a year."

Spencer looked a little lost. It was hard to follow Conner if you weren't familiar with the way he rambled. "I'm glad I don't have a dog then," he said.

Ian backed away from the tree. "I think we did it," he said. "It's straight, but how are we going to get the lights up on the top?"

"It's too late to buy a ladder. We'll just have to throw them up there," Spencer replied. "It shouldn't be a problem."

Katherine sighed and shook her head. "The lights are in *that* box," she said, pointing. "No, the *other* one," she corrected when he got it wrong.

When he had the lights out and ready to go, Spencer yelled, "Light stringing party!"

Everyone got to help throw lights. When we finished, layers of them covered the entire tree. Spencer connected the cords and plugged them into a surge protector. The tree lit up like the Vegas Strip.

"Impressive," Connor muttered.

Katherine pulled me aside. "We need to talk with you," she said. "Spencer is headed to the den now."

I'd been dreading this moment, but followed her out anyway.

Spencer was pacing in front of the window. I'd seen him like that before. He paced when he was nervous.

"Please, sit," Katherine said, offering me a chair. "You too, Spencer."

"I'd rather stand," he said.

"Sit," she ordered.

When he'd done as she asked, she turned to me. "We want to tell you how sorry we are for the way we treated you. We should have told you about your Falco grandparents, your inheritance, and that you're the Laurel clan chief now."

"Why didn't you?"

"The honest to goodness truth is that we were worried about you. Your mood kept switching from good to bad. From moment to moment, it was difficult to tell how you felt. We thought maybe you'd developed PTSD or something after you killed Sebastian. Your mother was worried about your mood swings, too. That's the main reason she let you go to Colorado."

At least I knew the last part was true.

"We didn't want to overwhelm you with details," Spencer said. "Especially when you were so adamant that you didn't want to learn about your heritage."

"We were waiting for things to settle down for you," Katherine added. "We weren't trying to manipulate you."

"I'm not sure I believe that."

Spencer leaned forward to explain. "We went about it wrong. And then when we found out that Maxwell was at the Ledges, I lost all perspective. You were right to call me on it. You can and should make your own decisions."

I looked from him to Katherine. They seemed to be telling the truth, but a part of me still didn't trust them.

"We will do better, if you can forgive us," Katherine said.

In her big speech, Phoebe said it was selfish not to forgive. When I thought about it, she was right. I was mad and thinking only about myself. Maybe I could forgive them, but that didn't mean I'd forget or that I'd put my fate in their hands again.

"Okay," I said. "Let's just move past it."

Spencer sighed with relief. "We'll talk more when the holidays are over," he promised.

"Deal," I replied.

Chapter Thirty-Seven

When Connor and his crew left and Ian's parents moved to a different room, Ian and I lay down on the floor and looked up at the lights on the tree.

"Do you think it will collapse from the weight?" I asked.

"What, the tree? Nah, it'll hold. It's practically nailed to the floor."

"It's snowing," I said, glimpsing snowflakes out the window. "Lillian said it would."

"Hmm…a grouchy old woman who sells smelly books is also a weather predictor. We should build her a profile on Match.com."

"Be nice," I said. "I think Lillian is actually coming around to you. She told me you can stay at her new house in Ystad. But only for three days."

"My life is complete."

I punched him in the stomach.

"Don't start something you can't complete, McKye," he said.

It was good advice. I was thinking about starting something.

At the pancake place, Theron said he wouldn't change how he'd felt about Amy. That the time he'd had with her was worth the loss. He'd loved and lost, but he was surviving. Given time, he'd get his groove back and look for love again.

Was I strong enough put myself through the same thing and come though it in one mental and emotional piece when it was over?

It was time to make a choice. Move forward or not at all.

I scooted closer to Ian. He put his arm out so I could rest my head on his shoulder. "Remember back at Theron's when I said I was going to make some changes?" I asked.

"Yep. You've made a lot of them."

"There's one more I want to make, and it involves you."

The muscle in his arm tightened. "Am I going to like it?" he asked tentatively.

"I hope so. What would you think if…I mean…how would you like…"

"Spit it out."

"Oh, crap," I muttered with my heart in my throat. "Do you want to, you know…date and stuff?"

He shifted a little. "Ah…did I hear you right?"

"I hope so, because I don't want to say it again."

"Well, if I say yes, would I get to take you to dinner and

then be able to kiss you good-night?"

"Maybe."

"Hm," he replied. "I'm not sure it would be worth it."

I pushed him. "Never mind," I said, smiling but feeling insecure at the same time. "I take it back."

"That's not how the game is played," he said, starting to tickle me. "No take-backs."

He tickled me until I couldn't breathe. Then he pushed some hair behind my ear and ran his thumb along my jawline. "Yes, you can be my girlfriend," he said quietly. "But only because you wore me down."

Then he kissed me until I lost my breath.

I went home that night feeling different. I had opened my heart to Ian. For a change, I was looking forward to what the future would bring instead of dreading it.

Flipping the light on in my room, I started getting ready for bed. I bent to untie my shoes and heard the crinkle of the letter in my pocket. I'd completely forgotten my mother had given it to me. Thinking it was another college application, I pulled it out and took it to the trash can. I was going to drop it in when saw the address was handwritten. That was unusual, so I opened it instead.

Inside was a scrawled letter. It read:

I don't know when or if you'll get this, Alison, but I have to try. I never thought it would turn out the way it did. I thought Sebastian only wanted to talk to you, but now I know it was much more than that. We never liked each other, but I didn't intend for you to get hurt. I may never go home now. After the way I betrayed everyone, I'm not sure I want to. All I can do is try to make amends. Sebastian is not dead. He was badly burned, but he survived the fire. He'll be watching you, waiting for a chance to take revenge. Watch your back, Alison.

It was signed, *Nikki Dawning-Truss.*

Acknowledgments

My sincerest thanks to all the wonderful people at Entangled who helped make this dream into a reality. Special thanks to Liz Pelletier for being my editor, fierce supporter, and wonderful to work with. Thanks to Robin Haseltine for her tireless work on this project. Much thanks to Meredith Johnson who I contacted more than once for reassurance and organization. Thanks to Heather Riccio for help with publicity.

Much thanks to my husband and daughters for putting up with me after sleepless nights of writing and editing.

Thanks also to the big guy upstairs I call God. Growing up wasn't easy, but he blessed me with a wild imagination and a library three blocks away to help me get through it.

Experience Alison's story from the very beginning in

Atlantis Rising

When a strange man told me I'm in danger because I'm a descendant of Atlantis, I thought he was crazy. Now I know he wasn't. But he left me with a warning. I'm being hunted by someone who will hurt, maybe even kill, those I love in order to control me.

So I've been hiding in plain sight, walking the halls of Fillmore High like a ghost. Now, two new students, Ian and Brandy, have discovered my secret. They've offered to teach me how to defend myself, but they want something in return…something I'm not sure I can give. And though I'm drawn to Ian, I can't act on my feelings. I might lose focus if I do.

The only thing I'm certain of is that I'm tired of hiding. It's time for the hunted to become the hunter.

Check out these other exciting reads from Entangled!

THIEF OF LIES
BY BRENDA DRAKE

Gia Kearns would rather fight with boys than kiss them. That is, until Arik, a leather clad hottie in the Boston Athenaeum, suddenly disappears. When Gia unwittingly speaks the key that sucks her and her friends into a photograph and transports them into a Paris library, Gia must choose between her heart and her head, between Arik's world and her own, before both are destroyed.

PERFECTED
BY KATE JARVIK BIRCH

Ever since the government passed legislation allowing people to be genetically engineered and raised as pets, the rich and powerful can own beautiful girls like sixteen-year-old Ella as companions. But when Ella moves in with her new masters and discovers the glamorous life she's been promised isn't at all what it seems, she's forced to choose between a pampered existence full of gorgeous gowns and veiled threats, or seizing her chance at freedom with the boy she's come to love, risking both of their lives in a daring escape no one will ever forget.

FORGET TOMORROW
BY PINTIP DUNN

It's Callie's seventeenth birthday and she's awaiting her vision—a memory sent back in time to sculpt each citizen into the person they're meant to be. In her vision, she sees herself murdering her gifted younger sister. Before she can process what it means, Callie is arrested and imprisoned, where she tries to escape with the help of her childhood friend, Logan. Now she must find a way to change her fate...before she becomes the most dangerous threat of all.

NEXIS
BY A.L. DAVROE

A Natural Born amongst genetically-altered Aristocrats, all Ella ever wanted was to be like everyone else. Augmented and *perfect*. Then... the crash. Devastated by her father's death and struggling with her new physical limitations, Ella is terrified to learn she is not just alone, but little more than a prisoner. Her only escape is to lose herself in Nexis, the hugely popular virtual reality game her father created. In Nexis she meets Guster, who offers Ella guidance, friendship...and something more. But Nexis isn't quite the game everyone thinks it is. And it's been waiting for Ella.

OBLIVION
BY JENNIFER L. ARMENTROUT

The epic love story of Obsidian as told by its hero, Daemon Black! I knew the moment Katy Swartz moved in next door, there was going to be trouble. And trouble's the last thing I need, since I'm not exactly from around here. My people arrived on Earth from Lux, a planet thirteen billion light years away. But Kat is getting to me in ways no one else has, and I can't stop myself from wanting her. But falling for Katy—a human—won't just place her in danger. It could get us all killed, and that's one thing I'll never let happen…

THE BOOK OF IVY
BY AMY ENGEL

What would you kill for?

After a brutal nuclear war, the United States was left decimated. A small group of survivors eventually banded together. My name is Ivy Westfall, and my mission is simple: to kill the president's son—my soon-to-be husband—and return the Westfall family to power. But Bishop Lattimer isn't the cruel, heartless boy my family warned me to expect. But there is no escape from my fate. Bishop must die. And I must be the one to kill him…